The dragon roared and came at Hellboy. Its claws, previously so light and elegant, scored channels in the concrete as it ran. The closer it came, the larger its teeth appeared.

Instead of turning to flee, Hellboy ran forward to meet it.

The dragon pulled up short, perhaps surprised by Hellboy's tactic, and gushed another wall of fire in his direction. But Hellboy was ready for that and did a long forward roll through the flames and out the other side. When he stood, smoldering slightly, he was only feet away from the dragon's head.

"That's not nice," he said, and punched the creature square on the nose with his heavy right hand.

The dragon roared, then whimpered. It reared up to its full height—big, very big, easily ten times as tall as Hellboy—and snorted.

"Again?" Hellboy said.

HELLBOY

UNNATURAL SELECTION

by

Tim Lebbon

POCKET BOOKS
New York   London   Toronto   Sydney

An *Original* Publication of POCKET BOOKS

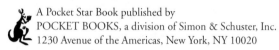 A Pocket Star Book published by
POCKET BOOKS, a division of Simon & Schuster, Inc.
1230 Avenue of the Americas, New York, NY 10020

This book is a work of fiction. Names, characters, places and incidents are products of the author's imagination or are used fictitiously. Any resemblance to actual events or locales or persons, living or dead, is entirely coincidental.

ISBN-13: 978-1-4516-6041-8

This Pocket Star Books paperback edition April 2006

10   9   8   7   6   5   4   3   2   1

POCKET STAR BOOKS and colophon are registered trademarks of Simon & Schuster, Inc.

Cover art by Mike Mignola

Manufactured in the United States of America

For information regarding special discounts for bulk purchases, please contact Simon & Schuster Special Sales at 1-800-456-6798 or business@simonandschuster.com.

Natural magic or physical magic is nothing more than the deepest knowledge of the secrets of nature.

—DEL RIO, *DISQUISITIONES MAGICAE*, 1606

HELLBOY

Unnatural
Selection

PART ONE

Old Memories

Temple of the Sun, Heliopolis, Egypt—1976

They had been digging for three days, and still the famed feather eluded them.

Three days underground, away from the sun and the heat of day, away from the darkness and the cool of night, timeless and airless and stuffy with the enclosed scents of history. They followed footprints left in the sand of subterranean passages millennia ago and compared their own feet for size. They drew their fingertips along the walls and sniffed the dust in wonder. Somewhere in each intake of breath was the skin of long-dead men and, perhaps, the sheddings of things other than men. Each time they opened their eyes after a short sleep, they were filled with awe. And every time they closed their eyes, their dreams were of greatness.

If only they could find the feather, these dreams would come true.

Richard Blake sat and consulted the ancient *Book of Ways* given to him by his father. Its author, Zahid de Lainree—doubtless a pseudonym designed merely to confuse—had been a man of mystery and obfuscation, and Richard had become adept at casting brief spells of course to wend his way through the man's writings and diagrams. If the ancient text said *left,* it sometimes meant *right;* if it said *up,* it could mean *down.* And occasionally, instruction to search in this world could hint at delving into another. This chapter, this very page, had already brought them to the secret entrance of the true Temple of the Sun, a place undiscovered by archaeologists and all manner of explorers who had torn this land apart.

The brothers knew that the Book was filled with arcane secrets, but that did not dilute their frustration.

"Gal," Richard said, "I'm reading this right, I *know* I am. I don't understand!"

Richard's twin brother, Galileo Blake—one wronged man named after another—was sitting several feet along the passage, casting his flashlight around him. The splash of light illuminated tool marks on the tunnel walls and ceilings, cracks in the bedrock, little else. "These damn tunnels are here for a purpose," Gal said. "Nobody builds tunnels from nowhere to nowhere. There's no *reason* for it."

"No reason . . ." Richard said. "Perhaps that's it! Gal, maybe we've spent three days looking for a reason. We've been walking through mazes looking for the middle, but maybe there *is* no middle!"

Gal shone the flashlight directly into his brother's face and smiled when Richard cringed back. "Sometimes, Rich, you're full of shit."

"Yeah, but magic shit." Richard smiled and closed the book so he could think. After a few moments, he cast another spell of course, then opened the book again. He held the penlight between his teeth, flicked to the chapter he had been staring at for three days, and began to read between the lines.

An hour later, they found the feather.

"I told you!" Richard said. "I *told* you!"

"Yeah, yeah, nobody likes a smart-ass."

"But just look at it . . ."

They had followed the lines scratched into the walls as described, choosing direction from the hidden messages of Zahid de Lainree's text, and it had taken them only another hour to find the right place. It was where the carved lines stopped. The creature that had made those lines so many years ago—its wings tucked in but still too wide for this narrow passage—must once have stood exactly where they stood now.

A sudden breath of warm air haunted the passage, a ghost memory from another world.

Ten minutes of digging unearthed the feather, as long as a man's forearm, a stunning royal purple flecked gold at its tip. Many centuries of burial had done nothing to dull its vibrancy or beauty.

And now Gal held it out before him, and they both stared. They could do little else. Here was evidence, here was proof, here was the first of many testaments to mythology they needed to find over the coming years. Their father would be waiting, lurking in exile and still mourning their murdered mother. Here, at last, in this feather from a creature that most would insist had never existed, the potential for revenge had found form.

"You send it," Richard said.

"Me?" Gal's usually gruff voice was tinged with a hint of trepidation. Even fear.

"Yeah, I've been reading the book."

"That's because you're good at casting the spell of course. You can divine hidden meanings. I just see ink on a page; you see whole worlds."

Richard sighed. "I make out the theory of the Memory

in Lainree's writing. You can actually *touch* it. You know you've always been better than me."

Gal sighed. "Well . . ."

Neither of them could look away from the feather.

Richard took it from his brother's hands. "Father will be so pleased," he whispered.

"Did you ever doubt him?"

"Did you?"

Gal smiled, still gazing at the plume. "Never. But I think perhaps he doubted himself."

"This will put an end to that." Richard offered the feather back to his brother. There was power in that gesture of sharing, and trust.

"Yes. This is the beginning of everything." Gal placed it on the floor of the passage, and Richard stepped back to give his brother the room he needed.

Gal drew a rough shape in the sand, closed his eyes, and whispered a series of gruff, guttural words. Eyes still closed, he sought out the feather, lifted it, and placed it gently within the shape. Its spine was so hot to the touch that, at first, it felt ice-cold. Instantly the sand around Gal's feet began to glow and skip, like a million tiny fleas striving to reach his outstretched hands. The glow expanded, remaining weak yet still bright enough to read by.

Then the heat truly arrived.

"Hot," Richard whispered. The passage grew warmer, his vision began to swim, and within seconds he was gasping for air, lying down and staring sideways at his kneeling brother. "*Hot!*" Each breath scorched his throat, and he wondered how his clothes had not erupted into flame. *Is this what it feels like to burn to death?* he thought.

Gal muttered louder, felt the world grow dim around

him, and as the phoenix feather flamed from this world and drifted gently through another, for a second he felt that other place. He sensed the Memory, the haunt of all mythical creatures, and he burst into an involuntary outpouring of grief and rage at the sadness radiating from there. It was a forgotten place whose very name emphasized the hopelessness of its existence. And it was dark, filled with drifting forms, many of them threatening and exuding menace, but only in the way that an old man will intimidate those younger than him with age, wisdom, and knowledge. They were fearful entities he saw, but ineffectual.

Ineffectual where they were now, at least.

The light faded, the heat withdrew, and Gal fell shivering to the floor of the passageway. If his hex of transmission had been right, the phoenix feather would be with his father even now. Given time, the light of revenge would begin to bleed into that darkened void.

As he withdrew from the Memory, he felt it shimmer with an echo of hope. *His* hope. And even through his tears, he smiled.

Baltimore, Maryland—1997

Abby Paris sat on the step of Edgar Allan Poe's grave and waited for the werewolf. The moon would be three-quarters full tonight; her own blood told her that, her own hunger. Yet she was certain that the werewolf would be here, clothed in its human form, but already planning the feast of a few days' time. Witnesses to the slayings said that the monster paid homage here after each killing. That made Abby un-comfortable, but, worried or not, she knew it was her job to try to talk it around.

That, or destroy it.

The afternoon was scorching. She sat beside Poe's grave, wearing black trousers and a black T-shirt, and she guessed she looked similar to a lot of visitors this particular grave-yard attracted. At least for once she wouldn't stand out from the crowd. Traffic hustled by and stank up the air, but the iron fence seemed to have a calming effect on the noise, as if the somber atmosphere of the churchyard were thick enough to soothe it. Abby watched a big dump truck pull up at the traffic lights down the street and belch brown coughs of exhaust fumes into the air. She wished she could avoid breathing for an hour or two. Then she thought of some of those dead things she had seen on her last mission with Hellboy, and she drew in a thankful breath. Stinking air was better than no air at all.

This was her first time out on her own, and she was nervous. Tom Manning, the head of the Bureau of Paranor-mal Research and Defense, had been hesitant about sending her out for a solo job, especially as this was such a personal assignment for her. "Send a monster to catch one!" she had said perkily, but Tom had frowned, and she had seen the troubled mind ever present behind his gruff exterior. Hell-boy, Liz Sherman, and Abe Sapien were all out of the coun-try on separate missions, and the significance of this had not been lost on Abby. There was a lot of stuff going on in the world right now. Weird stuff. BPRD stuff. Tom hated send-ing his agents out on their own.

But she had insisted, and he had relented, and now here she was sitting on Poe's grave waiting for a werewolf. She would recognize it when she saw it. She looked in the mirror every morning, after all.

Two young men entered the graveyard sporting identical black T-shirts, bald heads, and goatees. One was taller than the other, but other than that, they were peas in a Gothic pod. They even had the same look of reverence on their faces.

"Cool," one of them said. At first Abby thought he was staring at her, but then she realized it was the stone edifice behind her.

"She's pretty hot, too," the other one said.

"Well, boys, it *is* a bloody hot day." Abby smiled as she saw the effect her voice had on the men. The shorter one even stepped back a couple of paces as her throaty, sultry words faded into the street noise. She laughed quietly, knew the sound reached them, and she remembered howling at the moon and how that made her throat sore in the morning. But how wonderful it felt every single time.

She stood, stretched, looked around. *Can't let my guard down!* But there was no sign of the werewolf, and playing with these two would be fun.

The taller man was braver than his mate. "So you're hanging out with Edgar, too, huh?"

"Just somewhere cool to park my ass."

"Yeah, too cool."

The small guy asked, "Can you take our picture?"

Abby smiled and nodded. "Sure."

He stepped forward, probably totally unaware of the expression on his face: naked lust crossed with animal fear. He handed the camera to Abby. The taller man blinked at the length of her nails and the tattoos of claws along the lengths of her fingers. *Self-parody*, she wanted to say, but it would be lost on them.

The men skirted around Abby and positioned themselves on either side of Poe's tombstone. They looked nervous, their smiles forced, and Abby shook her head and turned away.

"Get yourselves natural, guys," she said. "Tell a joke. Ogle my ass. Remember the last time you got drunk together. I'll take your picture when you look like yourselves." She heard giggles behind her and took the opportunity to scan the street. Still no werewolf. Men and women, boys and girls, walking to and fro along the pavement. Abby sniffed. Smog, heat, sweat, but nothing like the wild musk she would recognize. Other than her own, of course. She could never shake that, however many baths or showers she took. She wondered whether the boys could smell her.

She spun around, ready to take their photo, and the werewolf was standing between them.

"Smile!" the man said. He was tall, pale, gaunt, yet his eyes were alive and strong, filled with exuberance.

He's just like me, Abby thought, amazed. *Except . . . he's not at all. Because he's tasted human flesh.* She looked at the men in black and wondered what they tasted like.

"I need to talk to you," she said. The man shrugged and sat down.

"What about our—?" the tall bald guy said.

"Scram," Abby growled. They ran off without their camera. She reckoned they'd run a long way.

"You're just like me," he said, smiling. There was utter confidence in his voice that even Abby found disarming. The way he sat, easy and graceful. The way he smiled, loose and friendly. Everything spoke of a belief in his own invulnerability.

First mistake.

"A little," she said. "But I don't kill people."

The man frowned. "Then what do you eat?"

"Deer."

"Holy shit!" He feigned disgust, stuck fingers down his throat as if about to vomit. "All that fur!"

"Some people are hairy."

"I rip off their skins first." He leaned forward, elbows on his knees. "That's usually after I've torn out their throats . . . usually. Sometimes I do it before. Fear adds to the flavor of that first bite, it really does. Something to do with the makeup of their blood."

"I'm here to stop you . . . stop you killing." Abby hated the nervousness in her voice, but he had unsettled her.

"You're BPRD?"

Abby nodded. She thought she hid her surprise quite well.

"Why didn't they send the big red guy?"

"He's off fighting dragons."

The man leaned back, laughing so loud and hard that he startled a flock of birds from the church roof. He patted his knees, wiped his eyes, shook his head. She saw the animal movements in every gesture, and she could not help feeling attracted to him. His power. His grace. Both were richer than hers, more emphasized. Was that because he ate people? Tasted human flesh? She glanced out into the street at the people wandering back and forth, and she could not help her subconscious throwing up the word: *cattle*.

"So they sent you to catch me," he said. "Well, what are you waiting for?"

"I wanted to talk you out of it, not catch you. You know I'm like you—a werewolf—but I control it. I have help, yes, but you can have help, too, if you—"

"You want to lock me up in a cage for a few days every month, feed me deer and sheep and cattle. You expect me to go for that rather than what I have here? This spread of tastes?" He waved his hand vaguely toward the street, but his eyes never left hers.

"Well . . ." That doubt and hesitancy again, and she was surprised that it was quickly making her hate this man. And she didn't even know his name.

"Think again," he said. "You have no idea what it's like. And if you did, you'd know why I have to do this."

She was ready. Maybe it was the training the Bureau had given her, or the way Abe Sapien had taught her to read someone's intention in his eyes, but even as the man came at her, she was twisting to the side, bringing her gun up out of its belt holster, and letting off a shot at his shadow.

He screamed as he landed across her legs. The bullet had taken him in the ankle, and his eyes went wide as he felt the silver bleeding into his system. "You bitch!" he hissed.

Abby closed her eyes at the stink of silver, felt her stomach heaving. When she looked again, he was gone, bounding over the perimeter fence almost before she could blink. *He's fast!* she thought. *Lord help me, he's fast even in his unchanged state.* She jumped up, readying herself for a long chase, but then she heard the squeal of brakes and the horrible impact of metal on flesh.

Perhaps she would be lucky.

Past Poe's grave, out onto the pavement, she saw the SUV slewed across the street. In front of it, writhing on the concrete road, the man squirmed in a spreading pool of his own blood.

"Oh, God . . ." the driver said as he got out of the vehicle. He stepped toward the wounded man, paused, and started backing away. "Oh, *God*!"

Abby walked out into the road and approached the werewolf. He was screeching, grasping at the side of his head where it had been caved in by the SUV's grille. Green-gray matter leaked out, spattering to the road and forming islands in the spreading blood. His eyes were red. His nose was bloody, but not from the impact. He was bleeding because of the change.

A circle of people was forming, all of them standing well back from this screaming thing thrashing about on the road. *I wonder if they'd still stand back if he was only a man,* Abby thought, and the answers she came up with scared her. *All that blood . . . all that gore* . . . She thought of the deer they gave her at the BPRD, delicate, shy creatures that barely had the sense to run when she went to tear out their throats. Their blood, pumping into her mouth. Their flesh, raw and rich and yet tasting so wrong.

She swayed on her feet, looked up at the sun, and went down on her knees.

"What's happened to his face?" someone said, sick fascination in his voice. "What's it done to his legs?"

Abby grabbed the .45 tightly in her right hand and opened her eyes.

The werewolf was up on his arms and legs. He was still screeching, and fluid and chunks of gore dripped from his ruined head. His tongue lolled from his mouth, longer than it should have been. His fingers stretched, and nails dug into the road surface. Clothing ripped, and his back seemed to expand, as if he had taken in the final, largest breath of his life. But Abby knew that was not the case.

"Down!" she said, aiming the pistol. The crowd gasped, but the werewolf uttered something that could have been a laugh. Blood slopped from his mouth as teeth gashed gums and lips.

"You think so?" he growled. Abby heard the words, but the crowd stepped back, as if they had just heard the first threatening snarl of a wild animal.

"I know so," she said, and jumped at him.

He knew what she was, and somehow he knew whom she worked for, but he was unprepared for her attack. Perhaps his wounds were just too much. She kicked out at his face and sent him sprawling, landed astride his chest, pressed the pistol muzzle into his right eye. He growled, then howled in anticipation of the silver bullet entering his brain.

"I will do it," Abby said, "I *will*!"

"What do you want?"

"Are you from Blake? Did he send you? Did he *make* you?"

"Huh?" The werewolf, fatal injuries bringing on his change, stopped squirming and ceased screeching. He lay still beneath her, left eye wide in surprise. And in that red eye, a glimmer of realization.

That was enough for Abby. She sat back, closed her eyes, and pulled the trigger.

The crowd scattered. The creature beneath her bucked once and then lay still. Abby walked away.

Rio de Janeiro, Brazil—1997

"That is one big worm." Hellboy had always wanted to take a trip to Rio, but not under these circumstances.

"Weird how people get used to things," Amelia Francis

said. She was a lecturer in Mythology in History at the local university and a BPRD adviser in South America. She had met Hellboy at the airport less than two hours ago. Now they were standing beside the road, staring up at the dragon that perched on the outstretched left arm of Christ the Redeemer. "Ask most people now, and they'll shake their heads and smile and say it's a joke."

"Even though that thing turned half of Copacabana beach into a sheet of glass?"

"People can't believe, so they choose not to."

"Huh." Hellboy rolled his unlit cigarette across his lips. He'd already searched through his jacket pockets for some matches and drawn a blank. He wished Liz were there with him. "What about them?" He pointed up the mountain at the colorful specks climbing its slopes. From here they looked like insects.

Amelia sighed. "They're not the first. The police are doing their best to deter the journalists, sensation seekers, and souvenir hunters, but it's a big place. They can't seal it off totally."

"Huh," Hellboy said again. He stared up at the dragon. "Souvenirs?"

"From . . . from what I know about dragons, it's . . ." She trailed off, staring up past Hellboy. "That's a *dragon!*"

"Sure looks like it." He glanced at the woman, looked away, back again. She'd hardly raised an eyebrow when he arrived at the airport; not the usual response he engendered. His lobster-red skin, horn stumps, and waving tail usually attracted some sort of comment, even from people he'd met before. Amelia had known of him—she had imparted that much, at least—but she'd already seen something more amazing that day.

He had to admit, it was quite a sight.

"So . . . souvenirs?" he repeated.

"You don't know about dragons?" she asked.

"They're lizards. They breathe fire. They're not nice."

"Actually, they were harmless once," the lecturer said. "Burned crops when people pissed them off, that was about their limit. Then Christianity turned them into demons, and they *became* demons, and they were hunted to extinction. At least, that's how the story goes. The story also says that if you eat a dragon's heart, you'll understand the language of birds."

"Useful," Hellboy said. "But that thing up there doesn't look extinct to me."

Amelia paled, leaned against the timber railing for support. Hellboy smiled and touched her shoulder gently with his big stonelike hand. Reality kept hitting her, surprising her with what she was actually seeing up there.

"What about the military?" he asked.

Amelia shrugged. "They've approached me, too. And . . . maybe it's my fault they're not doing anything. I told them that the appearance of a dragon was once thought to be an omen of good fortune."

"And is it?"

Amelia shrugged again. "They seem to think so. They left after I said that, and I haven't seen them since."

"Well, we can't just leave it there. I have to go up. See what that thing wants. Can't let it fly around and burn the place."

"How will you stop it?"

"I'll find a way, it's what I do. Will you drive me to the station?"

"Oh, yes, you bet!"

They heard a sudden screech, then a loud roar that spread out over the city. Hellboy looked up in time to see the dragon dip its head and sweep it across the rim of the plateau. Several waving shapes burst into flames and tumbled down the cliffs, their screams too far away to hear.

"Omen of good luck," he said. "You sure, Amelia?"

"Oh, those poor people . . ." She looked up into Hellboy's eyes, and for the first time he recognized her fear.

As Amelia drove her Jeep toward the mountain train station, Hellboy leaned out the window and stared up. The dragon was still there, perched quite comfortably on Christ's outstretched arm, surveying the view as if it owned the place. Occasionally it stretched its wings, stood up, and belched fire at the sky. Hellboy was not sure why until he saw the press helicopters hovering nearby.

So much for covert. He hated being the center of attention.

They followed the road around the slope of the mountain, and for a while a bulk of rock obscured the view. Hellboy sat back in his seat and chewed softly on the unlit cigarette. He wished—not for the first time—that he'd listened to Professor Bruttenholm when he had told Hellboy to spend more time learning. Maybe then he would know more about dragons, where they came from, what they wanted, what species this one was . . . and most important, how he could stop it. He touched the big gun on his belt and smiled. Bad shot though he was, he couldn't miss this sucker.

"Are you really from hell?" Amelia asked.

Hellboy scowled. "What's your area of expertise again?"

"Mythology."

"I'm no myth. Drive."

Amelia was silent for the next few minutes, but when they finally reached the station she stopped the Jeep and turned to Hellboy, her face stern. "I think it may be *Draconis albionensis*, a British dragon usually known as the Firedrake. Big. Strong. Weird that it's here, as most dragons were commonly sighted in Europe, North Africa, China, and Asia. I'm not aware of any dragon legends from North or South America. Very strange."

"How do I kill it?"

"Put on a suit of armor, and pick up a sword. They're not immortal, you know."

Hellboy frowned for a moment, then smiled at her. She was not mocking him. Far from it; she was trying to help. She shivered even in this heat, and he patted her leg softly. "Hey, I'm sorry," he said. "I didn't mean to be gruff. That's just me, and . . . well, I don't really like talking about me."

"I've always known about you, but in the flesh you're amazing."

"Hmph. I wish all the girls thought that way." Hellboy nodded his thanks and opened his door.

"Hellboy?" He looked back at Amelia. "That's a dragon," she said. "And that's impossible. A dragon . . . it's myth. A story. They don't really exist."

At that moment the dragon roared and let fly a breath of fire at a helicopter that had strayed too close. The aircraft veered away, paint blistered and rubber door seals smoking from the heat. The creature flapped its wings, stretched its neck, then settled back onto its roost.

"I think he'd disagree with you, Amelia," Hellboy said. "Hey, do me a favor? Wait here for me. I don't plan on being long."

She nodded. "Be careful."

"If I had a last name . . . 'Careful' would be my middle one."

On his way up the mountain in the deserted train, Hellboy called in to HQ. He asked to speak to Kate Corrigan, the BPRD's adviser on the paranormal, but she was busy somewhere else. So was Tom Manning, the director now that Professor Bruttenholm was dead. "Is there *anyone* there I can talk to?" Hellboy shouted, but the guy on the other end said something about being busy, having lots going on, and the world going to hell.

"Yeah, right," Hellboy muttered. He clicked off his satellite phone and tried to enjoy the trip.

The train clunked up the well-used tracks, taking him to a place where millions of people had previously journeyed to worship or admire or just to enjoy the view. He would be doing none of that. He flexed the fingers of his left hand, tapped the fingers of his right hand against the metal railing. They made a musical sound; if only he could identify the tune. And if he knew the tune, if only it had lyrics that would tell him more. Then he could sing along and learn the truth.

He had been called a dragon once. A Catholic priest in Ecuador had fallen to his knees when he saw Hellboy, clutching his rosary beads and prattling on in Spanish, shouting and screaming and generally acting upset. Hellboy was used to causing such a reaction, and he had smiled and shrugged and generally tried to exude benevolence. But even while he was being dragged away, the priest had raged, and the only word Hellboy had been able to make out had been *dragon*. That had offended him at the time, but later, sitting alone in the remains of a ruined church, he had looked at himself in a puddle of rainwater, and the offense had turned to sadness.

"Come on, dammit!" He thumped the side of the train car and left it dented. He shook his head. He hated these moments of calm before the storm, because they gave him time to muse upon his own nature. But then, he supposed that was good. Thinking such thoughts always got him in the mood for a fight.

Walking across the concrete esplanade, Hellboy was struck by the size of the statue of Christ. It was a magnificent effigy, beautiful, and he could only marvel at the builders who had constructed it so long ago.

Right now it was marred by the fire-breathing bastard sitting on its left arm. And below it, still steaming, dragon crap stained the hem of Christ's robes.

"Now that's just disrespectful," Hellboy said. "Hey! You!"

The dragon twisted on its perch and looked down at Hellboy. It was sleek and strong, its hide gray-green with shades of red on its throat, chest, and back. It moved without making a noise, and that unsettled him. Something so big and bulky should be clumsy, not graceful. Maybe he could learn a thing or two from this creature.

"We need to talk," he said. And for a second he thought that might suffice. The dragon put its head to one side, as if ready to listen. It dropped quietly from its perch, wings out for balance, and stepped daintily toward Hellboy, as if ready to parley.

And then it opened its jaws and sent a fireball his way.

Even as Hellboy rolled to the side, he was aware of the press helicopters homing in on this new confrontation. He hated the press. If they saw him trampled and gutted and having his insides burned out, they'd film, not help. He swore that today they'd get no scoop of that sort.

He stood and pulled the pistol, letting off a shot that punched a hole in the dragon's wing. It didn't seem to bother the worm in the slightest, and Hellboy saw why: its wings were giant sails, thick leathery skin strung between sinewy supports, and they were already full of holes. He'd wasted a precious round just to add another.

The dragon roared and came at him. Its claws, previously so light and elegant, scored channels in the concrete as it ran. Its tail waved behind it, ripping the steel hand railing from the edge of the esplanade. Its head swayed from side to side as it ran, and the closer it came, the larger its teeth appeared.

Instead of turning to flee, Hellboy ran forward to meet it.

The dragon pulled up short, perhaps surprised by Hellboy's tactic, and gushed another wall of fire in his direction. But Hellboy was ready for that and did a long forward roll through the flames and out the other side. When he stood, smoldering slightly, he was only feet away from the dragon's head.

"That's not nice," he said, and punched the creature square on the nose with his heavy right hand.

The dragon roared, then whimpered. It reared up to its full height—big, very big, easily ten times as tall as Hellboy—and snorted. A couple of weak flames came from its nostrils, and then only smoke. It snorted again. Blood flecked the concrete around Hellboy, and he wiped a glob of it from his eye.

"Again?" Hellboy said.

The dragon seemed to agree. It launched itself forward and fell on all fours, trapping Hellboy beneath its stomach and crushing him down into the concrete. Hellboy gasped, tried to twist away, lost hold of the pistol. And then the dragon began to move across the esplanade, dragging Hellboy beneath it.

"Crap. *Crap!*" His jacket was ripped, his skin scored by the concrete, and the creature above him rumbled with something that could have been laughter. "You laughing at me, barbecue breath?"

The dragon stood, and Hellboy immediately punched upward into its gut. It roared in pain and stumbled away, its swinging tail catching Hellboy across the chest as it retreated. Hellboy went sprawling, and as he came to a stop, he leaned over and picked up the pistol. "That's convenient," he said, firing at the dragon's head. The bullet ricocheted from the heavy scales above its eye and winged off somewhere over Rio.

That really pissed off the giant worm.

This is turning bad, Hellboy thought. Before he could stand, the dragon snatched him up in one of its claws and launched itself over the edge of the parapet.

The ground dropped away beneath Hellboy. Still clasping the pistol in his left hand, he was now loath to use it. Kill the dragon, fall a few hundred feet with ten tons of dead meat right above him . . . that did not appeal. And besides, there were houses down there, cars, parks, and people.

His only hope now was to wait and see whether this thing took him over open ground. Then, perhaps, a bullet in the spine.

Looking way, way down, he could see Amelia's Jeep parked in the station parking lot. He waved and almost laughed at the ridiculousness of the gesture, but he could not see whether the lecturer waved back.

The dragon flew hard and fast, and it took only a minute for the land beneath them to give way to sea. *Now,* Hellboy thought. *This is when I can—*

The dragon dropped him. They must have been a quarter of a mile up.

Hellboy wanted to scream, but then he'd lose the crushed cigarette in his mouth. He wanted to shoot, but his arms were pinwheeling in an attempt to keep himself upright as he fell. And he wanted, so much, to reach the water. Because he knew exactly what was coming next.

The dragon swept down at him and belched fire. Hellboy grimaced as the flames engulfed him, singeing his hair and goatee, stretching his skin, igniting his utility belt. When the flames guttered out, the dragon was already diminishing into the distance.

Hellboy had time to draw one puff on his newly lit cigarette before he struck the surface of the bay.

Venice, Italy—1997

Abe Sapien loved Europe. He loved the variety of the place, the mix of races and religions, food and drink, custom and tradition. He loved the fact that everywhere he went was different, and every place he visited gave him unique memories and distinct experiences to take back home. The differences spanned from east to west, country to country, and in some cases valley to valley. Some countries were as different from one side to the other as America was from north to south, and some cities were like microcosms of the whole world. In London he had been fascinated with its network of hidden streets, in Barcelona the architecture almost knocked him flat, and in Paris he had discovered a werewolf, and she had taken the name Abby Paris for herself.

Abby. He hoped she was all right. After today was over, he would get in touch with HQ and see how she had done. He'd had to rush away without really telling her to take care, or wishing her luck, and even after several years he still felt very protective toward her. And maybe a little more.

If Abe loved Europe, he *adored* Italy. Art was all here, and that was nowhere more evident than in the thrilling history of this place. Every building had a story to tell; most were older than him. And here art and science had truly come together in the form of one of his true heroes, Leonardo da Vinci.

And Abe's favourite Italian city . . . Venice. A paradise of one hundred and twenty islands linked by canals and lagoons. A city of romance and splendor, and so bound in with a watery existence that Abe had once thought to call it home. Maybe one day he would. Perhaps, if the time ever came when he found his own true history, he could begin creating a new future for himself here.

He only wished they could do something about their drainage.

And today the water did not seem quite so inviting as normal. Not with a thirty-foot alligator prowling the city.

Abe was riding in a police motor launch, crossing the choppy waters of the Grand Canal, and trying to ignore the stares of the two uniformed policemen accompanying him. The detective, Marini, was different. He could accept Abe's peculiarities, having already worked with another strange guy—Hellboy—on a case back in 1992. "Yeah, the old 'faces in the floor' case," Hellboy had said when Abe mentioned the detective's name. "That was a fun one. Never did catch that ghost." He had warned Abe to watch out for Marini's bad jokes, but so far the detective had been very quiet and subdued.

Abe stared unblinking at the two young officers until they looked away. He could always beat a human in a staring contest.

"And how many times has it been seen?" he asked.

"At least twenty times before yesterday," Marini said. "And then yesterday the incident near the Rialto Bridge, and there were dozens of witnesses. That poor woman . . . the German ambassador is already turning it into a diplomatic incident."

"He's blaming your government for a giant alligator?"

"The woman was his niece. At present, he only has an arm to send home for his sister to bury. I can understand the man's heightened emotions."

"Hmm," Abe said. "Quite."

The boat skipped from wave to wave, hull thudding with each impact, and Abe suddenly wondered how easy it would be for an alligator thirty feet long to tip them over. But this was a city built on water, it survived through water, and the first thing he had noticed upon his arrival was that the canals were as busy with traffic as ever. They could let this freak occurrence cripple them as a city, or they could defy it. So far, defiance seemed to be working.

"How is Hellboy?" Marini asked.

"Moody as ever," Abe said.

Marini lit up. "Ahh, not moody, Mr. Sapien. *Deep.* That's a very different thing. Hellboy has depths, I'm sure you know, and he frequently spends time trying to plumb them. That's where his moodiness comes from. That and the fact that there are no Italian shoes that fit him." He laughed at his own joke.

"He did tell me to beware of your sense of humor," Abe said.

"Did he really?" Marini shook his head and spoke quickly to his officers in Italian, still laughing. They smiled nervously, glancing at Abe as if he were about to bite their faces off. "Well, did he tell you about the time I painted an *L* and an *R* on his horns while he slept?"

Abe shook his head, aghast. "And you're still alive?" If Marini were telling the truth, he was lucky still to be in ownership of all four limbs.

The detective waved a hand, guffawed, then shook his head and looked down. "We only worked together for a couple of weeks, but we had much in common. I, too, never knew my parents."

I know how you feel, Abe almost said, but he let it lie.

The launch powered down and nudged roughly against the dock. The young policemen jumped up and secured the mooring lines, then stepped back and watched in fascination as Abe went ashore. Marini finally seemed to lose his temper with his subordinates. He fired a few harsh-sounding words at them, and they scampered off, ducking into the nearby police station and letting the door drift shut behind them.

"Forgive them," Marini said.

Abe raised one webbed hand and smiled. "Of course. I can hardly blame them."

"Now, to business. We will consult the incident map inside. I've plotted the location of every sighting, investigated possible hiding places, and from all that I think we can decide where would be the best place—"

"I think right here," Abe said. He had turned away from the detective to see what was causing a commotion out on the lagoon. A gaily painted tourist barge seemed to be floating at the whim of the tide, drifting sideways with the waves, and shadows and shapes waved and danced on deck. Screams of fright and pain came their way. Balancing on the edge of the boat, head thrashing from side to side, mouth filled with tourist, was the largest lizard Abe had ever seen.

"But what can you do?" Marini asked. Abe was perched on the edge of the dock, webbed feet just inches from the tips of the waves. The screams continued from across the water, and now he could hear the splashes of people leaping into the lagoon. Bad move. The alligator would love that, and if he didn't do something soon, then Marini would spend the time between now and his retirement pulling body parts out of Venice's canals.

"I'm not sure yet," Abe said, "but I have to try something. You have guns in there?" He nodded back at the police station.

"Of course." Marini pulled out his revolver.

"No," Abe said. "*Big* guns."

"Yes."

"Get them." Before Marini could say more, Abe launched himself into the Venetian waters.

As ever, he relished those first few seconds of immersion. He breathed in deep, aware of the tang of pollution in the water but enjoying the feeling of his gills opening and closing. This was really breathing. The water was murky and filled with muck, but no more so than the air up there. This muck was more visible, that was all. He kicked out and started swimming.

He could hear the sounds of the alligator attack. The human screams were muffled but louder than they had been above water. There were more than one. He could hear the frantic kicking and slapping at the water's surface as people tried to swim away and the calmer, more contented *thump, thump* of the alligator's great tail. Abe could also sense the grind of its jaws and the crunch of bones, and that was not good news. *Let's hope this one isn't an ambassador's niece,* he thought, but immediately berated himself. He'd been claiming for years that Hellboy's dry humor was rubbing off on him.

Abe struck out for the alligator. He kicked with his feet, pushed with his hands, slid through the water. Instinct steered him when sight could not; there was only a vague glow of daylight above him, and below and to the side the water was cloudy with oil and filth. He could barely see his hands when they swept out in front of him.

Instinct also judged his distance, and when he thought he was close to the tumult—the sounds were louder, the vibrations of violence stronger in the water—he surfaced.

He looked ahead first. The alligator was still propped on the side of the barge—good for him, bad for the tourists. The monster's small front legs were hooked over the gunwale, its weight tipping the vessel and making its remaining occupants slide toward its thrashing jaws. Blood smeared the deck. A few rags hung from the lizard's fist-sized teeth, the only remnants of the woman Abe had heard screaming from the shore. He turned in the water. Detective Marini was already jumping into the launch with his two staring officers, all three carrying something big and gray and nasty-looking.

Good. Abe would only have to keep this thing occupied for a couple of minutes, at most.

He ducked under and swam deep, passing beneath the alligator's swaying tail and hindquarters and pausing underneath the barge for a few seconds to check the situation. To his left Abe could see the dangling legs of the tourists who had flung themselves into the water. They hung there as if embedded in the lagoon's pale gray ceiling, some of them swimming away, many more simply doing their best to tread water. One or two were in trouble, but others seemed to be helping them for now. Abe's main concern was to his right: the staggering bulk of the alligator.

Its stomach was as wide as most creatures of this sort were long. Its rear legs were as long as a man was tall and tipped with claws that could rip Abe to shreds. Its hide was warty and thick, and Abe had no idea just what he could do to draw its attention.

Something scratched his foot. Abe looked down, and for once he gave thanks for humans' disregard for their environment. An old bicycle, wheelless and rusted, protruded from the lagoon bed beneath him. *Death by bike*, he thought, and the words were in his old red friend's voice. Abe could already imagine the conversation they would have over this one.

He could hear the buzz of the police launch approaching now. The alligator, consumed by its feeding frenzy, appeared not to have heard, and Abe wanted to keep it that way. He grabbed the bike, kicked away from the lagoon bed, and gave thanks when it plopped from the silt. No time to think. He turned and kicked out for the lizard, metal frame held out in front of him, rusted ragged and sharp, and a second before he struck the beast, Abe thought, *Not enough momentum, won't even scratch it.*

He was right. The frame sank into the belly of the beast, stretching its hide, and sprang straight back out.

Abe floated there for a second, wondering what the hell to do now, and then the alligator slipped from the boat and sank down to his level.

Its head was the size of a small car.

Oh crap, Abe thought, and he vowed to spend less time around Hellboy.

The alligator was incredibly fast for its size. It twisted in the water, bringing its wide mouth around to gulp him in, jaws opening, teeth ragged with torn flesh and snagged clothing. Abe dropped the bike and struck upward, passing just over the tip of the monster's snout, surfacing briefly before diving back down. Marini and his men had arrived and were taking aim, and it couldn't be soon enough for Abe.

No gunshots. His brief appearance must have confused them, and now they were holding back in case they hit him. *Shoot shoot shoot*, he thought, kicking hard and slinking beneath the hull of the barge. But the alligator followed, and within seconds Abe had led it to the other side of the barge, out of Marini's line of fire . . . and straight into the area of dangling legs. He felt it chasing him, the great pressure wave of water pushed ahead of it setting the webbing between his toes vibrating, and he knew that he had maybe seconds in which to act.

He spread his fingers and toes and stopped dead in the water. Turned. Kicked out at the shadow bearing down on him. The impact sent him spinning, but he felt the grumble of pain from the lizard as his foot glanced from its nose and scraped across its eyes. His kick had been lucky, and maybe he would not find that luck the next time. He struck upward and, with two powerful strokes, broke surface. He held onto the side of the barge for a couple of seconds until he felt the pressure wave of the alligator rising toward him, then hauled himself up onto the boat.

An immensely fat woman with purple hair and wearing a bright yellow dress screamed, and Abe screamed back.

Water erupted behind him and then settled again, and he closed his eyes, relieved that the gator had not simply come up out of the lagoon for him. It had tried to second-guess him, as he had hoped . . . but he was way ahead.

"Detective! Get ready!" Abe shouted as he crossed the barge, almost slipping in the bloody mess on the deck. Marini and his men aimed down at the water on their side, Marini glancing up nervously at him.

This was make or break.

Abe grabbed up the remains of one of the dead tourists—a bloody torso minus limbs and head—and lobbed it into the lagoon between the barge and the police launch.

A second later the alligator rose up and clasped the torso in its jaws, probably wondering why it did not taste fish-man flesh.

"Marini!" Abe shouted, but there was no need.

Marini and his men fired. The reports were tremendous, sounding over the water and echoing back from the surrounding buildings. Five shots each, six, and by the time the alligator sank out of sight, the echoes were crossing each other. One of the men continued firing until his rifle clicked on an empty chamber, and Marini had to press the man's arms down gently. The young officer was crying. He looked up at Abe and this time did not look away. Perhaps having faced the monster, he could recognize humanity when he saw it.

Abe nodded, and the man returned the gesture.

"Do you think we got it?" Marini shouted. "Is it over?"

The echoes of gunshots faded away, but the fat lady still screamed.

"Ask her to sing instead of screaming in my ear, and it will be."

Venice. Abe Sapien's favorite city. *Damn.*

Air Crash Investigation Center, Lausanne, Switzerland—1979

"It's a prediction more than anything," Richard Blake said. "The *Book of Ways* was written so long ago that Zahid de Lainree obviously couldn't have been specific, but he's quite clear in the implications." He and his brother sat on the hillside overlooking the acres of hangars and smaller buildings. Lake Geneva glittered in the distance, and the air was crisp, cool, and clear. And still. Waiting for something to happen. Richard had the *Book of Ways* opened on his lap, his hands shading it from the sun. Such old parchment, so brittle, found exposure inimical.

"So there's no way of saying for sure that they're the cause of every crash?" Galileo Blake said. "And it's all just supposition anyway?"

"No way at all. And yes, it's prediction and supposition on de Lainree's part. But why is that a problem? We've been chasing myths for years, and what are they if not supposition written down or passed on through word of mouth?"

Gal leaned back, raised his face to the sun, and sighed. "Nobody likes a smart-ass."

Richard ignored him and scanned the page of the *Book of Ways*. He closed his eyes and muttered a spell of course, and when he looked again, the words seemed to have altered. They led this way instead of that, said one thing and not another, and Richard smiled as he started relaying the relevant information to Gal.

"Small spirits, and minor," he said, "and yet possessed of flesh and blood and bone. Helpful to most, merely mischievous to others, they know the way of metals and powers, the stretch of tools and the magic of fixings. Their pleasure is in building, and in helping humans discover new ways and means. This manner may continue, and it may not . . . though if the humans disregard the spirits and claim their own inventions, the spirits may rise up. Mischievous will become nasty, creativity will give way to persistent deconstruction, and the humans will live to regret their ignorance and arrogance."

"Sounds about right," Gal said. He leaned over and stared at the page Richard was examining. The parchment was almost bare but for three curving lines, each spanning a different axis. At their center was what looked like an image of the sun. It glowed. "It says all that there?" he asked.

"In a manner of speaking."

"Looks like a lot of lines to me."

"That's why I read, and you send. I'm the brain, and you're the muscle." He grinned at his brother and rolled aside to escape the playful punch he knew would come.

"Let's go, then," Gal said, standing and brushing down his trousers. "No time like the present. And we haven't sent the old man anything in a while."

"He liked the dragon's tooth," Richard said. "That was a *real* treat for him."

Gal grinned as he started walking down the hillside. "And it'll be a real treat for someone else, too," he said. "*Such* a treat."

From Egypt the feather of a phoenix, from England a dragon's tooth, and now in Switzerland they sought something else entirely. They had not seen their father for four years, and yet they felt closer to him than ever.

When they were children, he had not been there. Benedict Blake—great scientist, philosopher, explorer of arcane mysteries, environmentalist, and naturalist—had never been a great father. Their mother brought them up and protected them, and she often told them what a wonderful man their father was. But not to them. For Richard and Steven—as a boy, he had not found cause to change his name, for he had not yet been wronged—Blake was simply an absence in their lives. He lectured around the world and wrote books and articles, but he had never once spent a Sunday afternoon in their back garden playing football, drinking lemonade, and planning the long walk they would take that evening. He had never ventured into the woods with them to help them dam a stream, or grabbed a kite and run into the wind out on the moor, or sat with them on either side of him while he read a bedtime story or listened to them talk about their school day. He was a great man wrapped up in his greatness, and it squeezed out true time. They watched him waste his life when he should have been living it. And their mother, beautiful and mournful, was as sad as they.

And then the fire, and the murder and accusations, and for the first time in their lives, their father had looked after them. They had run, and while on the run, he told them what he wanted to do. How he wanted to seek vengeance. And he gave them both something very special before sending them on their way, something that, in retrospect, did not surprise them one little bit.

He gave them magic.

The site was not especially well protected. There was a security fence, but something had burrowed beneath one section of it long ago—a fox or a dog—and Gal and Richard managed to squirm their way underneath. They paused while Richard cast a spell of haze at a couple of security cameras, waiting for a few minutes for the enchantment to take effect. When the lenses of the cameras whitened with cataracts, the brothers hurried across the open ground, coming to a standstill up against the closest hangar. They looked around, waiting for the shout or whistle that would signify their being sighted, but all was silent.

The air was still, as if nature held its breath. Perhaps soon it would. When they had collected everything their father needed, maybe then the whole *world* would hold its breath. And when Benedict Blake had finished with it, the planet would start to breathe itself clean once again. That's how Richard and Gal thought of it; they were helping the earth to clear its lungs. Humanity was the bad habit, and the planet needed to give it up.

The hangar was huge. They had to scamper around its perimeter for a while until they found an open door, but once inside, the scale of the enclosure became apparent. It was at least the size of a football field, the ceiling maybe a hundred feet high, and the open space it created was unhindered by columns or supports. At its center sat the charred remains of a passenger jet. The aircraft had plunged into the Alps a week before, killing more than a hundred people. If only the investigators could reassemble those lives so easily . . . but they did what they thought was the next best thing. Found out what went wrong, and why.

"If only they knew," Richard muttered.

"Even if they did, they'd never believe. That's their problem. They pay no homage to their Memory." Gal was haunted by Memory, that place, that emptiness where so much existed that should not. Every time he went there, he wished he were the weaker one, the translator his brother had become. He wished he did not have the strength it took to dip into the Memory, because he hated that place and what it represented, and as each year passed, his rage at the ignorance that had created it grew.

"Let's go," Richard said. "No one here. Maybe they're out to lunch?"

The men darted across the floor of the hangar and hid amid the separated and labeled wreckage of the airliner. They could still smell the fire that had consumed the fuselage, and though much of it had been reconstructed on a framework of steel supports, the floor was still strewn with unidentified parts. *Like body parts,* Richard thought. *Bits they can see, many more pieces they can't identify. The plane came apart like the bodies inside, and people only have themselves to blame. If they'd opened their minds—if they'd given the little spirits credit for their talents—the gremlins would have never turned on humanity.*

"Over here," Gal said. Richard followed him to the tangled mess of one of the massive engines. It had been gutted by an explosion, and its mechanical guts hung out as if seeking escape. Gal traced his finger across the blackened surface of the metal, sniffed the soot, shook his head, and moved on. "Closer," he said. "Getting closer." He repeated the process here and there, and Richard joined in, touching and sniffing, looking for that trace of something that was not mechanical or electrical, something that had once had life and thought and emotion.

They found it on the outside of a smashed door.

The door was so twisted by fire that it had not yet been reaffixed to the body of the plane. Molded around its exposed handle, cauterized hard by the conflagration, was a layer of greenish material. Neither brother even had to touch it to know what it was. Flesh, the fat of a spirit, the trace of a gremlin.

"There it is," Richard said, and, as ever, he was filled with wonder at what they had found. Every search started with belief and little more. And every search ended with discovery. They were doing something right, and not for the first time he wondered who, or what, might be steering them.

"You take it, I'll send it," Gal said.

Richard used a penknife to take a slice of the material. When he cut it, it bled.

Gal sketched a sigil in the soot on the hangar floor. He knelt, closed his eyes, started to mutter the invocation that would open the Memory to him, and he dropped the gremlin flesh onto the sigil. The world around him receded to little more than an echo. The sigil grew warm, as if flaring with the flame of the crash once again, and the gremlin flesh sizzled and popped as it faded out of this world and into another. It passed into Memory and, as always, Gal had an instant to watch it go. He felt the depth of that place and the emptiness, the loss and the rage, and he fell back crying into the arms of his brother.

"There," Richard said, rocking his brother back and forth. He never got used to the tears. "Come on . . . you're back."

Someone ran toward them across the hangar, shouting words the brothers could not understand, and Richard smiled at the irony. If he answered the query, his response would also be beyond understanding.

What are you doing here? the guard was probably saying.

Saving the world, Richard would say.

Saving the world.

Tsilivi, Zakynthos, Greece—1997

Liz Sherman was hot. Her friends at the BPRD sometimes joked that she should be used to the heat—sometimes, when they thought that such joking would not hurt her too much—and she would smile and shrug and say that being used to it didn't mean she had to like it.

She never thought they were very funny.

No, Liz liked it cool, misty, raining. She liked it grim. She preferred it when the weather didn't seem to be doing its utmost to remind her of who she was. Her dreams did enough of that.

Here on Zakynthos, the sun was burning the ground dry. Heat sucked moisture from the plants. What greenery there was looked pale and wan, covered in dust, and forests of dead olive trees cut funereal swaths across the rocky hill-sides. Some of them seemed to be blackened, as if the tips of their branches had caught fire. Liz blinked, shook her head, and still did not believe.

"Dimitris, are you seriously trying to tell me that a phoenix came down from the hills and ate those cattle?"

"Yes, Miss Sherman."

"Call me Liz." She stamped her cigarette out in the dust and leaned back against the police car. Its metal was hot to the touch. And dusty. "So did you see it yourself?"

"No, Miss Sherman."

"No," Liz said, shaking her head. "Well . . ." She didn't know what else to say. She had seen a lot during her time at the BPRD—and she'd been through too much herself to let doubt cloud her mind. But something just didn't feel right about this, and she could not quite put her finger on what that was. She wished that Hellboy were here with her, because he had a knack for cracking mysteries like this. He'd add two and two and come up with an impossible five . . . and then, likely as not, he'd take that five and kick the crap out of it until it reverted back to four. A basic approach, but one that invariably worked. Liz was thinking too much, too deeply, and she closed her eyes and tried to coax herself into viewing things under a simpler light.

She opened her eyes again, and Dimitris was offering her another cigarette. She smiled, let him light it for her, breathed deep. Christ knows what brand he was smoking, but she welcomed the sting of the rough smoke on her throat.

They were parked on a roadside overlooking the holiday resort of Tsilivi. To their right the sea was an inviting blue, and directly below them the long narrow beach was spotted with tourists, pale Europeans who had just arrived and the brown or red shapes of those who had been here for a week or more. The holiday makers spilled off the beach and into the sea, and Liz could hear the constant buzz of motorboats and Jet Skis bouncing from wave to wave. They drew white lines in the sea behind them, like aircraft trails in a deep blue sky.

To the left lay Zakynthos. Tsilivi itself was a long, relatively narrow band of restaurants, hotels, bars, and holiday homes twisting and turning away from the sea, mostly following the road but spreading out here and there where builders had moved outward into the countryside. Away from there, the glaring white of other buildings dotted the landscape. Hotels that lay away from the main drag often had two or three pools and plenty of land, and farther up the hillside toward where Liz now stood were occasional farms and more salubrious holiday homes.

Here and there the hillsides had been smudged, as though they were mistakes on a charcoal artist's masterpiece.

Liz looked out to sea and back again, and, yes, there was a definite pattern to the marks across the landscape. They were narrow at the top and wider farther down, as if fire had tumbled from the hilltops, spreading as it went.

"Anything could have caused those fires," she said, nodding toward a darkened stain on a neighboring hillside.

"No, Miss Sherman. Only the phoenix."

"You know that a phoenix is a mythical creature, Dimitris?" Dimitris smiled and raised his eyebrows, as if used to being patronized. "Oh shit, Dimitris, I'm sorry," Liz said. "I didn't mean anything by that, it sounded awful."

"I've heard worse, Miss Sherman. Yes, I know it's mythical, and yes, I know that mythical creatures don't exist. But the coelacanth was once considered mythical, and the mountain gorilla, and . . . well, I know who you work for and who else works for them. The big red one. My father worked with him a long time ago, back in America in seventy-eight. Something to do with pods, I believe."

"I haven't known him that long, but I do know how he'd react to being called a myth. And call me Liz." She took another drag on the cigarette and looked at Tsilivi through the smoke. If what Dimitris said was anything to go by, this was a view that a lot of people could be seeing in the very near future.

The phoenix had first appeared several days before. It had swooped down from the hills, slaughtered some cattle, and then flown away. Many people had seen it happen. A day later another visit, and this time the great bird's rage-filled attack had left several goats dead and, Dimitris had said with a note of regret, completely inedible. The following days saw two attacks each, and though no one had yet been hurt, Dimitris was worried that the bird would clap its wings and incinerate a busload of tourists. Bad for business,

he had said when he first met Liz at the Tsilivi police station, and even then she had detected a note of defense in his
voice. Here was a man used to being condescended to, and
he had developed a built-in defense of dry sarcasm.

"So why hasn't anyone been up into the hills to look for
it?"

Dimitris averted his eyes, shuffled his feet. A cloud of
dust rose and settled on his trousers. They seemed used to
it. "Afraid," he said. "There are a couple of small cafés up
there, and a farm, and we can't get in touch with anyone
who lives there."

"Isn't that a good reason to go up there yourself?"

The policeman kept his eyes averted, and Liz stamped
out her cigarette. Sweat dribbled down her sides, trickled
into her eyes, and she cursed the heat once again.

"He's a god of fire," Dimitris said. "He's a relative of the
sun, and something has enraged him, something has driven
him mad. He can clap his wings and raise fire! Those people
up there are dead. Cinders. Ashes. I have a wife and child; I
have no wish to mix my own ashes with theirs."

"Don't hit me with that ancient god bullshit!" Liz said.

Dimitris turned away, shaking his head. "You don't understand," he said.

Now who's being condescending? Liz thought, hackles rising. Her skin burned, and not just with the sun. She was
getting angry. *Yeah, god of fire*, she thought. *Wait until he
gets a load of me.*

"Dimitris, I'm sorry, but you're right, I don't understand.
What I do know is, I've been called for by your superiors to
help out here. I need you to take me up the mountain so
that I can see for myself."

"My wife? My child?"

"I promise you that today will not see them without a father."

"How can you promise that?" Dimitris took out another cigarette and popped it into the corner of his mouth.

Liz shrugged. *What the hell.* She reached out, summoned a flame from her fingertip, and lit his cigarette for him.

"Aren't you a little too old to believe in monsters?" Liz asked.

They were following the road around the slope of the mountain, throwing up a cloud of dust behind them. That, Liz noted grimly, seemed to be a theme of this place: dust. Grit, too, grinding between her teeth. And muck; dust damped by her sweat turned into a grimy layer that ran in rivulets beneath her clothing. Dammit, why couldn't she have been sent to Iceland to deal with a snow demon?

"I'm old enough to be able to believe again," Dimitris said. He glanced sideways, Liz frowned, and he smiled at her. She liked that. He had a nice smile, and it made her feel good. "What I mean is, I'm old enough to be able to accept that things aren't all that they seem, and that there are mysteries in the world. I'm still talking to you after you conjured fire. Proof enough? I have accepted you and what you can do. I'm *old* enough to accept that. Once mysteries are revealed, they're no longer mysteries. A monster is only a monster when it can't be categorized or photographed."

"You think science can explain everything?" she said.

Dimitris shrugged, sending the car clunking over the gravel beside the road. "I'm sure it can say why you make fire. Something's only supernatural if it *isn't* explained. Ghosts, for instance. If they really exist, then they aren't supernatural, because nature allows them to exist. See?"

"I see exactly what you're saying," Liz said. She plucked a cigarette from his shirt pocket and lit it with her finger. "But even in the short time I've been around, I've seen things that nature does not allow. And they still exist. And nature abhors that."

Dimitris stared wide-eyed at her cigarette. Accept it he might, but he was still amazed. And probably scared. Liz nudged his arm and pointed ahead, and the policeman turned just in time to save them from a long, long drop.

"Eyes front," she said.

"What do you mean?"

"I mean I don't want to end up as fish bait when you drive us off this mountain."

"No, Miss Sherman, what do you mean when you say—"

"Call me Liz." She rested her arm through the open window and looked up the gently sloping mountain. She'd been rude, cutting off the conversation like that. Especially as she liked Dimitris. His naïveté was appealing, and there was a certain innocence about him that actually made her jealous. Liz had been innocent once, but it had come to an abrupt end back in '73 when she burned her family to death. Ever since then, she had craved a return of innocence, but she knew that finding it again was about as likely as becoming a virgin.

She glanced at Dimitris, but he was staring ahead with grim determination. Maybe she'd already ruined this potential friendship even before it had begun. The British had a saying for it: she'd pissed on her chips.

The policeman drove them higher. Dust swirled through

the car, the road became rougher, and he started to mutter under his breath. Liz thought he was praying, and she wished that she could, too.

"I told you so," Dimitris said a few minutes later. He stopped the car, and Liz nodded a silent admission that, yes, he had told her.

The building had been white once, but fire had scorched it black. Tiles had shattered from the heat, and charred roof timbers sat exposed to the sun. They were still smoking gently, as though fire were hiding in their depths just waiting for the right moment to erupt again. Masonry had cracked, one wall had tumbled to the ground, and a blackened mass lay twenty feet from the ruined building, buzzed by flies. It had no discernible human features, but Liz knew a burned corpse when she saw one.

"You need to leave me here and go back down the mountain," she said very slowly.

"Not now that I've come so far," Dimitris said.

"Dimitris, you really need to go. A phoenix is no dragon; there's no reason for it to be doing this. Fire accompanies its death and rebirth."

"You believe me? Well, then, I can't just leave—"

"Dimitris!" Liz looked at him and saw that perhaps he did care. "Please . . . I've handled worse than this. Go back down, and when I come down later, how about I buy you a drink?" She gave him her best smile, the one that made her eyes look as though they were aflame.

"Miss Sherman, if you're sure . . . ?"

"I'm fireproof. Usually."

Dimitris uttered a short bark of a laugh, reached out to touch her hand, and then the phoenix landed on the car and started to prove Liz right.

Now she was hot.

The roar of the fire was tremendous. It had come after a loud clap above them, the sound of the phoenix striking its wings together. Liz wished she had taken more time on the journey over to read up on phoenix mythology, but the drinks trolley had been stocking a good single malt, and whiskey took away her memories.

Shit!

Fire bathed the vehicle like a flaming waterfall, melting the tires, igniting rubber seals, warping and cracking metal, shattering glass, and the sounds were worse than the heat, rocking the car from side to side as every air pocket exploded and the metal shell split in two. They were surrounded by the flames. The stench of burning was awful, a nightmare, *her* nightmare, and Liz opened her mouth to scream against the memories being dredged up. But there was no air in the car, and her scream remained unborn.

Something grasped at her arm, and she saw the skin on Dimitris's hand bubble and blister as he squeezed.

Liz kicked open her door and rolled out into the flames.

The fire stopped. It died out as quickly as it had come, leaving only the ruined car in its wake. Metal pinged and cracked as it continued to expand and rupture. Tires were black puddles in the dust. Glass ran. And at last, Liz found the air to scream.

The phoenix sitting on the car roof looked down at her almost casually. It had curled its claws through the metal, and now it shifted its footing so that it could turn to face her head-on. It was beautiful. Coppery plumage, merging to a gorgeous deep plum color on its wing tips. Huge wings, narrow and graceful, and a long curved beak that looked as finely crafted as a musical instrument. She caught its eye, and it tilted its head to one side, as if waiting for her to speak.

Liz stood, brushing her hands subconsciously over her smoldering clothes. The bird watched, tilted its head some more, and then it bowed three times. *Damn, I wish I'd read more!* she thought again, but regrets could do her no favors. She bowed three times in return, never taking her eyes from the phoenix.

The giant bird opened its wings and stood upright on the car, calling into the blazing sky and shaking its head. Liz cringed down, expecting it to throw its wings together again. *They only conjure fire to destroy themselves.* At least, that was what she seemed to remember. And it was this fact that had been bugging her all day. If this really was the phoenix of myth and legend, how come it was conjuring fire at will?

What had pissed it off?

"We need to talk," she said. The bird looked down at her again and opened and closed its beak. Then it screeched, the sound so loud and forced that its body shook with the effort, claws squealing against metal where they had pierced the car's roof.

Liz looked down quickly, pleased to see that Dimitris was moving. He didn't look too good . . . but at least he was not dead. Yet.

And then she had an idea. She'd always hated the saying "Fight fire with fire," but if this thing was screeching like this to show off—as a display of power—then she, too, could play that game. So long as it didn't get the wrong idea and turn this into a mating ritual.

"Here!" she said. "Fiery ass!" She closed her eyes, picturing Dimitris's skin melting as he had squeezed her arm, and when she looked again, her hand was clothed in flame.

The bird stilled its strident calling and seemed shocked for a few seconds, standing there with giant wings unfurled and head tilted as it stared down at this other firestarter.

"I have this," Liz said. She turned her hand over, and the fire consumed her arm, moving up to her neck and curling around her throat like a pet snake. "It's a true power, isn't it? And it's beautiful. Feels like a cool kiss on my skin." She played with the fire. The familiar thrill came to her, unbidden and mostly unbearable. She hated what this curse had done, yet she loved this gift. Hellboy had once told her that something could be both, and he should know. You only had to open your mind to see the ugliness and beauty in everything.

The phoenix was watching the fire twist and coil around her arm, transfixed. Liz could hear its breathing above the sound of the car cooling. *If the fuel tank goes up . . .* she thought, but there was little she could do about that. Dimitris's best chance was for her to distract this thing, or even to calm it down. Anything else—more fire, more flames, more rage—and he would die.

The bird's breath was like the whistle of a tuned flute. It sang to her, or to her fire.

"No rage or anger here," she said. "Nothing to hurt you, nothing to hate. Just the fire we both know so well. Let's look at the fire for a while . . ." Liz stared at her own hand, bewitched. Control was good, but at times like this, she knew that there was really no such thing. She could funnel her power but never truly manage it. It was untamed. Like a wild animal performing tricks in a circus, it was merely obeying her command. Deep down where it really came from, down in the depths of her mind that she had never been able to plumb, it was ferocious.

And as her curiously becalmed mind acknowledged that, the phoenix began to laugh.

Liz dropped her hand and let the fire gutter away to nothing.

The bird was snorting through nostrils high on its beak. It shook, but with mirth this time instead of rage. The car vibrated below it, Dimitris crawled out, and the phoenix looked down at his blackened head, the clothing scorched from his body, his olive skin turned red, split, weeping . . .

"Liz," Dimitris croaked, raising his hand as if to hold on to her memory.

The phoenix reared up, clapped its wings together, and conjured the greatest conflagration it would ever know.

Liz retreated into herself. Even the heat of this mythological fire could not mirror the fury of her own memories. She was eleven years old again, living with her family, and something went wrong, and everything was heat and light and pain—physical pain for the people she loved, mental pain for her. Anguish that would last a lifetime, and beyond. Guilt that would swallow her up and spit her out many times over. There was screaming and melting and dying, and it was all because of her and through her.

From outside, other fires came in. They merged with her experience and became memory, and there was a single new scream—brief but intense—that added itself to her gallery of screams, all those exhalations of terror that she had heard through the years, all those cries that came because of her, and what she was, and what she could do. She collected screams, and in her nightmares she viewed this collection.

When Liz surfaced, the new phoenix was rising from the remains of the old. It shrugged itself from the scalding remains, testing its new wings, their colors fresh and vibrant even through the layers of ash. It looked at Liz, and she was sure it was staring down at her hand. She flexed her fingers, and fire danced there.

The phoenix turned away and gathered its mummified father into its claws, ready to launch itself for its fledgling flight to Egypt. Then it took off without sparing Liz another glance.

She stood shivering in the heat, gathering the remnants of her scorched clothing around her, crying. The tears washed a clean route through the soot on her face. They burned.

"No!" she exclaimed. "Oh, no!" She almost went to him, but she knew there was no need.

Dimitris was little more than a greasy stain on the road.

Somewhere over the North Sea—1997

The rukh drifted on air currents high in the sky, its massive wings spread wide to catch the updrafts. Its great beak cut through the air, so streamlined that there was no noise as the atmosphere parted around it. Although it was more than strong enough to carry the weight of the two fully grown cows, each claw hung low beneath it, and wind raged around them. They were dragging it down, and every now and then it beat its wings once and soared a hundred feet higher. One of the cows still bayed helplessly. The other was dead, the bird's talons having pierced its heart upon lifting it from the ground.

Hanging from the rukh's beak were the fleshy remnants of the rest of the herd.

It drifted northward. The slate-gray sea far below offered no points of reference, and yet the bird knew exactly where it was going. Home was a bright point in its mind. The sea was shaded by different tides, varying temperatures, and here and there white smears told where waves had broken and given birth to brief white horses. Clouds wisped the air below and around the bird, and sometimes it dipped itself through the tailing edge of a cloud, reveling in the coolness the moisture bestowed upon its warm body. The effort of flying so far had tired the rukh; even though it had just eaten, the flight had been long, and the cows were growing cumbersome.

Way overhead, the deep, dark blue of the edge of space. A mile below, the shaded gray of the North Sea. And around it, the wide open sky.

At last, in the distance, a blur appeared on the textured sheen of the ocean. The bird cawed once, cracking the air like thunder. It tilted its wings and drifted lower. The surviving cow, ears shattered by the rukh's call, bayed one more time and then died. The rukh twitched one wing and turned a few degrees to the left, aiming for the blot on the ocean, delight filling its impossible mind.

The blot grew to a spot, the spot to a definite shape. Long, and from this distance still narrow and small. Behind the shape lay a smeared white line in the ocean, evidence of where the shape had just been, pointing at where it had yet to go. The rukh drifted lower and adjusted its grip on the dead cattle. It would have to drop them before it could land.

The shape resolved itself into a boat, and it grew larger and larger as the rukh approached. And larger still. The boat dwarfed even the huge bird. Fifteen hundred feet long, more than two hundred feet wide, the former oil tanker had lost all trappings of its previous existence. No slicks accompanied this vessel's movement across the ocean. No port of registration appeared anywhere on its hull, for it was its own home, and it had not rubbed against a dock in almost twenty years. And its true name appeared only in the minds of its inhabitants, human and otherwise. The *New Ark* was a whole new world in itself . . . and what a world.

The rukh cried out again in delight and prepared to make its landing run. One set of the ship's great hold doors was lifting, the vessel opening itself up to the bird, and it could see shapes scurrying across the deck in preparation for its arrival. The horn blared as if to answer the rukh's call.

On the parapet surrounding the high bridge, unmoving and yet more visible than any other living shape on the ship, the rukh could see its father.

As it neared the vessel, the bird could make out the hidden protection that had kept it secret for so long. Just as the ocean seen from on high had different shades, so did the sea in the immediate vicinity of the hull. Great shapes drifted below the surface, their direction and speed having nothing to do with temperature, or depth, or the raging currents. These shapes—some of them almost a third the size of the massive ship—dictated their own direction. Some kept pace with the *New Ark*, others moved farther afield, and some rose from and dived to depths that light never reached. Their shapes were concealed, their true nature unfathomable. They were shadows on the sheen of reality.

The giant bird approached the *New Ark*, hovering lower. Downdraft from its wings disturbed the waters around the hull, creating whirlpools and eddies. When it was directly above the hold, it dropped the two cows down into the belly of the ship—that strangest of places, that dark hole where the light of creation burned fiercely and this world no longer really existed—and looked up at the bridge.

The rukh's father was there. And he was smiling.

The rukh called out once more, its joyful cry winging across the North Sea like a spirit only recently set free, and then it settled itself into its home once more.

The man on the bridge continued to smile as the hold doors closed slowly above the giant bird. A unicorn galloped along the deck, and his smile broke into a grin. A mile to starboard the sea erupted as something huge and bright red broke the surface for a few seconds. A forest of tentacles slapped at the air as the thing dived for unknown depths, and Benedict Blake's grin erupted into a laugh. Nowhere near as loud as the rukh's call, still it filled the sky and winged its way out over the waves. Soon his voice would at last reach the ears of those who mattered. And then it would be his time once again.

Baltimore, Maryland—1997

It was nighttime, and it was hot, and Abby Paris should have been back at BPRD headquarters hours ago. Instead she was walking the streets, just another face hiding an anonymous life behind averted eyes. Most people wandered in pairs or groups, chatting and laughing, shouting and giggling. Light and noise spilled from bars and restaurants. The smell of food permeated the air, steak and seafood and sweet stuff all adding their own signatures to the night. She tried to shut out that sense, but she could not. Heightened smell was another part of her curse. As was hunger; but not for this. She stopped by a street vendor and bought six doughnuts, ate them, then vomited them back up ten minutes later. She held on to some park railings and heaved, splashing her shoes. A passerby paused for a moment and watched, then moved on. A police cruiser slowed and sped up again, and she wondered what the policemen had seen that had prevented them from stopping and arresting her. Just another drunk? Or something else entirely?

Abby wiped away her tears and looked at her hand, but there was no change there. It was several days until full moon, but as always she wanted meat.

She had reported in to BPRD after killing the werewolf. He had reverted seconds after she put the bullet through his brain, but she knew that many of the bystanders had seen what she had seen, heard what she had heard. She knew also that the human mind had a way of ignoring such strangeness and relegating it to the stuff of nightmares. Most of those present would shake their heads, look down at their

feet, assume that the shock of what had happened had conjured fanciful images in their minds. Those who doubted
their eyesight less would still say nothing, through fear of
ridicule. And if there had been one man there, or one
woman, who truly believed what he or she had seen, that
person would be called insane.

For all anyone cared, Abby had killed a man in cold
blood and then walked away.

She had spoken to Tom Manning. He had told her to
come in, she had agreed, then she had gone for a walk. And
now she was still walking, and it felt good. It was good to be
out from BPRD, free for a night. They were her family, but
they were also her prison guards, keeping her locked away
for her own protection and the protection of those around
her. These people here, swaying along the pavement and
paying homage to the alcohol in their blood. Those people
there, sweating and grunting in a shadowy doorway. Inno-
cents all of them, cattle going about their daily lives of eating and drinking and rutting without realizing that monsters lived among them.

"Monsters like me," she said, but she shook her head so
hard that she cricked her neck. No, she was not a monster.
She had shed that name the instant she escaped from Blake.

*The man knew who I was talking about. Blake! He denied
it, but in his eyes I saw that spark of understanding . . . and
something else. Something that could have been recognition.*
And that was why Abby walked. Because of Benedict Blake,
and what he had done, and the secret that she had carried
from the second Abe Sapien set his strange hand on her arm
in Paris and rescued her from the night.

———————

She could remember few details of her life before Paris. There was Blake, the force in her mind and the physical presence that had nurtured her, and there was her escape from him. Plunging through the night into the ice-cold embrace of the ocean; the panicked swim; those massive things moving beneath her, deep down and yet so huge that they seemed to exert a fearful gravity, pulling her down with them. Something touched her legs more than once on that long swim, but it never held her back. Fear drove her on, fear of what Blake was and what he might one day do. Somehow she *could* fear him—the others did not—and that was another secret she had dwelled upon ever since. After that, there were only fleeting memories of Paris, none of them good. None, that is, until Abe Sapien touched her arm. His touch had seemed to welcome her to the world, unnatural thing that she was. And Abe had welcomed her into his life. *We have like minds,* he had said as she coughed the Seine water from her lungs.

But he did not know her. And deep down, she hoped that he was wrong.

She had plenty of guilt to walk off. She could pretend it was culpability at the killing of the werewolf, but that was not true. When she thought of that thing lying in the road as she put a bullet through its eye, she felt nothing. This was a deeper, sicker feeling, one that stank of betrayal. Betrayal of her friends. They had taken her in and cared for her, and she had told them nothing. She had lied. She found it strange that freedom only increased that sense of guilt.

She passed a burnt-out building and paused for a moment, wondering whether she should go inside and find somewhere to sit for the night. A man and a woman passed her and averted their eyes. She stared at them, hoping they would say something that would change her mind. But they walked on, wrapped up in their own small world. Sometimes Abby scoffed at such narrow-mindedness, but most of the time she wanted to be just like them.

Her satellite phone rang, and she sighed. That would be BPRD asking where she was. Tom, probably, the concern in his voice barely masking the worry he had about her being out on her own. She plucked the phone from her pocket.

"Hello."

"Abby? Tom. Where are you? I thought you were coming in."

"I . . . I am, Tom. I'm still in Baltimore. Walking. Couple of things about the guy I killed I'm still trying to work through in my head."

"Hmm. Well, can you work them through back here? The shit's really hitting the fan right now, and I could do with your help."

"What's happened?"

"Sightings," Tom said. "Lots of sightings."

"Sightings of what."

"Well . . . things. Dragons. Sea serpents. Other weird stuff."

"Where?" Abby already felt a chill, the sweat on her brow cooling.

"Everywhere," Tom said. "Abby, come home. Abe's on his way back, and I'm hoping to hear from Hellboy and Liz soon. I think we're in for a busy couple of days."

Abby cut the connection and pocketed the phone without agreeing to return, hoping that Tom would take that as a yes. *Dragons . . . sea serpents . . . other weird stuff.* She closed her eyes and allowed in the memory of her dreams, and they were filled with bad things.

Blake.

And she suddenly knew that she would not be returning home.

Abby Paris remembered her dreams, and she knew that the dreams were memories in disguise. In those memories she was nameless, because she had yet to be named; she was empty, waiting to be filled with history; and she was unsettled.

Yet still she remembered herself as Abby, because to remember herself with no name was like being nothing.

She walks through the *New Ark*, a young girl in a world she does not understand, and yet she regards it as normal. She knows nothing else. She is a teenager, but she can remember nothing of her childhood. She knows the reasons for this—the evidence is all around her—though she does not understand that, either. Understanding is for Blake; her job is simply being. That is what she had been told. *You exist, creature, because I give you my will to exist,* Blake told her. *You are here because I brought you, you breathe air because I allow it, and in your creation there was a pledge of faith to me. Wander the ship, but do not wonder. See what is happening, but do not question. Your time in the Memory is over, and now you have a new home in reality. Accept that, accept me, and your future is one of triumph.*

That was the only time Blake ever spoke to her. She has seen him many times since then, working at a vat or wandering through the ship. But although he always offers her a smile and a nod, he never speaks. He is a tall, thin, ghostly figure, and for some reason he always reminds Abby of her time before memory began. That is a dark time, and Blake carries darkness with him. It is also a deep, hollow time, filled with nothing but space, and when she looks into the tall man's eyes—past the light of passion, past the shades of madness—she can see the hollowness that lies at his core.

The hollowness of her own mind has its ghosts as well. They are knowledge and intelligence, things that she was born with but that are not exactly hers. Her first memory is of Blake staring down at her, smiling as he uses a rough old cloth to wipe fluids from her eyes, clearing them, ensuring that he is the very first thing she ever focuses on. Even then she has a strange awareness, and yet everything this aware-ness brings up feels as though it has been left behind in her mind by someone or something else. Her life is new, her mind old. She screams. Blake steps back, still smiling, and she thinks her first true thought: *He's more than used to this.*

Experience with no history; life with no true birth; knowledge without a past. She accepts them all and yet yearns for something more: understanding.

The hollowness inside her, haunted though it is, needs filling. And this is when she first perceives her need for es-cape.

On the day she leaves, there is one goodbye to make.

Few of Blake's creations speak any sort of language that Abby can understand. They fly or crawl, walk or slither, sleep or scream, but there is only one other creature whom Abby has any sort of communication with, and she never sees him. He—she assumes it is a he, simply because of his voice—is contained behind a heavy steel door, and the only space through which he can talk is a narrow grille at its base. Abby first noticed him soon after her birthing, when she wandered naked through the ship trying to find who she was, and since then she has been back at regular intervals to talk with him.

Her voice feels like an alien in her throat, the thoughts that conjure it strangers in her mind. It is the hidden creature—Voice, as she has come to know him—who helps her come to terms with herself. His words are few, but their meaning is always deep. He has built her from nothing to something, and years later she realizes that it was Voice who made her something more than Blake ever intended. He gave her the thirst to fill her potential. And he made her free.

On that final night, she sits on the floor and leans back against the door. She can hear him breathing on the other side, and she likes to think that the metal is warmed by his breath. Some contact, at least. Some affection. Without really understanding or knowing why, that is something she has always missed.

"It's so dark in here," she says.

"It's made that way."

"You told me years ago that he locked you away because of what you think, and what you know. Why doesn't he lock me away as well?"

A snort comes from behind the door. "Because I made no secret of my doubt. I've told you before, you're unique here. You're a bright mind among stupidity. You're *human*. The fact that Blake didn't take that into account shows just how mad he has become. He has these things he has brought out of the Memory—you and me included—and because of that, he has begun to doubt the facility of humanity. He's committed the very crime that put everything in this *New Ark* into the Memory in the first place, except that he's committed it against humans. He doubts them, looks down upon them, and that has made him underestimate them."

"And *I'm* human?" Abby doubts that, because there is something else deep down that drives her. Like a blazing fire behind a locked door, it surges for release at frequent intervals.

"As human as anything aboard this ship, Blake included."

"And you, Voice?"

Voice is quiet for a long time, and Abby begins to think he has fallen asleep. But then she feels movement at her back, a subtle vibration transmitted through the metal of the door, and when he speaks it sounds as though he is crying. "Abby, it's time for you to leave. Escape. You're looking for a life, and you'll never find it in here. Here, there's only death waiting for the right time to visit."

"Voice?" Abby is shocked, but it is more at the way he seems to be reading her mind than anything else. *Escape*, she has been thinking for weeks. *Escape is the only way.* Perhaps seeking Voice's approval is the impetus she really needs.

"Go," he says, and that is the last she hears.

Abby stands. She has been planning this for some time, never really believing that it would happen; it was a fancy, a daydream, a glimpse of a future that would never be. Now that she is actually going through with it, she finds herself calmer and more composed than she has any right to be. She is leaving home for the first time, with only the good wishes of someone or something locked away from the world to see her on her way.

The stern will be the best place for her to jump from. Even if she is seen, it will take hours for the *New Ark* to halt and come back to look for her. And it seems fitting that, at the moment of her plunging into the sea, she and Blake will be parting company at the greatest speed possible.

"Goodbye," she whispers at the metal door. But it will be years before she knows whether or not Voice even hears.

On this, her final walk through the other world that is the *New Ark*, she takes in everything and commits it to memory. *One day*, she is thinking, *it may all be useful.* She never intends to return to Blake's realm, yet she knows that a part of her will never be able to leave.

She heads through the maze of rooms and cells at the bow of the great ship. It is dark in here, occasional lights flickering and blinking as the troubled generator soldiers on. A drone passes her, and she pauses to watch it go. She has never discovered the source of these things, and Voice claims not to know. Of one fact she is certain: they are not born out of the vats. Blake has created these creatures, not dragged them out of the Memory, and to Abby's mind that makes them more of a travesty. Gray, short, sallow, strong of muscle but weak of mind, the drones run the ship and do all the work that is necessary in keeping Blake's creatures alive and well. She has never seen them when they are not working. She has never seen a drone resting. She has never even seen a dead drone, though there are plenty of places where corpses can be disposed of inside the *New Ark*.

"Hey!" she says. The drone stops and turns, pointing its doglike face her way and averting its eyes. They *never* meet her eyes. Blake has made them less than the other things aboard the huge ship, and they seem to know their place. "What do you do to rest?" she asks.

"Huh," the drone says.

She has never been able to make any sense in the noise, and even now she is still unsure whether there is any intelligence behind it at all.

"What do you eat?"

"Huh."

"What do you like to do?"

"Huh."

"Touch your toes." The creature bends and fingers its toes. "Stand up." It stands. "Why are you here?"

"Huh."

Abby feels tears blurring her vision, and she wipes at them angrily. She knows nothing other than what she has been born with, yet this thing pains her, *offends* her. It is nothing so shallow as mourning the creature's rights or feeling upset at the abuse; it is more as though she senses the fallacy of the drone's existence. Everything else on this ship—all the creatures she is about to pass by for the very last time—has risen out of rightness. Cast as they have been into the Memory, still they had their time, and they take up a space in the world that was once meant for them. These drones that Blake made are simply wrong.

"Get the hell out of here," she whispers, and the drone turns and leaves. She continues her final walk to the stern.

The first of the chambers is hot and humid, bustling with activity. Drones dash here and there, fussing about the huge steel vat that stands at the center of the chamber. Abby feels a thrill of power as she hides back in the shadows to watch. She came from a vat—perhaps even this one—drawn out of the Memory and given life. That was natural, and that was also magic, and she has spent the years since her birthing struggling to come to terms with both. She walked, she thought, she talked with Voice, and she dreamed, but she could make out no true dividing line between what Benedict Blake plucked out of nature and what he forced back into it. Magic was a bending of its rules, but it was far less simple than that. There were complexities and subtleties, and however many birthings she witnessed—scores, perhaps a hundred—she never understood what she was truly seeing.

"One last time?" she whispers. "Shall I try to comprehend what I'm seeing one last time?" Her head tells her to flee, now that the idea of escape is upon her. But her heart bids her to stay, to watch. Because in truth, each birthing is beautiful. And every new creation she witnesses makes her feel more justified in being alive.

The vat—huge enough to hold Abby a hundred times over—is starting to shake and smoke, and several drones dash out from beneath it, squealing. Something has pattered down on their gray hides, and patches of skin seem to be fading into nothing. *The Memory is leaking*, Abby thinks. She tries to make out shapes in the darkness beneath the vat, wondering what can be slipping through between sheet-metal whose rivets have been weakened over the decades. Shadows flail, another drone runs out, its rear half already seemingly vanished.

"More hydrochloric acid!" a voice roars. Blake is in the room.

She sinks farther back into shadows, kneeling behind a pile of discarded crates. What they contain she does not know, but they stink of fish and chalk. She peers between two crates and watches the man walk down a metal staircase.

His long coat swings around his feet, giving the impression that he floats rather than walks, and his gray beard reaches his chest. His shoulders are narrow, his hands splayed as if it hurts for his fingers to touch. Blake's face burns with excitement, and his eyes catch the weak electrical light and reflect it back as a fierce glare. "More acid, damn you!"

Two drones scamper up steps set into the side of the vat and swing on a metal wheel. It squeals and then opens, letting a spray of fluid down into the vat. The smoke and vibration lessen, and the drones close the wheel and drop back to the deck.

"Bring it through too soon, and it'll never coalesce," Blake says. He reaches the bottom of the stairs and stands with hands on hips, staring up at the vat even though he cannot see what it contains. The drones fuss around him, but he ignores them. The vat shakes again, as if whatever it contains senses Blake's presence, and Abby realizes that he is the center of the *New Ark*, its heart, its tainted soul. There is nothing grand or even intimidating about his appearance— he is an old man—but he seems to exude a power that keeps the vat turning. "Not long now," he whispers, and his voice fills the chamber. "Not long now, and the next of my children will be through."

What this time? she thinks. Hidden away behind the crates, she thinks of all the strange creatures this ship is home to, and she tries her best to imagine what could be forming in the vat even now. Does it have wings or horns? Does it breathe air or water? Can it make fire or ice? Her hackles rise as a noise erupts from the vat—boiling liquid, or the growl of something already there—and she feels her own hidden strangeness aching to break out.

Blake hurries to a control panel set in the side of the vat. He taps some dials, shades a display from the flickering light, and moves in close so that he can read it. He seems happy with what he can see. "Coming along fine!" he shouts, and Abby wonders whom he is talking to. The drones? Unlikely.

Me?

She shifts uncomfortably. She's still certain that Blake does not know of her presence; he must be talking to himself. After so long out here, he must crave company. She wonders for the thousandth time why he has never spoken to her since her birthing, though she is one of the few "children" of his possessing intelligence enough for the gift of speech. The potential answer—that he does not truly care— hurts her as much as ever.

"Crazy," she whispers. "He's a crazy old bastard." Even on the verge of escape, she almost goes to talk to him.

But then something rises from the vat, something black and huge and monstrous, and Blake steps back, arms wide, face split by a maniacal smile, and he cries out in joy. "Black dog! My black dog!"

The dog—five times the size of Abby, coated with slime and still spitting weird green ectoplasm at the shady air of the vat chamber—opens its mouth and barks for the first time in living memory.

Later, rushing through the ship, everything she sees crushing in on her, Abby at last realizes the importance of everything she has seen and known. It is as if leaving has given her sight, allowed her truly to perceive the very *wrongness* of all this. These creatures are terribly real and yet awfully redundant, their purposes on this world having long since faded away. They have had their time. Evolved out of humankind's collective mind, these things have been relegated to something darker and more distant than simple memory, a place where even legends no longer live and the memories of legends are less than sighs in a hurricane.

Abby is one of those legends, and rushing through the ship, she feels that more keenly than ever. The knowledge cuts her, stabs her to the quick. It almost carves out her heart. But Abby has a mind, and she has a soul, and being here, though not of her own devices, is something she cannot deny. She is here, and she wants to continue being here. Life is precious. Perhaps, she thinks, even legends can find their own places in the world once more.

Later, when she realizes that she has been fooling herself all along, the memory of her last contact with Blake will seem like the last time she has ever been alive.

Abby runs the entire length of the ship, from compartment to compartment, hold to hold. She rushes past the compounds and cages and cells, hearing their occupants screeching at her passing and growling at her meaty presence. She shoulders by things milling in corridors, creatures with dripping maws and the blistering stares of memories given a second chance. She even speaks to some of the things in the ship—a man who lives by drinking blood, some women with the tails of fish bobbing in a huge water tank—but she is nothing like them. They are blanks upon which Blake has

cast his anger and rage. However smart they may seem—
and in one room there is something like an angel, singing
songs of deliverance and growling the threat of vengeance
falling from above—Abby is running with her own mind,
not standing around waiting in tune with the mind of another.

She wonders briefly why that can be, but dwelling on it
will make her just like them.

She hopes that news of her impending escape will not
reach Blake's ears. By its very nature, the ship contains
things that run, fly, or squirm their way back and forth, and
she does not seem to attract any undue attention. Yet intent
is there, and she hopes it will not mark out this particular
running woman as something different.

At last, at the giant ship's stern, with the cold night pressing in and the promise of colder water already tingling her
skin, she hears the voice she has wished to never hear again.

"You can't leave me," Blake says.

Abby pauses, panting, and turns to face her father. "I
can. I am. I'm not like you, not like any of *them*." She waves
her hand back the way she has come. She is terrified. She
has no idea how he got here before her—the last she saw of
him, he was bending over the black dog back in the birthing
chamber—but there is still so much she does not understand.

"No, you're not," Blake says. "You're unique. Every one
of you is unique."

"I'm not a monster."

Blake steps forward, and a light on the bulkhead stutters
on. He is unruffled and calm, though he looks older than
she has ever remembered. "What *is* a monster?" he says.

"Something . . . something that . . ."

"Yes?" He moves closer still, and she sees what he is trying to do. Shadows flit at the extremes of her vision, and though she cannot see them, she can sense the drones creeping into position. Soon they will grab her, and then she will find herself imprisoned until freedom is Blake's choice, not her own.

She steps to the rail and curves one leg over. The cool metal sits across the underside of her thigh, and she realizes this is the first time even a part of her has been beyond the ship.

"Full moon soon!" Blake says, glancing at the sky. "The hunger will be upon you. The griffin will come in with your food, and you'll rip and tear and thank me. But if you go . . . what then? What will a werewolf eat in a world she doesn't know?"

"Stay away from me!" she says, holding up a hand. The nails are longer, fingers more muscled. Full moon tomorrow, yes, but tonight the tides are already at war in her blood, and her flesh is weak.

"Look at me," Blake says. "I'm no monster. I bring my children back to the world simply because they've been forgotten, allowed to fade away. That's no way to treat a child."

"They're not children!" she snaps.

Blake shrugs, and she sees a glimmer in his eyes—amusement. She is amusing him. He's talking to her, biding time while his drones prepare to grab her, and he's finding this humorous.

"You're mad," she whispers.

Blake raises his eyebrows and holds up one hand. "Ahh," he says. And then he nods.

Abby falls sideways to the deck, and the first drone passes over her, crashing into the railing. She kicks out and sends it shrieking into the sea. The second drone grabs her arm, but she twists away, snapping at its throat and ripping flesh and sinew. She spits. The blood is rank, like old oil, and the flesh tastes bland and insipid. There is nothing to these things. Two more drones attach themselves to her, Blake laughs . . . and instead of fighting them off, Abby goes for the old man.

The next few seconds are a confusion in her memory. Blood and screams, the impact of flesh on flesh, her teeth crunching together, and a long, desperate howl that can only be her own as she falls from the ship and splashes into the water. She swims hard, kicking against the flow, pulling with her hands, knocking aside the drones that fell with her, and hearing their panicked squeals as they are sucked into the giant propellers. Seconds stretch into minutes, and at last she floats on her back, riding the swell and surprised that she can swim. She looks up at the shadow of her father, standing at the railing high above and staring down at Abby. Believing, perhaps, that she is dead. He says nothing. He does not move. Abby floats, staring up past her father at the waxing moon, and even as the tanker moves quickly away, she sees him standing there, looking back at her with mad eyes she hopes she will never see again.

Abby sat in the shade of a huge, anonymous building in Baltimore and cried. She remembered swimming ashore at last and finding her way to Paris. Freedom had never tasted the way she thought, and soon the Seine served to drown her sorrows. And then Abe was there, giving her a place in the world, whereas Blake had only given her a life . . . and that was too painful to dwell upon as well. Because she was about to betray Abe—him and everyone at the BPRD—simply because she could not face admitting her lie.

Her tears were not for herself but for that girl she had been. Innocent, unknowing, ripped out of myth and given something that resembled life by Benedict Blake, all to further his own madness and feed his hate. She cried also for what was to come. Because if the werewolf she had killed really was from Blake, then the other things even now being sighted across the globe were probably his as well. And that could mean only one thing: whatever insanity he had been courting over the decades was soon to come to fruition.

And she knew exactly what the *New Ark* contained.

"Help us all," she sobbed. "Oh, God, whoever, help us all now that he's here!" Unable to calm herself, she gave in to the tears. Once she was cried out, she knew, she had to leave to find Blake. He was her creator—her father—and only she had an inkling of how he could be stopped.

Having escaped, and lied, Abby Paris felt responsibility crush down upon her.

Bureau of Paranormal Research and Defense Headquarters, Fairfield, Connecticut—1997

Tom Manning, director of the Bureau of Paranormal Research and Defense, was having a very bad day.

"Where the hell is Hellboy?"

"I don't know, sir." The man running the Bureau's communications that day, Chris Moore, shrank down in his seat, offering Manning a smaller target.

Manning seemed to grow, pumped up with disbelief. "You don't know? How the hell can you not know? The guy's seven feet tall and red. Someone in Rio must have seen him!"

"I've got a lecturer on the phone," Moore said. "She was with Hellboy when—"

"Is it Amelia Francis?"

"Yes, sir."

Manning closed his eyes and breathed deeply. He held out his hand without looking at Moore, still breathing slow and deep. "Here. Let me." He felt the communications officer place the headset in his hand, sensed him rise and walk away, and Manning silently cursed himself for losing his cool. In this job, cool was essential. "Thank you," he said. He looked at Moore; the poor kid was pale as chalk, his shirt patched with sweat. "Do me a favor, Chris, and bring me some coffee."

"Decaf?"

"Full-fat. Strong as you can get. I want a bucket of coffee I can float a horseshoe in." Manning was pleased to see Moore break a smile as he left the room.

"Amelia."

"Tom . . ." She sounded scared; bad sign number one. And number two: there was screaming in the background.

"Amelia, what's going on there? Where's Hellboy?"

"He's fallen into the bay," the woman said, her voice crackling with emotion and static. "The dragon just picked him up and dropped him in the bay . . . horrible, it must have been a thousand feet high . . . and then it flew away."

"What's the screaming?"

"Now that it's gone, people are starting to believe it was really here."

Manning rubbed his eyes, frowned. "Wait a minute. You called this in more than twenty-four hours ago. You're saying that it waited till Hellboy got there, kicked his ass, then flew off into the sunset?"

"Well . . ."

"Amelia, get Hellboy to call me as soon as you can."

Silence. Even the screaming had calmed down.

Manning smiled. "He'll be fine, Amelia. He's . . . hard. But really, do your best to find him and get him to call in. Something's going on."

He clicked off the phone, redialed, and was grateful to hear Liz Sherman on the other end.

"Tom?"

"Liz, how did it go?"

"Bad."

One word, but it spoke volumes. Tom almost wished he could sign off, but there was so much more going on today. Abby Paris still hadn't returned from Baltimore, and Moore had not been able to track her satellite phone signal. Abe Sapien had called in to report his encounter with the giant alligator. And other BPRD agents were investigating other sightings, every report only confusing the picture and making it more terrifying. Kate Corrigan was due in soon, and for that Manning gave endless thanks, but already he could discern a purpose forming in these sightings. What he and the rest of the Bureau had to do now was find out just what that purpose was.

"Are you all right?"

"I am." Liz emphasised the "I," and Manning decided not to ask.

"Liz, do you want to come in?"

"Should I?"

"Not unless you really have to. Because I have to tell you, there's seven shades of shit hitting the fan at the moment, and if you can go to Madrid, I'd be most grateful."

"What's in Madrid?"

"A griffin. It started carrying off horses, but now it's eating *people*, Liz. There's utter panic there, and the Spanish government is on the verge of calling in NATO."

"Oh, that'll help," Liz drawled, and Manning smiled. He loved her sardonic humor, even though he knew it masked such depths.

"So will you go?"

"Where's HB?"

"Just got his ass kicked by a dragon in Rio."

"Oh. Sure, I'll go."

"I'll e-mail you the contact details in Madrid. Thanks, Liz."

"Don't mention it."

Manning signed off, and Moore came in with a huge mug of steaming coffee and placed it on the desk. It looked as though it could be used to lay felt roofs, and Manning sipped and sighed luxuriantly. "Chris, do you have anything urgent to do at home in the next few days?" he asked.

Moore smiled and shrugged. "This is my home, sir. I'm a geek for weird stuff."

"Ha!" Manning smiled, though he could not shake the feeling of unease that had settled over him. Perhaps it was having most of the field team gone from Bureau HQ. "Well, I think your addiction is set to be well fed over the next few days."

"Sir?"

Manning shook his head, sipped more coffee. "Chris, just see if you can raise Abe. I need him back over here. We

should follow up on that Ogopodo report from Canada."
While Moore tried to contact Abe Sapien, Manning took
the opportunity to finish his coffee. Looking at the map on
the wall—red pins signifying recent sightings of things
weird, wonderful, and deadly—he decided he was going to
need some more.

Rio de Janeiro, Brazil—1997

Hellboy liked fishermen. They led difficult lives, they
worked hard, and they were more accepting than most people of strange things. Every fisherman he had ever had cause
to speak to was full of stories about a weird catch, last week
or last year. And even though most of them never managed
to retain any evidence of what they had hauled up from the
depths, Hellboy usually believed them. The sea hid many
bizarre things—he had never forgotten that shark thing in
'75—and fishermen were witnesses to their discovery. Un-
like most listeners, Hellboy was always willing to believe the
story about "the one that got away."

Of the four Brazilian fishermen in the boat, three sat
staring at him with undisguised fascination. The only reason
the fourth was not staring was that he was steering them
into the busy harbor, but he glanced back every few seconds, as if to make sure the big red guy was still there. They
had pulled him from the bay and sat him in the corner, and
he was grateful they had not bugged him since then. The
staring he was used to.

The cigarette was a soggy mess in his mouth. Wet ciga-

rette tasted terrible. But pride prevented him from spitting
it out.

His chest and face still ached from the impact with the
water. He'd tried to turn as he fell so that he could part the
water with his hands, but he'd never been particularly graceful, and the echo of his belly flop had rung in his ears even
as water rushed in behind it. The impact had dazed him for
a couple of minutes, though he'd been conscious enough to
swim to the surface and tread water. For a while, up was
down and down was up, and he had spent a confused
minute trying to work out why the dragon had been flying
away upside-down. Then his senses had returned, just in
time for the real pain to kick in.

His skin was redder than usual, and his belt had been
scorched black in several places. One pocket had burned
through, and he had placed its remaining contents elsewhere: a Peruvian life crystal on a silver chain, a concussion
grenade, and a ball made of rubber bands. He'd doubtless
lost something, but he had no idea what. He rarely knew
what he carried in his belt, so he'd never miss it. He hoped.

One of the fishermen had been smiling at him for ten
minutes, nodding his head, muttering something Hellboy
could not understand. At first Hellboy had smiled back, but
the guy had cringed, averted his eyes, mumble turning to
shout. So Hellboy sat out the ride looking as glum as he felt,
slowly working the muscles in his neck and shoulders, trying to stretch out the aches and pains that had settled there.

Damn dragon! It had whipped him, discarded him like
just another turd, and that made him angry as hell. With no
sign of a rematch with the dragon apparent, that anger simmered inward. His satellite phone buzzed—incredibly still
working even after its immersion—but he ignored it. Let

them wait. Hellboy was angry and pissed off, and whoever was on the other end would only end up getting the sharp end of his tongue. That thought took him back to the dragon, and the time *he'd* been called a dragon, and he had to clench his fists to prevent them from taking a swing at something.

The smiling fisherman and his friends were starting to get on his nerves, too. They may have pulled him from the sea, but that gave them only a certain amount of license to gape. That license was rapidly running out. Hellboy stood, walked to the bow without glancing at the men, and tried to make out who'd be waiting for him at the harbor. Whoever it was, they'd know that he had messed up.

Something nudged his hand. He spun around, and the man cringed but still offered up a small wooden box. Hellboy smiled, nodded, and the man gave him a toothless smile in return. "Sorry," Hellboy said. "Hasn't been a good day. But thank you." He took the box, opened it, selected a cigarette, and presented the open box back. The man raised his eyebrows and took a cigarette as well. "Got a light?"

The fisherman nodded. He lit Hellboy's cigarette and his own, and the two men sat and smoked contentedly as the little trawler edged in toward the dock.

The harbor was a riot of activity. Hundreds of boats of all shapes, sizes, and colors bobbed against jetties and docks, and the sound of rubber rings squealing against timber bumpers provided a constant background to the hubbub. They sailed past a selection of yachts that probably cost more than Hellboy could even imagine. Scantily clad women lounged picturesquely on recliners, while muscled men swam and dived and strutted their stuff. Hellboy would have laughed, had his ribs not ached so much.

They docked in the fishing harbor, a place filled with the smell of the sea and the sound of forklifts transporting cooler boxes to and fro. Trawlers sat two or three abreast against the dock, and fishermen bustled about, repairing nets, loading provisions, and washing down guts-strewn decks. Others sat in their boats, smoking, drinking, laughing together, or staring sadly out to sea, as if they had left a part of themselves out there.

Hellboy thanked his rescuers again and accepted another cigarette from them for later. They seemed much more animated now that he was about to leave. He touched his horn stumps in an unconscious salute and turned quickly away as the men's eyes strayed there, and stayed.

Along the stone dock, just before it hit the mainland in a chaos of warehouses and fish markets, he found two men rooting through a spread of containers set out across the ground. At first he thought they were sorting their catch by size or grade, but on closer inspection he realized that they were weeding out bad fish and throwing them back into the sea. Hellboy paused to watch. The two men had not yet noticed him, and he waited until one of the discarded fish was close enough for him to grab from the air.

"What's this?" In the palm of his big right hand lay the discarded fish. It had two heads. "What the *hell* is this?"

One of the two men looked up. His brief surprise at seeing Hellboy faded quickly, countered by the sadness that tainted his voice when he spoke. "Bad fish."

"Damn right it's bad," Hellboy said. "Jeez!" He looked closer, but suddenly the smell hit him. Not only was it mutated, it stank. "Why?"

The man looked up, waved his hands at the air, and for a second Hellboy thought he was blaming God. But then the man crossed himself and shrugged. "Filthy air," he said.

"Pollution?"

"Yes." He turned from Hellboy and carried on with his task.

Hellboy walked away, listening to the intermittent *splash, splash, splash* from behind him as bad fish were returned to the harbor to rot. As human as he tried to be, he had never been able to understand the streak of self-destruction that seemed to pass through most of humanity like a seam of crap in a gold mine. They had it all, and they were slowly but surely throwing it all away. He glanced back at the posh yachts moored farther out and thought how such riches should really lead to better things, not worse. The women preened while the men posed. The more money they had, the more inward-looking they became. He shook his head, but much as he tried to believe he was just like them, he knew that he was not. It was not superiority or moral egotism. It was a simple fact. However human he made himself inside, Hellboy knew that there was so much more to be.

"Hellboy!"

He stopped and scanned the bustle of the harbor front, and there, waving like a mother welcoming her son home from the sea, stood Amelia Francis. Hellboy was immensely grateful that it was she rather than anyone else. She knew how hard dragons were, and his beating by the giant worm would give her no cause to gloat. He hoped.

He worked his way along the dock. People mostly got out of his way. He liked that. The satellite phone went off again, and he cursed, taking it from his pocket, popping its back, and ripping out the battery. It would have been simple to turn it off, but that would not have the same therapeutic value. In moments such as this, symbolism said a lot.

"Amelia," he said when he reached her.

She stared at him, as wide-eyed as when they had first met a few hours before. "I thought you were dead for sure," she said.

Hellboy shrugged and winced. "I'll be sore in the morning, but I've been through worse."

"I spoke to Tom Manning. He said to get you to call him. He said something's going on."

"Perceptive as ever," Hellboy said. He looked around the harbor, sniffed the air, and shivered. "Mind if we get away from here? The stink of fish is starting to piss me off. It'll take forever to get it out of my coat."

Amelia looked him up and down. "You're soaked. And burned."

"I'll dry, and heal. Don't worry, it's my ego that's most wounded."

"Well, it *was* a dragon," she said, and Hellboy could have kissed her.

"So," he said, "is there somewhere close where we can get a decent meal and a beer?"

Amelia stared at him, and he noticed for the first time just how pretty she was. It was an unassuming attractiveness, something that came to her naturally and didn't have to be worked at. "Aren't you going to call Tom?" she said.

"No," Hellboy said. "He can wait. I'm in a bad mood. What I *am* going to do is take you for a drink."

"Why?" Amelia's suddenly flushed cheeks suited her.

Hellboy shook his head and looked down at his feet. *Oh crap*, he thought. "*Because* I'm in a bad mood, and I need one. And because you're an expert in mythology, and I've just had my ass kicked by a damn dragon."

"Oh," Amelia said, glancing away.

"And because blushing suits you."

Amelia looked back at Hellboy, and this time she held his gaze. "Your color gives you an advantage."

"I promise, you'll know when I'm flustered. My tail twitches."

She smiled, but it soon slipped from her face. "A *dragon*!" she said. "There were paramedics going up the mountain when I saw it take you away, and ambulances lining up. I don't know how many dead there are . . ."

"Well, it's gone for now," Hellboy said. "And after we've had that drink and talked it through, I'll get some more of my guys down here to make sure it doesn't get away again."

"You think it'll come back?"

Hellboy shrugged, took a slow draw on his cigarette, and looked up at the sky. He blew a smoke ring and watched it disperse, adding itself to the pollution. He frowned, stomped out the cigarette. Looked down at Amelia and made her avert her eyes once again.

"Let's go," he said. "You lead the way. We need to drink and talk."

"Just don't make me blush," she said, turning away.

"Me? Look at me. Do I look mischievous?"

The bar was called Zero's. None of its furniture matched, the main window out onto the street was hazed with decades of smoke and beer breath, the timber floor was pitted and scarred, the bar had been built from old railway sleepers, the barmaid was three hundred pounds and almost as wide as Hellboy was tall, the clientele ranged from teenage gang members to a grizzled old man who could well have been pickling himself to save the embalmers time, and there was a signed photograph of Burt Reynolds on the wall from when he had visited in 1979.

Hellboy loved it.

Amelia directed him to a private table in the corner, looking as though she knew the way. A few heads turned, a couple of conversations paused for a second, but by the time they sat down, everything felt normal again. She had a small, smug smile on her face, and she tapped her fingers on the heavily marked table. Evidently she was not going to be the first to break the silence.

"So long as they have soft toilet paper," Hellboy said. Amelia laughed out loud, and he found that he liked the sound she made—a girlish giggle, unconscious and unaffected.

"Hellboy, they serve the best chili you'll find anywhere in Rio. As for the beer, you can take your choice: there's Budweiser in cans or a selection of stuff brewed locally. It has a bit of a kick to it, I have to say."

"I always like to support the local economy." He caught the eye of the barmaid—not hard to do, as she was staring right at him—and raised an eyebrow. She sauntered over, a moving mountain of flesh and attitude. A cigarette hung from the corner of her mouth. By the time she reached them, the ash was almost two inches long, yet still it hung on tenaciously to its former shape.

"Look at that," Hellboy said, quietly enough so that only Amelia heard. "Damn, I've seen some stuff, but—"

"You're that *Hellboy*?" the barmaid said.

"No, my name's Kevin."

The woman laughed, and every bit of her shook. "No, you're him. So are you really from hell?"

Hellboy scratched the table with his big right hand, adding his own signature to a hundred others. "Do you want to find out?"

The woman laughed again, fleshy ripples overlapping with those from her last outburst. "Fair enough!" she said. "Chili's good today."

"Chili's good every day," Amelia said. "We need two bowls and—"

"Four," Hellboy said. "And a large bowl of nachos, heavy on the guacamole. And a pitcher of the strongest local brew you do, which is called . . . ?"

"Old Devil." She laughed shrilly.

Hellboy winced. "Well, I can't argue with that." He and Amelia watched the barmaid waddle back behind the bar and disappear into the kitchen. "Please tell me she doesn't do the cooking as well?"

"Don't know who does, but it's divine."

Hellboy made a show of looking around. "Nice joints you frequent, Ms. Francis."

"There's an American chain pub two blocks down," she said. "There've been two murders there in the three years I've been in Rio. Here . . . never even seen a fight. Most people are too drunk—or too filled with chilli—to bother."

"Hmph." He fished the satellite phone and battery from his pocket, toyed with them both, and ended up leaving them to one side. Tom could wait another hour. Hellboy was sore and thirsty and hungry, and this was nice. Just . . . nice.

"You're sure you're all right?" Amelia asked.

"I'm fine. Aching, but as I said, I've had worse."

"So I imagine. Some of the things you've seen . . . some of the things you've done . . ."

"I guess as a lecturer in mythology, you'd be interested, eh?"

Amelia shrugged, then smiled. "Damn right! The reason I started advising the BPRD is that I dream of becoming a field agent. When they approached me back in—"

"But do you believe?"

"Huh?"

The barmaid came with their pitcher of beer and two glasses, fired an incoherent quip at Hellboy, and left.

"Do you believe?" he asked again. "That was a dragon back there, and you still seem a bit shaken up about that."

Amelia poured the beers and took a long swig of hers. As she put the glass down, she was frowning, staring at Hellboy's chest but seeing right through. To the dragon, perhaps. Or back to herself, reliving her reaction to the creature's appearance. "Myth is myth," she said. "Or so I've always believed. There's always an element of truth behind every myth, but . . ."

"How much have you done with the BPRD?"

"I've answered a few questions over the phone."

"This is the first time you've actually seen anything?"

She nodded. And then she smiled sadly, and Hellboy realized that he was busy trying to deconstruct the meaning of her life. Questioning her beliefs when she had just had them challenged so violently—and so comprehensively—was insensitive of him.

"I'm sorry," he said. He touched her arm with his right hand, and she withdrew. "Hey . . . sorry."

"The thing with mythology is, it's safe," she said. She

drank some more, finishing her glass and letting out a dainty burp. "It's secure. It's a land of stories and legends that affect humanity down through the ages, but for me it's always been just that: stories and legends. I can tell as many students as I like about vampires and werewolves and dragons, and how terrible they can be, and how awful they are. But when I go home at night, I'm not afraid, because the world I've been talking about doesn't really exist. It's theoretical. Some people believe, many more don't, but it's always very safe. Mythology isn't as dangerous as murder, or as immediate as pollution, or as vicious as the drug gangs that control part of this city. The ideas within it are, for sure, but when I close my books at the end of the day, that's where the ideas stay. And I avoid the places where the drug gangs rule, and I wear my smog mask, and everything is right with the world."

Hellboy drank and watched and said nothing, because he knew the real truth. And he was watching Amelia discover it now, for herself. There was no reason for him to go in heavy-handed and smash it home for her.

"Now I can't close my books anymore. The myths have escaped. I've seen the dragon, I've seen it kill people, and life will never be the same again." She looked up at Hellboy, and he could see the weight of realization in her eyes. "Do you see what this is?" she said. "Do you understand why today is the first day of the future?"

"Isn't every day?"

"Not like today." Amelia shook her head and drank more beer. "No way, not like today. Stuff like this has always been hinted at, that's all; fuzzy photos in tabloid newspapers, secondhand accounts of the supernatural. But today . . . there were cameras up there. That was prime time! News companies the world over were feeding those images into people's living rooms. Kids at school in America were watching those pictures over their amazed teachers' shoulders. Adults in Europe were settling down to be numbed by another evening of soap opera, but they saw the world changing instead."

"You think? What about the people here, in Rio? You said yourself, they could hardly believe what they saw, even when it was standing up there on Christ the Redeemer and shitting down his soapstone robes. People have a way of compartmentalizing stuff like this. It'll cause a fuss, but it'll die down. People need to eat, pay their mortgages, have affairs. Personal stuff will always take over."

"That's so cynical," Amelia said.

"Cynical?" Hellboy was surprised, because he'd never seen himself as a cynic. Perhaps Amelia was right. "Maybe. But didn't you know what the Bureau did when you agreed to advise?"

"Yes, but I always thought it was a lie."

"Why?"

Amelia shrugged. "I thought that's what the government did. But dammit, Hellboy, *dragons aren't real!*"

"You'd say magic isn't, either, but—"

"But the two together . . ." Amelia looked into her glass and swilled the beer, and Hellboy could see that she was working something through. She watched the bubbles, touched them with her finger, tasted, never really seeing or tasting the beer at all. She was miles away. Hellboy thought that when she came back, something would have changed in her life forever.

He refilled his glass and drank, keeping his motions slow and measured. A few tables away, a young man and woman were making out, hands everywhere and too much on display; if they'd heard of the dragon, they were unconcerned. Close to the front window, there was a card game going on, three old men gambling pennies and sharing a bottle of whiskey. They couldn't have helped but notice the commotion in the streets outside, yet their game went on. The amazing happened every day, but the next day things were back to normal. Hellboy was witness to that, and he could list a dozen days in history that *should* have changed the world but had not. At first, back in the '50s and '60s, he'd put it down to the resilience of the human spirit. But lately, as time went on and his own spirit dwelled in as much mystery as ever, he had begun to believe it was apathy.

"Why would a myth suddenly come to life, Hellboy? It wouldn't, unless something forced it. It's like magic. Some people believe in it, but it isn't real."

She paused and watched Hellboy, but he said nothing. Perhaps she saw the truth behind his eyes . . . but he had an idea she was getting there pretty well on her own.

"But what if magic—an untruth—and this thing of mythology—again, untrue—were forced together?"

"What if they were?" Hellboy considered for a moment, trying to discern Amelia's logic, but it evaded him. Perhaps it was the Old Devil, which was already going to his head. "Crap," he said.

"Crap? Who's just been dropped into the bay by a dragon?"

Hellboy shrugged. "Well, combining the two—magic and mythology—implies a force to do it. Cause and effect. So what's the cause?"

Amelia looked at him brightly, raised her glass, and finished it off in one long swallow. "I have no idea," she said. "I'm a lecturer, not a preacher." She smiled.

Hellboy sat up straighter and lit his second cigarette from the stub of the first. He frowned, trying to clear his head, but then he let it ride, enjoying the fuzziness of the alcohol instead of fighting against it. Because something Amelia said had struck a chord, and he suddenly wished Abe were here with him. Abe could think straighter than Hellboy. He glanced down at the satellite phone and its spilled battery, wondering what Tom Manning would have to say.

"It's obvious, really," Hellboy said.

"It is?"

"Sure. If you're right, the cause is an insane megalomaniacal madman, messing with this stuff for his own ends."

"How do you know?"

Hellboy puffed on the cigarette and drained the pitcher. Damn, he was going to have to call. So much for his date with Amelia. "Because it always is," he said quietly. He reached for the battery and the phone and prepared to blow apathy out of the water.

Puerto Plata, Dominican Republic—1984

Richard Blake felt sick, and the smell—drying seaweed, the rolling ocean, dead things on the beach—was making him feel worse. His stomach seemed to roll with every wave that came in, and he hoped that the old myth about every seventh wave being a big one was wrong.

His brother, Gal, walked by his side, quiet and contemplative. His hands were clenched into fists, as if he had the relic already in his grasp.

"I'm still not sure I really believe this," Richard said.

"You know what the old man said."

"Yeah, but the old man was a drunk. He's ninety if he's a day, and he's been stuck on this island for thirty years drinking moonshine rum. He's pickled his body, and his brain's fried by the sun."

"What is it with you?" Gal paused atop a sand dune and looked at his brother.

Richard shrugged. "I feel as sick as a dog. I'm shitting through the eye of a needle, and—"

"Enough information!" Gal said. He squeezed his eyes shut, laughed quietly. "Damn, you're my brother, but that's just a bit too much. You want me to go alone?"

Richard shook his head. "Hell no. What if I wait here and you really find it? I'll never forgive myself. Besides, if it really is there . . . you'll need me around for when you send it."

Gal nodded his thanks. "It's getting harder."

Richard could think of nothing to say. Each time they found a relic and Gal sent it to their father, his brother seemed a little weaker afterward. Mentally he was just as strong—arrogant, angry, justified—but there was no hiding the physical change. Much as he tried, Richard could not simply put it down to Gal growing older. Magic was taxing, and one day it might come to a point where he could no longer send. His forays into the Memory were draining him.

"Let's go on," Richard said.

Zahid de Lainree's tome was of no use in this instance. They had heard the rumors, and tracked down the rumormongers, and questioned them, and now there was a site and a target in mind. There was a good chance that it was all false, but if it were true . . .

They had already sent their father some true treasures from the Memory. Each time Richard felt there could be nothing more amazing to find—a phoenix, gremlins, a dragon, other incredible discoveries—but then they would find something else, and his wonder grew. If the rumors were true, this could be the most powerful yet.

"There's the cave," Gal said. He unshouldered his ruck-sack and brought out two heavy flashlights. Their beams were strong, and, if necessary, they would double as weapons.

"It's so exposed," Richard said. "Anyone could wander in there. How come this hasn't been found before?"

Gal looked around, wiped sweat from his brow. Clouds were gathering in the distant hills in preparation for the regular afternoon downpour, and the air was heavy and humid. "This is off the beaten track," he said. "No tourists down this way, and the locals probably don't bother. Especially as there are rumors. Maybe kids come down here sometimes and dare each other to enter, but I doubt they go in too far. If what the old sop said was true, this cave is deep."

"And we have to go all the way in."

Gal smiled. "All the way, brother."

"Damn, now I feel sick as well."

Gal laughed and led the way. They left their heavy ruck-sacks just inside the cave entrance, out of the sun but still in daylight. That comforted Richard. With everything he and Gal had done over the years since their mother's murder, he was still afraid of the dark. He dreamed about that night sometimes, and when he woke up screaming, it was the darkness itself that was bearing down upon him, not what was hidden within. The darkness, the great unknown, still stalked him when he was awake. He supposed that was partly the reason he was doing his best to uncover some of what it concealed.

That and revenge.

Gal's flashlight beam flooded the cave when daylight faded away. Richard turned his flashlight on and combined the beams, shining them into the cracked walls and rugged ceiling. The floor here still consisted of sand; the sea must flood in here sometimes, and he hoped their calculations about the tide had been correct. Perhaps there were other ways out of there . . . perhaps . . . but he had no desire to find out.

In there for three days! the old drunk had said. *No light, no food, drinking my own piss. Three days! And I heard it calling to me every minute of every hour of those days.*

They worked their way into the cave, squeezing through a couple of narrow openings where the rock walls and ceiling had been scoured smooth by water being forced through at pressure. The sand floor eventually gave way to rock, and all signs of the sea—smashed shells, dried seaweed—vanished. The cave headed up, then down again, turning left and right. Cracks led off to the left, but Gal and Richard chose the easier route. The drunk had tried giving them direction, but he had been so flooded with rum by then that his words had been slurred beyond recognition. *Stray un*, he had said, *Jus go stray un.*

It took half an hour to reach the cave. It opened up suddenly, and the space took their breath away. The flashlights were powerful, but even they could not fill the cave with light; there were always shadows evading the beams. Richard felt as though they were being stalked.

"There," Gal said. "Do you hear that? Is that what the old fool meant?"

Richard opened his mouth to try to calm his breathing. His beam shook, and he placed the heavy plastic flashlight on the ground, propped against a rock. "Yes," he said.

Something was whistling at them. Gently, consistently, so low that it was almost below their level of hearing. It was sensed rather than heard; Richard felt the tiny hairs in his ears reacting to it, his skull vibrating slightly with the sound. And it seemed to be coming from all around.

"He thought it was the kraken's ghost," Gal said. "Stupid old shit."

"And it isn't?" Richard said. "Are you really sure of that?"

"We're not here to find a ghost," Gal said. He walked into the center of the cave and looked around, turning a slow circle and splaying his beam across the lower walls. "There!"

The two brothers hurried to the light patch in the dark rock wall. Something glittered in there. Like treasure seekers, they felt their excitement rising, but this was not any traditional treasure. It was evidence of the past they sought, proof of a myth. And like everything else they had spent the last ten years searching for, its discovery delighted them.

"It's huge!" Richard said.

"Imagine the size of the thing this came from . . ."

"How did it get in here? What's that it's buried in?"

Gal stepped back and aimed the beam wider. "Whale," he said. "Dried, fossilized. Maybe this cave was under water. Earthquake could have closed it in, raised it, who knows? Who cares? Father will be so pleased with this. We've sent him things of the air and the land, now he'll master the sea as well."

Richard produced his knife and set to work prizing the barb out of the hardened whale hide. The barb was as long as his hand, and it was set in a definite circular scar on the whale's skin, a sucker mark. Richard could have stood within the diameter of that circle with room to spare. *The size of this thing!* he thought. But soon he would not have to imagine it any longer. Soon his father would bring it back from the Memory. That scared him, but it thrilled him as well. With so much power at their disposal, how could they not find the vengeance they sought?

It was all going to be so easy.

Two hours later they emerged back into the sunlight. Gal had one arm slung across Richard's shoulder. The sending had tired him more than ever, and there was a small smudge of dried blood beneath his nose. Richard had pretended not to notice.

The rains had come and gone, and the trees along the back of the beach steamed in the afternoon sun. It was hot, humid, sweaty, but they were both glad to feel the sun on their skins once again.

As soon as Richard had removed the sucker tooth from the wall of the cave, the whistling had stopped. Gal said it had been a draft of air moving across the tooth, but Richard wondered. Perhaps it really had been the ghost of the kraken, singing into reality from the vagueness of the Memory, silenced now in anticipation of what might come next. Silenced and ready.

Bureau of Paranormal Research and Defense
Headquarters, Fairfield, Connecticut—1997

"A dragon?"

"Yeah. A Firedrake, apparently."

"And I thought my giant alligator was hard work." Abe Sapien sounded impressed, and Hellboy loved him for that. He hadn't yet mentioned the fact that the dragon had beaten Hellboy off, and for that he loved him more.

"You got to see Venice, at least."

"Hey, you went to Rio. I would have seen Lake Okanogan, too, if Tom hadn't called me in."

"Tough on you. Hey, I found a good bar called Zero's."

"And?"

Hellboy raised an eyebrow. Abe could read him like a book. Maybe that's why they were such friends, though sometimes Hellboy thought they were friends in spite of that. "And . . . ?"

"Amelia Francis?" Abe smiled.

"She's very nice. Didn't know you'd met her."

Abe shrugged. "I haven't, but I spoke to her a couple of years back when I was looking for the Loch Ness Monster."

"Never did find that one, did you?"

Abe stared. Blinked. "So what happened with the dragon?"

Hellboy slapped his friend on the shoulder, and they both laughed. They had a close friendship, and when they went on separate missions, Hellboy was always pleased when they met up again. He guessed they saw something familiar in each other, some inexplicable thing that science had yet to unravel.

"Hellboy, Abe, good to see you again."

"Hi, Kate." Hellboy turned to the woman who had just walked into the conference room; Kate Corrigan, professor of the supernatural and consultant to the BPRD. He always enjoyed Kate's presence, though it usually meant that something big was going down. Tom Manning strode in behind her, face grim, and his single glance confirmed Hellboy's suspicions. "Tom," Hellboy said. "Good to see you again."

"Abby is missing," he said. "I've asked Liz to get back here as soon as she can; she should be here by the end of this meeting." No questions about Abe's time in Venice. No questions about Hellboy's Rio adventure or how he felt after his drubbing by the dragon. All business and no small talk. *This,* Hellboy thought, *could be bad.*

"When did you last hear from Abby?" Abe asked.

"Yesterday. She was in Baltimore. She'd made contact with the werewolf and killed him. Out in the street, in broad daylight, I might add. She sounded confused and upset, and I told her to come in, but she never showed. Her satellite phone has been turned off ever since, and there's been no more contact. An hour ago I listed her as officially missing with the Baltimore Police Department, but . . ."

"But if she doesn't want to be found, she won't be," Abe finished.

"Hey." Hellboy touched Abe's shoulder. He knew there was something special between Abe and Abby, though it was more of a paternal concern than anything sexual. Abe had pulled the werewolf girl from the bottom of the River Seine, dragged her back from suicide, and though it had taken time, her gratitude had grown. There was a love between them now, something profound and deep. "Hey, she'll be all right."

Abe nodded. "I know she can look after herself," he said. "I'm just afraid that one day she won't want to. Some people accept the mystery of their lives, others never can."

"We'll find her, Abe," Tom said. "In the meantime—"

"Who have you sent after her?"

"No one."

"What?"

"I can't spare the manpower." Tom stared at Abe and Hellboy and indicated that they should take a seat. They did so, waiting to hear what Tom and Kate had to say. Even Abe said no more. There was a heavy atmosphere in the room, loaded with awful potential like a breaking news item on TV. "You may all want to take a drink," Tom said. "This could be a long one."

"Not thirsty," Hellboy said. "Abe?"

Abe made a rude gesture.

Tom sat at the head of the conference table, and Kate took the seat next to him, opening her briefcase and spreading a slew of papers across the polished oak surface. Photographs, photocopies, a few CDs; her eyes seemed to dance from one to the other and grow more serious with each second.

"I've got a bad feeling about this," Hellboy said. He had a thing for bad feelings. His tail twitched and scratched at the timber floor.

Tom rapped his knuckles on the table and sighed. "Guys, the shit has really hit the fan. The missions you've just returned from are the tip of the iceberg. Liz had what sounded like a nasty encounter with a phoenix in Greece, and other agents have been investigating other sightings across the globe. They've all been highly visible occurrences. Hellboy, the dragon you met was a case in point. It's been splashed across the media all over the world. Abe, the alligator you tackled is already on Italian TV. The list is long, but so far we've had unicorns running through the streets of Manila, a troll pulling trucks off the Sugg Gate Bridge, mandrake plants sprouting in banana plantations in South America, sirens luring ships onto rocks in Newfoundland . . . and the list goes on. Very visible, very filmable, and all pretty nasty. Death tolls from each separate occurrence hadn't been high and were mostly a result of press or curious publics getting too close."

"You said *hadn't* been high," Abe said. "Has that changed?"

Tom bit his lip and looked down at the table. Kate shuffled papers nervously.

"What?" Hellboy said. "Hey, Tom, we're big boys. Abe and I have been through enough crap—"

"Not like this," Tom said. "Hellboy, this is all new. This is *different*. We're used to fighting things that are between the lines or below the radar of normal perception, powers that work behind or beyond reality to achieve their own ends. What we have now . . ." Tom shook his head and rubbed his eyes. "Kate?"

Kate Corrigan forced a smile and stood. "The shit that Tom talks about hitting the fan shouldn't be real, but it is," she said. "In the past twelve hours, four airliners have been brought down over Europe, one of them crashing into Zagreb. Almost two thousand people have been killed. Flight recorders and radio transmissions received from the first downed aircraft talked of little men running across the fuselage and smashing their way out of panels in the cockpit."

"Little men?" Abe said.

Hellboy frowned. "Gremlins."

Kate nodded and continued. "Six hours ago in Paraguay, hikers entered a village to find its entire population dead, totally drained of blood. Many of them had been killed in their homes, but there were a few in the streets and a concentration of corpses in the village church. Several dead creatures also lay in the streets, brought down by gunfire. Bats. Huge, bodies as big as a fully grown adult, with unnaturally long canine teeth, and their stomachs were distended with the amount of blood they'd drunk."

"Not good," Abe muttered.

"Yeah." Hellboy stood and paced over to the window, looking out at the HQ's gardens. "Is there more?"

"Believe it," Kate said. "More than a hundred men have vanished in the Azores in the last day. Some of their bodies have been washed up on beaches, minus their sexual organs—"

"Ouch," Hellboy said.

"Quite. Their throats are ripped out as well. The ones who hadn't already been got at by normal marine life displayed signs of human teeth marks on their wounds."

"Human?" Abe said. "Mermaids?"

Kate shrugged. "Who knows? But men are still disappearing, and women are patrolling the beaches with shotguns."

"Daryl Hannah was never that nasty," Hellboy said.

Tom stood. "We saved the worst until last," he said. "This one's . . ."

"Beyond belief?" Hellboy asked.

Tom shrugged, then turned and used the remote control to open the doors on a digital projection screen. "I could tell you, but I think seeing it would be easier." He said no more, falling silent as he scrolled through commands on the screen and prepared the footage. It started to play—an aerial shot of a cruise liner, huge, long, sleek—and he paused the film. The picture froze, jerking subtly back and forth as if the ship sought to escape being viewed.

Hellboy knew that it was going to be bad, and he wondered what every person on that ship was doing as the actual scene was shot. There would be couples making love in their cabins; people playing sports; others watching films in the ship's movie theater; families eating in the various restaurants onboard; mothers reading on deck while fathers showed their kids the wonders that such a cruise ship would contain. The frozen moment in time should have screamed happiness and joy, instead of dread and doom. He closed his eyes, not wanting to see, but knew that he would open them again when he heard Tom press play. That was his job: to see the doom and gloom of things, instead of the joy and happiness.

"Here," said Tom Manning. "This is where it changes. This was shot by a press helicopter doing a feature on this new cruise ship. The footage was impounded before it could leak out. You'll see why."

Hellboy opened his eyes.

The cruise ship moved on its way, all instances of happiness on board moving on as well, and seconds later the scene began to shift from reality into disbelief. The sea around the liner—previously disturbed only by the boat's wake—began to stir. Ripples turned to waves, and waves spun into swirling whirlpools that spat spray. It was as if the sea were heating up, reaching boiling point in a matter of seconds, and then something burst from its depths. Calmness gave way to violence. Peace gave way to terror. And the kraken surfaced.

A huge gray tentacle rose from the water, tip waving, feeling up the side of the ship. It twisted onto the deck and slapped down among dozens of tiny shapes fleeing its appearance. As it rose it revealed several bright red splashes on the deck. It smashed down again, swatting a dozen more vacationers into the pale timber. Several more tentacles rose to join it, and then on the other side of the ship, three more came into view. They curved up and over the superstructure, slapping, waving, punching down. Glass exploded out from windows, scurrying shapes were crushed or sent plummeting into the sea, and several lifeboats were knocked from their moorings. They fell, crashing into the churning waters, saving no one.

The liner, massive engines still powering at the waves, began to lift.

A huge gray body surfaced beside the ship, and one eye—twenty feet across—clouded as it emerged into sunlight. The tentacles still raged across the decks, exploding parts of the superstructure and sending showers of timber and metal to splash into the sea. People ran here and there, sometimes in groups, more often alone and lonely in death. Tiny shapes floated in the sea around the emerging monster. Arms waved, but the unfortunates did not remain on the surface for long; the huge swells drove them down, and when they bobbed back up, they were lifeless, drifting at the mercy of the waves.

The kraken rose further, the liner now firmly in its grasp. Only a minute had passed between the first tentacle rising and the monster basking in the sun with the liner lifted almost clear of the sea. The ship's huge turbines still pumped spray, forming a rainbow at its stern. The sea boiled as if in fury at the kraken's appearance. Or perhaps the fury was directed at the ship itself, an invader here, a construct slicing the ocean and leaving only an oily wake behind. Because as the kraken suddenly rose higher and slammed down—breaking the ship's back, crushing it, spilling passengers like innards for the carrion creatures of the sea to pick off—the waters seemed to rise in celebration. Huge spurts erupted on either side of the ship, driven by the unbearable pressures of air escaping the crushed hull. Shapes rose and fell, forming desperate waving stars with arms and legs. Several small explosions blew out sections of the hull, but the worst destruction belonged to the kraken, and the kraken alone. It shook like a crocodile trying to drown a gazelle. The liner—gleaming white and proud once, now broken and sad—came apart.

After the kraken sank back below the waves, it took only a few minutes for the remains of the great ship to go under. None of those in the BPRD conference room spoke; none of them wanted to break the silence, because there was really nothing to be said. The helicopter must have swung in close then, because the view suddenly began to change. Instead of specks seen from a distance, the survivors in the water were suddenly real people—men and women, boys and girls. A few bobbed here and there—those flung free by the kraken's thrashing tentacles—but mostly the survivors clung on to ragged wreckage. The helicopter passed low across the disaster scene. Desperate faces turned upward, pleading to be saved.

"Turn it off," Hellboy said. He had closed his eyes, but he still felt the thrum of tension in the room. "We don't need to see any more."

Tom clicked the remote control. "That's about it. The helicopter left the area because it was running out of fuel.

When the U.S. Coast Guard arrived three hours later, they found fewer than a hundred survivors."

"How many were aboard?" Abe asked.

"Almost three thousand, including crew." Tom's words hung in the room, accompanied only by the whir of the projection-screen doors enclosing it once again.

Hellboy whistled, looked around the room at Abe, Tom, and Kate, but for a while none of them had anything else to say. Tom poured some water, Kate leafed through a file, and Abe stared at Hellboy, his big eyes more watery than usual.

"So what's happening?" Abe said at last.

Tom looked at Kate and nodded.

"I don't need to tell you all just how wrong this is," she said. "All the creatures we've seen here are from myth and legend. Some of them go back thousands of years—the dragon, the phoenix—while others are more modern. Gremlins are a creation of the age of technology, an excuse for machines going wrong."

"Not an excuse any longer," Hellboy said.

"Maybe. We've all seen things here, things that most people wouldn't or couldn't believe. We know what exists beyond the everyday, behind the veil, and in the dark. And some of us can shift that veil. But what we're seeing here is a complete manifestation of a whole slate of myths, not just one aspect. It's not just a dragon or a demon, it's a Who's Who of world mythology, from the beginning of time up to the modern day. It's true. It's all here. There's a hundred hours of film of these things, and both of you have just returned from brushes with creatures of myth and legend."

"Brush? More like a hammering." Hellboy flicked at his arm as if still clearing water from his skin. He struck the floor with his tail and looked down at the table, angry.

"So where does all this come from?" Kate asked.

"Memory?" Abe said. "Collective subconscious?"

"Ah, the Memory." She picked up a sheaf of notes and began flipping through them, but Hellboy could not help thinking that she was not really seeing anything written there.

"Kate?" he said. "Is it just me, or did you say that with a capital *M*?"

She looked up at Hellboy and smiled. "There's a book," she said. "It's a map to the Memory, where humankind has relegated many of the most wonderful things that ever lived—allegedly. It tells its owners how to find that place, how to dig down through layers of the veil that overshadows this world until they break into the pure darkness of that other. It's a plane in itself, the Memory, a whole level of existence. A sad place but a temporary place as well, because one day it will be touched upon from this side, and those creatures shunned by humankind will find themselves once more."

"Seems to me this Memory leaks," Hellboy said. "We've all been dealing with this stuff for years."

"Maybe it does," Kate said. "But it's only a minor leak compared with today. The book is the key and the map. Again, allegedly. It was written by a man called Zahid de Lainree, but there's no proof anywhere that he ever existed."

"A book is no proof?" Abe said.

"Even if it existed, would it be proof enough? No one has ever seen it or met anyone who has seen it, but its existence is mooted by cultures and societies all across the world. Some think it's a guilt thing; having turned their backs on creatures of imagination, people have to manufacture a belief in something that can explain what happened. Others think it's just a story made up and carried down through time, designed to explain why these creatures of myth don't exist in this world anymore."

"And you?" Hellboy asked. "You're a lady with strong opinions. What do you think?"

"Yesterday I'd have said it was make-believe. Today . . . ?" She shrugged and threw down a batch of photographs that fanned out across the table: a dragon, a herd of unicorns, a still from the destruction of the ocean liner by the kraken. "Today I'm starting to wonder."

"But who could be doing this?" Abe said. "Supposing the book even exists, who would have the knowledge to know how to use it?"

"A megalomaniacal madman," Hellboy muttered. Everyone turned to look at him, and he smiled grimly. "Isn't it always? Something I talked about with Amelia Francis down in Rio. For her, the dragon she saw was impossible, so she deduced that something impossible must have created it: magic. Reverse logic, I thought, but maybe—"

"Benedict Blake," Kate whispered.

"Huh?"

Kate was not listening. As if she were alone in the room, she flipped the lid on her laptop and started tapping at the keys. A minute later she sat back, shaking her head. "But he's dead. He *must* be dead. Especially after so long . . ."

"Sorry, Kate," Hellboy said. "I don't want to crash your party, but who the hell is Benedict Blake?"

"An insane genius who knew magic, and mythologies were his love," she said. "After what was done to him and his family, it'd be only a small step to add 'megalomaniac' to his résumé. If he were alive, of course."

"Sometimes being dead's no obstacle. You know that," Hellboy said.

"Tell us what you know," Tom said. "I'm tired, Kate. This could well be the worst time we've ever faced. So if there's any chance that you have any idea at all about what's going on here, stand up and cough up. Because I sure as hell don't. Abe?"

"Lots of monsters, and we can't fight them all," he said.

"Hellboy?"

"Just got my ass kicked by a dragon."

Tom nodded. "Right. Kate . . . the floor's all yours."

Kate Corrigan stood and opened her laptop wider. She glanced down at the screen for a few seconds, frowned, and then began.

"You have to remember, this all happened when I was a little girl. Everything I know about this man comes from re-ports written at the time, and you'll see from what I say in a minute that those who wrote the reports . . . well, they all had their own agendas. But I've read everything I can about Benedict Blake, and I know as much about him as anyone. A few years ago he became something of a fascination for me, though I haven't really thought about him for some time." Kate scrolled down the file she was looking at and turned the computer around. "Haven't really had cause to." She showed them all a photograph of Blake, standing be-hind a lectern, delivering a speech or lecture.

"Looks like a regular guy," Hellboy said.

"To start with, he was. Blake was a scientist and some-thing of a magician. The scientist side people respected; his research into cell reconstruction was second to none, and he was one of the first to catalogue the genetic changes being caused in the natural world by humankind's pollution of the planet. A sort of roster of defects, which back then was pretty much doubted or ignored by many people. The

magic . . . well, that made people nervous. For such a serious scientist to dabble in arcane matters meant that he was
effectively ostracized from the rest of the scientific commu-
nity. It didn't stop his research, or his messing with magic,
but it did mean that he lost several major grants from uni-
versities and government agencies. Blake went out on his
own, and in 1969 he went underground."

"Disappeared?" Abe said.

"Vanished. Nobody knew where he was or what he was
doing. And in many ways, nobody really cared. His wife and
two boys went with him. There was no big hoo-ha, no fuss.
A few people here and there wondered where he was and
what he was doing, but he soon just faded away. Another
nutty professor. Those few who cared thought he'd probably
had enough of the mockery and ridicule and found himself a
quiet place in South America to continue his research.

"But then something happened. In 1970 certain U.S.
government agencies started trying to track him down—
nothing official, all covert. I've collected files and letters over
the years, all of them pointing to the fact that, suddenly, the
government wanted him. There are few hints about why,
but one of the main reasons seems to be something to do
with what he left behind. Someone took an interest in his
research, broke into his home, and found something there
that scared them."

"Who broke in?" Hellboy asked.

"I don't know."

"What did they find?"

"Again, I don't know. But there seems to have been a
tremendous amount of energy and resources expended in an
effort to track down Blake and his family. They didn't find
him."

"So that's it?" Hellboy said. "It's hardly conclusive."

"That's not all," Kate said. "The best is yet to come. Blake came back of his own accord, and he'd changed. He set up home in New York, but he never seemed to go back to work. Instead he launched a bitter series of verbal assaults on the world's governments' disregard of the environment. He warned of the end of the world being brought about through pollution and climate change. He predicted holes in the ozone layer, dead seas, and the air being denuded of oxygen because of deforestation. He was raving, expounding all sorts of apocalyptic theories that most people ignored or just laughed at. On the surface he became something of an object of ridicule." She tapped her finger on the table and stared down at Blake's image on her computer.

"On the surface?" Abe said. "What about underneath?"

"Beneath the surface certain people were very scared. Blake was scorned by his peers and vilified by governments, but he kept on ranting through every possible public forum. He went from delivering lectures on TV to standing on street corners, raging about the death we were bringing down on ourselves, claiming that humanity had already wiped out most of the wonder in the world and now was ready to destroy what was left. 'Slow suffocation' is the phrase he used. He claimed that we had destroyed all that was good in the world, and now we were suffocating."

"He wasn't far off on some points," Hellboy said. "The pollution stuff, at least."

"It wasn't something that governments wanted to hear."

"Still isn't now. Too much money involved in saving the planet. So what's all this building up to? What happened to Blake?"

"Official version first," said Kate. "He killed his wife and children, burned down his house, and went off somewhere to commit suicide." She opened another computer file and showed them all the image of the blackened house, the framework a charred skeleton.

"And the true version?"

"Conjecture on my part, but I'm pretty certain that his wife was killed in a state-sanctioned hit that went wrong."

"Oh crap." Hellboy leaned forward and looked closer at the ruins of the house. "Not very subtle."

"You said they killed his wife?" Abe said. "What about his children, and Blake himself?"

"Back underground," Kate said. "So far as I can tell, nothing has been heard or seen of them since. They've gone. Where, when, or why I was never able to find out."

"So," said Hellboy, "why does this guy leap to mind for you now?"

"Your comment about magic and myth," she said. "And the fact that Blake's last real lecture was entitled 'When There Were Dragons in the World.' "

"Right," Hellboy said. "Dragons."

"As I said, he believed that humankind had purged the earth of all that was good. Drove away the wonder. And he spoke of the Memory, using the exact same terminology as the legendary book by Zahid de Lainree."

"And you think what, Kate?" Abe said.

"I think that when he disappeared in 1969, he went to find the book."

The room was silent for a while, all thinking their own thoughts. *When there were dragons in the world*, Hellboy thought. *Damn, that's now!* He flexed his arms and tensed his neck, feeling the stiffness settling in there from his fight with the Firedrake.

"Aren't we adding two and two to get five?" Tom said. "I mean, there's nothing here to say it's anything to do with Blake, is there? And this all happened . . . when exactly?"

"His wife died in 1973. If Blake were still alive now, he'd be almost ninety, and his boys would be in their late forties."

"And you think this is all revenge?"

Kate shrugged. "I never knew the man. But yes, vengeance for his wife. And to prove that he was right."

"Maybe he's just mad."

"That too."

"It leaves so much unexplained," Abe said. "Where are these creatures coming from? How are they suddenly appearing again?"

"If he has the book, he has a map to the Memory."

Abe shook his head. "It's all too woolly for me," he said. "And even if it were true, it gives us nothing. Hellboy? What do you think?"

"I think we have to find where this butthead is and have a chat with him."

"He's been missing for almost twenty-five years," Kate said. "How do you expect to find him?"

"Ask. Tom, do you have a list of recent sightings of these things?"

"Cryptids," Kate said.

"Huh?"

"I call them cryptids. Cryptozoological creatures."

Hellboy nodded his head sagely. "Classy," he said.

Tom slid a computer printout across the table in Hellboy's direction. "What do you mean, ask?" he said.

"I have my ways," Hellboy said. He used one finger to position the paper in front of him and started scanning down the list. "Cryptids," he muttered. "Classy."

"Hellboy . . ." Abe said.

"Hey, buddy, I know. You need to go after Abby. Tom knows that too, though he didn't say anything. Just keep in touch. I'm here if you need me."

Abe nodded his thanks and stroked the flared gills on his neck.

They were standing in the entrance foyer of BPRD headquarters, waiting for Liz Sherman to arrive. She had called in from the airport to say she was on her way, and Hellboy had not liked the tone in her voice. She was vulnerable at the best of times, but today she had sounded defeated. He wanted to see her, talk to her, take her with him. The way she sounded, being alone would be the worst thing for her.

"I'm afraid for Abby," Abe said. "She doesn't belong out there any more than we do, not really. But we've adjusted. We've *accepted*. I still don't think she has."

"Accepted what?"

"That we're different. Abby's a werewolf, Hellboy. Ninety-nine people out of a hundred would call her a monster, and that's never likely to change. She hasn't come to terms with it yet. Her being out there on her own . . . I'm scared of what will happen."

Hellboy nodded, looked up through the atrium's glass roof at the night drawing in.

"Full moon in two days," Abe said.

"Right."

They stood in silence for a while, two friends feeling the weight of worlds on their shoulders. Hellboy flexed his huge right hand, flicked his tail at the floor, shrugged his shoulders to twist away some of the stiffness. Kate's ideas were still sinking in, but at least now he had an aim and a purpose in mind. Sitting around was fine, but as far as he was concerned, it never got anything done. He needed to be out there. And as soon as Liz arrived, he would be. "You have any idea where she might have gone?" he asked.

"I'm not sure," Abe said. "I'm thinking maybe Paris."

Hellboy knew what had happened there, how Abe had rescued her from suicide, and he did not like the tone of dread in his friend's voice. But there was little he could say that would be of comfort. "You go," he said. "Find Abby. Hell, we need her now more than ever."

"Tom—"

"Tom will live with it!" Hellboy said. "And if he's got a problem, he can talk to me."

Abe smiled. "Yeah, I can see that. But things are really kicking off, and my place is here."

Hellboy squeezed his friend's arm. "Abe, after what we saw in there, I'm not sure *where* our place is anymore. That dragon wiped the floor with me in Rio, and that damn kraken . . . you really see yourself being any good up against that?"

Abe shook his head. "It's all so much," he said. "What are we going to do? What if all this gets worse?"

"Guns," Hellboy said. "Lots of very big guns." The front doors opened, and Liz walked in. "Oh crap. She looks worse than I feel."

"HB, Abe," Liz Sherman said. "I really need a drink."

They took one of the Bureau's Humvees. Liz drove. For the first few minutes she had been annoyed at not being able to stop, freshen up, and take that drink she so craved. "There's a bottle of Jameson's with my name on it in my room, dammit! she had said. But then Hellboy had filled her in on their chat and what they had seen, and Liz had fallen silent.

"Made me sick to the stomach just watching it," Hellboy said. "It wasn't the size of that thing, though that was bad enough. It wasn't even the dread we all felt when we watched it happening. It was the specks of color in the sea, the splashes of red on the deck. The people, all of them dying. There are a lot of grieving people in the world tonight."

"I met up with a policeman in Zakynthos," Liz said. "He was a nice guy. I think he wanted to buy me a meal, you know? When the phoenix set itself aflame, it took him with it. It *melted* him, and now I'll never know what his favorite childhood memory is, or whether he has a scar, or what meal he wanted to buy me that evening. Every death matters so much, HB. We've got to do our best to make sure the grieving doesn't spread."

"You all right, Liz?"

She nodded, and in the dusky light he saw her break a smile. "I'll be fine. Now tell me where the hell we're going and what we're going to do there. I've already assumed that this will end up with you beating the crap out of something."

"Don't prejudge," Hellboy said, affecting a wounded tone. "It is my intention to drive to New York, capture the banshee in Central Park, and have a friendly chat with it."

"Yeah, right, a chat. And if it doesn't want to chat?"

"*Then* I beat the crap out of it."

Liz turned up a ramp onto the freeway and took the Humvee up to ninety.

New York, New York—1997

New York is the city that never sleeps, and Hellboy had
never felt so awake. There was so much going on that his
thoughts were darting all over. He wished he could have just
one problem to dwell on, not a million. He wished he had a
better idea of what was happening in the world tonight. He
wished he could hit something.

They went south and drove in over the Queensboro
Bridge, and New York slapped Hellboy in the face as hard as
ever. He knew of no other city that was just so damn *visible*.
It was a great wall of civilization, reaching up for the sky
and peppering the night with lights. Darkness never truly
fell here, not completely, and the city itself never went to
sleep. It did have its dark areas, that was for sure, places
down narrow alleys that were haunted by death, and deeper
mysteries beneath the city: abandoned subway stations, col-
lapsed drains, the guts of the old city, still grinding and
churning but blocked with effluent, human and otherwise.
Hellboy had visited a few times over the years, the episode
with those giant insects that mimicked humans being the
most recent. That was bad. But he'd been able to hit something, at least.

"Damn, this place gets to me," he said. "So many people."

"Behind every light is a person," Liz said.

"And for every person there's a hundred rats."

"Charming."

"I'm in a mood. I feel like I need to punch in every direction at once, but I won't hit anything."

"Take it in steps, HB. Just think about this job for now.
Don't worry about things you can't do anything about."

"But Abby, and Abe, and that madman Blake—"

"Abe's a big boy, he'll look after Abby. And Blake may not exist. I know I wasn't there, but Kate's reasoning sounds full of holes."

"Maybe."

They crossed the bridge and passed between the first of the towering buildings. The streets were alive, people flowing in both directions and painting the sidewalks every color imaginable. Manhattan was the whole world condensed into one area, its good and its bad. A car horn blared, and a boy helped an old woman cross the road. A man slumped in a doorway with blood running from his nose, and an old beggar with no legs counted up the generous dollars that would pay for his meal that night.

"Will you look at that guy," Liz said, and Hellboy looked. The man was standing on a street corner juggling flaming sticks. A small crowd had built up around him, kids clapping and adults looking suitably impressed, and the crowd gasped in unison as he plucked a stick from the air and swallowed its burning end. Liz parked at a red light and watched, and Hellboy saw the spinning flames reflected in her eyes. For a few seconds she seemed to forget that he was there. He let her.

The light changed, and they drove on.

"How do we find this banshee?" Liz said.

Hellboy shrugged. "Met one in Ireland once," he said. "Far as I can tell, they only visit families of Celtic or Gaelic descent. That pretty much rules me out, but the report Tom had said that everyone who lives within two blocks of Central Park can hear it at night."

"I'll bet it's zeroed the crime problem in the park, at least."

"Maybe the NYPD will sign it up."

"You think it'll talk?"

"We can but try. Trouble is, I figure if Kate's idea does hold any shred of truth, and this thing is from Blake, it won't be too keen to reveal the fact."

"Banshees are spirits, right? Not flesh and blood?"

"You're asking me?"

Liz smiled. "You're not as dumb as you make out sometimes."

"Actually I am, and now you've hurt my feelings."

"Big red jerk."

"Done it again."

Liz laughed, Hellboy back at her. He and Liz worked well together, and they were good in each other's company. He sometimes thought it was because they distracted each other from too much introverted misery. Occasionally he believed it could be something else. But they'd known each other too long, and been through too much, to do anything that would risk such a precious friendship.

The traffic stopped and started, worming its way north and south, east and west. Hellboy wanted to start at the bottom and work up, and it was almost midnight by the time they reached the southern extreme of Central Park. The roads and sidewalks were just as busy here, but as Liz parked and turned off the engine, they noticed how quiet the crowds were. So many people, so little noise.

"They're like zombies," Liz said quietly.

Hellboy opened his window and looked at the faces of those passing by. A couple of people glanced up, most did not. Many held hands or had their arms around each other, a comfort for both. "They're scared," he said. And then he realized why.

The wail rose in the distance, growing louder and louder as if the wailer were drawing closer. It was an appalling sound—a wolf in pain or a child screeching for its lost mother. It changed from a wail to a scream, lessened to a sob, rose again, and it echoed between the buildings and along the streets and avenues, giving the impression that its source was everywhere. Hellboy looked into Central Park, and it seemed much darker than normal.

"Oh shit!" Liz said. "What the hell *is* that?"

"That's the voice of the banshee," he said. People were hurrying from the streets now, trying to lose themselves inside or behind buildings in the hope that the wail would not find them there. They were crying, but their sobs were merely human. "Let's go," he said.

"Out there? Into that?"

"It's what we came for. Easier to find it if we can hear it crying. Once it falls silent, it'll be just another shadow."

Liz frowned across the front seat at Hellboy, then reached out for his hand. She closed her fingers around two of the big fingers on his right hand, squeezed, and he loved her then because he knew there was no awkwardness in the gesture. He smiled, nodded. Then they left the Humvee, and the banshee's wail rose to a piercing shriek.

Liz covered her ears. Hellboy bit his lip. They crossed the street together, not needing to look out for cars because no one was driving here anymore. Those who were still in their cars were covering their ears, burying their heads in their hands, or shouting in an effort to drown out the dreadful noise.

"Why isn't someone doing anything about this?" Liz shouted.

"We are," Hellboy said. "Someone in the know at the

NYPD called the Bureau a day ago, and I guess we just put them on hold for a while."

They walked into the park. Hellboy turned his head left and right to try to make out where the banshee shriek emanated from, but echoes confounded him. Liz held on to his arm, cringing toward the ground as they walked. Darkness nestled beneath the trees and strove to reach out against the streetlights, and it felt as though they were leaving the whole city behind them. Hellboy had been in Central Park once before, and it had felt like a whole new world within a world, a place totally separate from Manhattan. Now, as the darkness was split by the wails and the lights of the city receded behind them, he was more nervous than ever about what they would find.

They passed a fenced baseball area, and more fencing enclosing a basketball court and a kids' play area. The pale concrete path curved away from them, catching some of the sparse starlight and showing them the way.

The wail died down into a moan. *She's giving birth to pain,* a woman in Ireland had told Hellboy the last time he'd heard a banshee. *She's pregnant with agony, and it births itself, so it's never ending for that poor spirit.*

"This way," he said. Liz let go of his arm and walked beside him, slightly more relaxed now that the screaming had died down. They still heard groans and sobs, and at every corner Hellboy expected to come across the banshee. The sounds were so intimate, so close, that he thought perhaps it was following them, drifting through the shadows beneath the trees, and teasing them for sport. It was crying from the left, sobbing from the right, and all the time its weeping abraded his ears.

"Damn, it sounds pissed," Liz said.

"It's not a happy bunny, that's for sure."

They walked on, passing the shadows of rocks hunched down like cowering beasts. When the angle was right they could make out splashes of graffiti on the stone, exhorting love and hate and the wonder of drugs. They kept to the path, steering deeper into the park. The sobs of the banshee surrounded them, neither drawing them in nor pushing them away, and Hellboy wondered whether it even knew that they were there. It would soon. He planned on tracking it, holding it down—he had charms and trinkets in his belt pouches that would aid him in that—and quizzing it about why it was here, where it had come from. It would not be easy. And it would not be nice, putting this wretched spirit through more pain and uncertainty. But the banshee's was a small part in a much larger play. Hellboy needed to see the whole act.

Something flitted past them in the dark. Both Hellboy and Liz spun around and looked the way they had come, but there were only motionless shadows behind them. The wailing continued, though it had not seemed to grow any closer.

"What was that?" Liz said.

"Dunno . . . saw it from the corner of my eye."

"Bat?"

"Bigger."

They walked on, glancing nervously behind them in case whatever it was came in for a second run.

It did, but not from behind.

A shadow emerged from the darkness before them and wrapped itself around Liz's head. She screamed, but her voice was muffled and then drowned out completely as the banshee screeched. Its sound was thunderous and desolate, and it drove Hellboy to his knees. Liz thrashed around, desperate to keep her footing, waving at her head and pummeling at the hazy shape that enveloped her. It coalesced into the image of a woman, and as Liz stumbled out from a tree's shadow, moonlight illuminated the spirit's face. It was an old woman, face gray and heavily lined, mouth open wide, and lips pulled down into an image of abject misery. It looked directly at Hellboy and cried, its voice vibrating through his bones and setting his right hand shaking. He screamed, clasped his fingers tight, fisted his hand, and punched at the ground. He did not hear the impact. The banshee's voice was everything.

"Liz!" Hellboy shouted. "Down onto your knees!" But even his booming voice was drowned out by the spirit's wail, and he forced himself to stand and stumble into Liz. She sprawled to the concrete path, hands still flapping at the ghost wrapped around her head, legs kicking, and Hellboy began to wonder whether she was able to breathe in there. *Slow suffocation,* he thought.

Something shimmered around Liz's hands and feet, and it was not starlight.

"Oh, lady, now you've pissed her off," Hellboy said.

The banshee seemed to grab on tighter, and then it rose slowly from the ground, Liz still wrapped in its arms and legs. Hellboy leaped and grabbed its wrinkled gray cloak. Still the banshee and Liz rose, their ascent slowed but not halted by Hellboy's grasp. They were above his head now, his arm pointing straight up, the spirit's cloak wrapped in his big hand.

"Oh, no you don't!" he said, and pulled down sharply. He felt his feet leave the ground, and a sudden sense of panic shocked him. He did not know were it came from—

he'd been dropped from heights before—but his hand snapped open, and he felt the tickle of the cloak passing across his palm. "Oh no you *don't!*" Hellboy squatted, bunching muscles, and jumped as high as he could. This time he grabbed hold of Liz's ankles, one in each hand, and his weight brought her back down. The banshee shrieked again, its voice changing from miserable to angry.

And then something in Liz gave way. Whatever dam she maintained, whatever pressure valve she had been able to apply to her curse over the years, finally broke. The flickering flames on her feet and hands bloomed into expanding balls of fire, crawling up her legs and down her arms. She still batted at the insane creature hanging on to her head, but the spirit was slippery and insubstantial, not something that could be simply punched away.

Hellboy let go and dropped to the ground. This was Liz's show now.

The banshee rose again, taking the burning Liz Sherman with it. Flames erupted all across the firestarter's body, engulfing the banshee with no apparent effect, and for the first time Hellboy truly feared for Liz. The higher she went, the harder she'd fall, and while her furious fires could aid her in some instances, in this case . . .

The banshee breathed fire. Its cloak erupted in flames, its hair became a burning snake dance, and its eyes grew wide before popping and melting from its head.

"Oh, that's gotta hurt," Hellboy said. He shifted to the side, positioned himself below Liz, and seconds later caught her as she dropped from the banshee's grasp. Her flames wrapped themselves around him, scorching his skin and sizzling his goatee.

"Hey, put out the fire," he said. Liz's eyes sprang open—

he saw the terror in them, the rich flame of panic—and it seemed to take several seconds before she recognized him.

"Someone's going to die!" she said. "The banshee . . . it told me. Someone in my family is going to die!"

Hellboy sighed, kissed Liz on the forehead. There was nothing he could say.

"Bitch!" Liz spat. "That bitch! It knows, it knows about my family, and it's *teasing* me!"

Hellboy looked up at the flaming thing a few feet above them. The banshee spun in the air, twisting and thrashing as the flames ate into its ghostly self, and he could feel no pity. "Yeah, I think it was," he said. "But now it's time to ask it a question or two."

He set Liz down and delved into his belt pouches.

"What are you looking for?" Liz asked. She stayed close to Hellboy, reluctant to lose contact with him. He could feel her fingers around his arm, her skin hot against his.

"I've got it here somewhere." Hellboy did not need to check to see if the ghost was still there; he could hear its cry, see the flames flickering across the ground, and he could even smell it. He had never smelled a ghost before. That's one of the things he liked about his job: no two days were the same.

"Er . . . HB?"

Liz's voice told him there was something terribly wrong. He looked up.

The banshee had stopped screaming and was now smiling. It was a grotesque expression; the grimace had suited it more. Its melted eyes were sliding down its cheeks, bloody sockets aflame, and fire curled from its ears and nostrils. The few teeth that remained in its mouth dripped flame like thick saliva.

"Oh crap," Hellboy said.

The banshee came at him. Air rushed into its mouth and through its hair, agitating the flames and giving it a whole new roar. Hellboy turned and ran away from Liz, hoping to lure the spirit after him. He still dug in his belt, looking for the binding charm given to him by the African witch doctor back in the '70s. He was sure he still had it—couldn't remember using it, at least—but each pocket he delved into gave him nothing.

He could still hear the banshee behind him, so he ran hard. He left the path and clomped across the damp grass, heading for a huddle of large rocks that shone with reflected moonlight. He was glad the park was abandoned. That meant he could do whatever he wanted to the spirit bitch.

"Come on," he whispered. "Come to Hellboy, come on, you flaming old hag, come—"

The banshee struck him between the shoulders, driving hot fingers into his skin. He felt nails puncture his flesh, pretty sharp for an apparition. He pretended to fall, cried out in false pain, and as he rolled across the grass he brought up his hand. The eyes were resting in his palm. The old witch doctor had told him they were from a river demon, gouged out a century ago and fossilized from being buried with the bodies of a mother and her stillborn child. They bound spirits, the witch doctor said, and they held that power between them, an overwhelming magnetism. Hellboy dropped one under his tongue and readied the other.

The banshee came at him again, wailing through its terrible smile. With his sidearm Hellboy was a terrible shot. With the fossilized eye of an African river demon, he was spot on. He lobbed the eye, and it sailed straight into the banshee's throat. Its screech was cut off into a cough, its burning eye sockets went wide, and it clasped its hand to its neck. It gulped and swallowed.

"That's it for you," Hellboy said. He stood, reached for the banshee, and threw it down at his feet.

It tried to escape, and he let it. Still flaming, the banshee rose and scurried off across the grass, fast at first, then slowing, then coming to a stop before tumbling back to Hellboy's feet. It took off and rose into the air, streaming fire behind it, but it fell back down. Left or right, however hard it ran or flew, it would roll or fall back against Hellboy's steady legs.

The banshee turned to him at last, and although its eyes were ruined, he could see the fear that had appeared on its face.

"Demon!" it spat.

"That's rich." He almost kicked it, because he hated being called a demon. But then Liz was there, and he didn't like losing control in front of her, because she was someone who exercised more control than he could ever hope to possess. A single flame still fluttered at her left ear, like a butterfly settling on her skin. It wavered out as she spoke.

"So what has it got to say?"

"It says I'm a demon."

Liz glared down at the banshee. "You," she said, "had better answer Hellboy's questions. He's not real fond of being called that—"

"Or dragon," he muttered.

"—and people who call him a demon tend to end up having the living crap beaten out of them. Or the dead crap. Whatever. So."

"Demon's bitch!" the banshee said, then uttered a laugh that rose into another terrible wail.

"Oh, can it!" Hellboy shouted. "People are trying to sleep!" He punched at the flailing spirit, the impact sounding nothing like stone on flesh. The banshee flipped on the ground, the scream lessening, and it only stopped moving when Hellboy raised his fist again.

"Sorry," he muttered to Liz.

"Hey, it deserves it."

"You're bound to me by the eye of the river demon," Hellboy said. "That means you can't escape me, ever, unless I will it. Now, why did Blake send you?"

"Who's Blake?" the banshee said.

"Hmm. I was hoping that one would get you." He smashed the spirit across the jaw with his left hand. It felt like hitting thick smoke, but its head flipped around, fire splashing from its eyes like fresh blood. "So now, tell me why you're here, and where you came from, and why it is you're keeping the good people of New York awake tonight."

"Good people? *Good* people? Stinking dirty people, hateful hearts, blackened souls, rancid breaths, and polluted lives, killing the land and sending me, sending me away to that dark place."

"Polluted lives?" Hellboy said. "That's enough for me. Liz, move off a bit and call HQ. Tell them Kate was right about Blake being responsible for all this. Meantime, I'll stay here and find out where he is right now."

"Blake?" the banshee said. "Blake? I don't know Blake. Who is Blake?"

"Methinks the lady doth protest too much," Liz said, and she smiled as she turned away. "Remember, you demon ghost bitch, answer the nice red man, or you'll be in a world of hurt."

"Charming," Hellboy said.

"I charm when I need to, and only then."

"Charming."

Liz walked away, and Hellboy went back to work on the banshee.

Liz sat on a park bench, called her report in to Tom at HQ, and lit a cigarette. She could hear the commotion in the distance as Hellboy and the banshee had their chat. She was pleased. She hoped he hurt it. *Someone is going to die!* the creature had hissed. *Someone close to you is going to die.* Liz had instantly thought of Hellboy, but then somehow the banshee had forced her to replay those terrible memories she had tried to put down for years. Her mother, her father, her little brother . . . those were the faces she saw as the banshee wailed again. And it could have only been doing that to gloat.

She smoked her cigarette, looked around at the lighted buildings surrounding the park, and it sounded to Liz as though New York were coming back to life.

A few minutes later Hellboy approached across the grass. Liz could no longer hear the banshee. HB took out a cigarette and lit it, breathing in deeply and looking up at the stars. "Beautiful night," he said.

"Like no other."

"Hard old hag."

"Did it speak?"

"Of course it did. It said *London.*"

"Right. I'll call that in, then I guess it's back to HQ for us."

"I guess."

"And the banshee?"

Hellboy puffed at the cigarette, and its glowing tip lit his face redder than ever. "Back in dreamland," he said. "Let's go."

Baltimore, Maryland—1997

After so many years, so much time trying to forget her genesis, and after all the help she had received from her friends at the Bureau to forge a new life and existence in a blinkered world, Abby Paris found herself drawn once again to the Memory. Even in her dreams she had never thought to visit there again. Even in the deepest nightmares, when visions of Blake's unnatural *New Ark* haunted her, she had never found herself tempted back to that dark place that had once been her home. It was partly fear, and a desire to disassociate herself from anything Blake had been, but it was also terror at the idea of revealing her deceit to Abe. She had told him and the Bureau that she had no memory of her early life, and she had weathered the tests they had conducted. As far as they were concerned, she was a blank slate upon which they could help her create a whole new history. In fact, Abby knew that her slate was already tainted, and the writing there was dreadful.

There was treachery, and lying, and in the end she supposed she had always known that there would be betrayal. But that did not make it any easier.

She sat in the ruined church and felt the lure of the full moon closing in on her. Deep inside her burned a small fire, one of desire and animalistic freedom, and it was slowly growing. The side of her she could not control was coming to take charge, and in two days she would no longer be herself. Or, she supposed, she would be more herself than ever before. She would be pure Abby Paris, not the restrained, re-created Abby Paris she had lived her life as since escaping Blake.

She looked down at her hands and clenched them. Her fingers were long and fine, graceful, and her nails were short and functional. There were no hairs sprouting from her tattooed knuckles yet. No stretching of the nail beds, no thickening of the nail, no bulking out of her hand and palms to create the pads of feet. She closed her eyes and felt that fire inside simmering, but she knew there was still time. Her betrayal of her friends was cutting deep, but at least she would have a chance to lessen its impact. She would visit the deep blackness of the Memory, do her best to discover where Blake was now, and she would kill him. Simple to say . . . but she did not wish to dwell on the practicalities.

Then she would return to Abe and the Bureau, and her future would be her choice. They could accept her back into the fold—the werewolf they knew about, the liar they did not—or they could let her go out into the world. Any other possibilities did not bear thinking about.

She closed her eyes and tried to calm her mind. It was too busy and too stretched, so she started breathing deeply, concentrating on one point of light, filling herself with its source, and letting it out with each breath. She let her mind wander where it would to begin with, knowing that to rein it in too soon would be detrimental to her efforts. Soon her slowed breathing became more natural, her heartbeat dropped, and the point of light in her mind's eye suffused her bones, flesh, and muscles. She felt illuminated, and her mind drew back and wallowed in the sensation. Such freedom gave her confidence, and that confidence gave her peace of mind, for now at least. The future was always a dark place, so she did not look that way. The past was mostly pain, so did she not look that way either. The present, the here and now, was where she could truly find salvation. Every second of every minute of the next few hours could provide her with an opportunity to validate her life, and she guessed that was all anyone could ever really hope for. Some could merely exist, and some could *live,* and she wanted so much to live.

Something touched her leg, but Abby ignored it. A cat or a rat, it would move on, finding nothing of interest here. Water dripped on her head from the broken church roof, but she reveled in it, an anointment from history. She became separate from the outside world, existing deeper inside her own mind than ever before.

Then, when she felt the time was right, she went further.

As a true creature of the Memory, her way back was relatively easy to find. Abby moved forward into the light, pressed deeper, and when she emerged from the other side, darkness prevailed. This was the primal darkness, the place that was the everywhere and nowhere before creation had come to build upon it, and its vastness terrified her. She hung back for a while, sheltering in her own mind and aware of the light behind her. It no longer shone, but it was there, as much a presence as her own mind. It comforted her, and in this place comfort was hard to find.

This was the landscape of Memory. A great blankness,

deep and endless, to which forgotten things had been relegated, imprisoned. They existed here as conceits, not physical presences, and though they had minds, there was no past
and future, no now and later. Abby's time here had been
long, but she could remember nothing of it, other than a
sense of being known by no one but herself. That strange
solipsistic existence had not been painful, as such, because it
had allowed consideration of no other. But its memory was
still there, painted on the black backdrop for her to draw
upon, and now that she knew so much more of life, its im-
plication was horrendous: she could have stayed here, a
mind festering forever. Blake had pulled her through from
the other side, and for that she wanted to feel grateful. But
his reasons for doing so . . . they had been all his own.
There was only selfishness in his mind. Freeing the creatures
of Memory he might be, but for his own ends, not theirs.

Abby moved on, leaving the light behind. She knew that
it was there for her should she need it, and she had a very
definite sense of being attached to her sleeping body, back
in that ruined church in Baltimore. That was her physical
side, and it was very important to her, a link to the world
that she would never willingly break. She might have been
re-created for someone else's gain, but she was all herself
once more. If ever a time came when she would be relegated
back to the Memory . . . then she would rather die. That
way at least she would be remembered, rather than being
sent back here so that everyone could forget.

Out in the darkness little stirred. She felt intimations of
presences around her, but none made themselves apparent,
and she was surprised at how reduced this place felt, how
empty. She drifted through the Memory, questioning the
dark but receiving only blankness as an answer. Perhaps

anything out there was keeping to itself, shy of her intrusion and unsure of how to respond to this presence, one of them and yet linked to a place beyond. She tried to project kinship, but in truth she felt none. This had once been her place, but that was no longer the case. She had a new home now.

Help me, she thought, and the idea echoed in the dark. *I was once here and always will be.* The echo to this was smaller, as if the darkness itself could see the lie of her statement. *A man took me out, and now I seek him.*

The man! something shouted. Its voice was loud and broken.

The scientist, Abby thought. *The magician.*

He pulled he hurt he tore!

And did he not take you?

He pulled he tried he broke he shouted he left me all alone!

Where are you? Abby thought. She looked through the blackness but saw nothing, sensed nothing other than the vague outlines of things that once were. Echoes of presences, that was all. Most were the ghosts of memories made whole again by Blake, but some drifted, so faint as to be almost invisible even to her. Some were lost forever.

I'm here, I'm lost, the echo said. *I'm here forever.*

Why didn't Blake take you through?

He tried, it hurt, he failed and moved on. Left me here with them.

Them?

The old ones, the oldest ones. The ones even he could not try to touch. And now that so many others have gone, their shapes become more apparent. Can't you see, stranger? Can't you taste them, invader?

I'm no invader, Abby thought, but she knew that was not

the case. She looked further, deeper, but saw only taints on the empty blackness. *What were you?*

A god and a demon, and now barely a memory.

And if I promise to remember? Will you help me then, will you tell me where the man is?

I'm here hurting, I'm here nowhere, and you want me to give you a place?

An idea at least, Abby said. *You'll become my memory, I promise.*

If there could be laughter in Memory, the thing uttered it now. It was a hollow sound, dry and empty and devoid of character. *Don't offer what you can't deliver,* it said. *I'm way beyond Memory now. Too old, too faded . . . too terrible.*

But you can tell me, can't you?

The thing was quiet for a time, and at last Abby sensed something starting to drift closer. *I could hold you here,* it said. *The pain would go, the hurt would go, because you would be my own memory . . . my own waning dream . . .*

I exist, Abby thought, and she suddenly had no fear. *I'm a part of the world, no longer just faded history. I have friends.*

And I can never be a friend, the thing said.

Darkness grew out of darkness, a bulk formed from void, and it was growing closer. Abby began to feel its weight, its gravity, and it was tremendous. She sensed age, eons of time, and an endless stretch of experience and knowledge. *A god and a demon,* the thing had called itself, and she shrank back at its approach. It was not only size and weight but import and presence. She began to think she had been fooled. If this were only an echo, the true source of this Memory must be terrible indeed.

Yes, terrible, it said, and then it laughed for real.

Abby fled, but as she drew herself back out of Memory

and into reality again, the thing she had touched gave her something. Whether intentional or accidental, she fell back into her own body with an image, and a sense of place, and an idea in her mind that showed patterns and designs where there had previously been nothing.

Abby cried out and sat up in the old church. It was fully dark now—the street lamps around the ruin had gone off—and rain pattered down through the open roof. For a few seconds the terrible weight of that thing was all around, pressing down on her body and squeezing breath from her lungs, blood from her veins. She felt the fire of her soul deep inside lessened by the presence, and she screamed against being snuffed out. But then she was alone in the church again, eyes blinking back Memory even as it faded away like an old dream, so complete and solid upon waking and little more than an echo once life and time took over once again.

She was alone, and all that watched her now were the eyes of a ruined Christ.

She hurried from the church. The streets of Baltimore were all but deserted now, occupied only by shuffling nighttime people. A bum pushed a loaded cart down one street, pausing here and there to snatch up something from the gutter and stuff it into one of his already bulging bags. A police cruiser drifted by, wheel hissing along the wet concrete road. It slowed as it passed Abby, but she walked with purpose and confidence, and the cruiser moved on. Three women passed her going in the opposite direction, none of them looking at her or saying anything. They were well dressed and seemed intent on keeping themselves dry with oversized umbrellas. Abby paused and turned to watch them go, wiping rain from her eyes as though that would make her vision clearer.

She was trying to make sense of what she had seen in the Memory. As she tumbled back out of that place, the huge presence had given her something, an image or a smell, a location or a direction. She was struggling to get hold of it and translate it before it faded away, a dream gone to shreds. Blake was somewhere in there, she was sure. If she could make sense of what she had been given, she was certain that it would tell her either where he had been or where he was now.

She ducked into a doorway and pulled a small notebook from her pocket. There was the nub of a pencil in there too, and she bent forward, shielding the paper from the rain as she started jotting, doodling, letting her mind run off at whatever tangents it chose.

The moon tugged at her. She glanced up and saw its pale image behind the rain clouds. If only clouds would hide her from the moon in a couple of nights' time. She worried about that—what she would do and to whom—but it was also a fascinating prospect. Back at Bureau HQ it had been deer, and before that on the *New Ark* there was nothing she could remember, and she was happy keeping it that way. But now she was faced with true freedom for the first time, and though she was terrified of what she would do, she was fascinated as well. *Will I be a murderer?* she thought. She hoped not. But if that was her destiny, then she would embrace it, become who she really was, be herself for the very first time—free of Blake, free of the Bureau, liberated and unbound.

Abe had tried to help her create a history, when in reality she was the only one with the power to do that.

She glanced down at the paper and saw that while she had been thinking, her hands had been doing their own thing. There were words and phrases jotted there, smudged lines that could have been something else. She turned the page and carried on, trying to make sense of what that huge presence had left her.

She thought of Blake and her time in the *New Ark* and what might have come before. She had little memory of being birthed, though there was a sense of time beginning, a point at which life had started. Blake had created her from the Memory, and it had been a pure creation, not a resurrection. Abby was not a werewolf that had lived before but rather a creature constructed from the faded memories of all of humanity. She was born of old superstitions, given life where before there had been only potential. She was like a never-ending dream brought into reality. And instead of fading away as time took hold, she had taken on true form.

Blake was the nearest thing she had to a father, but she had no love for him. She had seen his mind and known its madness, understood what he was capable of. She had always known that this day would come. She should have told Abe . . .

"No!" she said. "Dammit, no!" Her dilemma was growing, because she was aware of what would be happening around the world by now. She knew what was aboard the *New Ark*, and her brief visit to the Memory had shown her how much had been taken from there, how *empty* that place of myth and legend now seemed. The world was full of monsters tonight, and she had spent her life swearing that she would not be one of them. She could tell Abe and Hellboy what she knew, but that would draw them in deep and fast. They would die. She had no doubts about that. She would not consider other possibilities. Betray them, yes, but she would not kill her friends.

She looked back at the paper, and whatever the Memory presence had given her had been channeled through her hand. While she was distracted by her own deep thoughts, information had risen from the depths. She had written of intent, though she had an idea of that already. She had sketched ideas of vengeance and intervention, an image of the world gathered under a pair of spread wings, Blake taking the world under his own control. That, too, she had suspected. What she had never known was how and where, and here was a rough map, drawn in her own hand, of a place she could not yet recognize.

But she would find out.

She had gone to the Memory seeking Blake, and something he had left behind had given her a map. She should have been pleased, but she knew what was to come. This information only took her one quick step closer to her doom.

Abby left Baltimore in the dark, rain still sheeting down, and as she sat in the back of the taxi, the world opened up to her. At the airport she would buy a map and sit drinking coffee until she could figure out where her sketch would lead her. Then she would fly, and during the flight she would prepare herself for whatever was to come.

She looked out the rain-smeared window and saw the moon peering from behind the thinning clouds. Her nemesis and her hope, her devil and her comfort. Her breathing was shallow, and she was terribly aware of the taxi driver's hot blood coursing through his veins.

She could hear the beating of his heart.

Time was running out.

Bureau of Paranormal Research and Defense Headquarters, Fairfield, Connecticut—1997

Hellboy and Liz returned to HQ at daybreak. They stood in the parking lot and watched the sun rise, sharing a silent moment.

As they entered the building and signed in, Tom Manning hurried across the lobby, coffee cup in one hand and sheaf of papers in the other. "We think we know!" he said. "It's flimsy, but it seems to tie in with what's been happening. Come on, Kate's waiting."

"Have you told Abe?" Hellboy asked.

Tom paused and glared at Hellboy. "Considering he's gone off on his own, I'm not sure that's relevant."

Hellboy reared up, rising onto the tips of his hooves, tail swishing at the floor. "Of course it's relevant," he whispered. "Tom, don't piss me off on this one. You know where Abe's gone, and you know why. And it's not as if he's avoiding anything. Do you really think he'd want to be dropped into the Caribbean to fight a kraken the size of Iceland?"

"It's not right," Tom said. He stood his ground without averting his eyes, and Hellboy was quietly impressed.

"It *is* right, it just doesn't follow your rules."

"Rules are what make us—"

"Don't screw with me, Tom. Kate's classy *cryptid* word can apply to anyone here, you know that. Even you, Tom. Honorary cryptid. Like that?"

Tom shook his head, but he smiled tightly, and it did something to drag the exhaustion from his face for a while. "I'll call Abe and fill him in. Of course I will. But you're wrong, Hellboy."

"About you being—"

"No, that's good. I like that. But you're wrong to lump yourself in with the things screwing up the world today. I'm a human being. So was Hitler. See?"

Hellboy growled at the name and everything it conjured, but he knew why Tom had used that analogy. And yes, he saw.

"So let's work out what we can do about all this. If what Kate's come up with is right, you and Liz will be jetting off again very soon."

"London?"

"London. But we wanted to talk it through with you first, show you some more pictures that have just come in. If you and Liz agree we're on the right track, I've got lots of phone calls to make while you're en route."

"Selling your shares?"

"I wish. No, I'll be speaking to the president and to the prime minister of the U.K., asking them to mobilize their armed forces."

"What'd I tell you?" Hellboy said to Liz. "Lots of very big guns."

Liz lit a cigarette and offered Hellboy a light. "Why do I feel we're going to have a busy few days?" she said. "Damn, all I want to do is sleep."

Tom waved them on with his handful of papers. "No rest for the wicked," he said. "Let's go."

Kate Corrigan had changed her clothes since their meeting the day before, but her eyes held the same tiredness. If she had slept, Hellboy thought, it had been a rest troubled by dreams and images that would haunt her for a long time.

The footage of that ocean liner being taken apart was enough to disturb anyone's sleep.

"Hellboy, Liz," she said in greeting. "Have a coffee."

"Caffeine," Liz said. She stood at the coffee machine in the corner of the conference room, poured and drank a cup, then prepared another one.

"Are you all right?" Kate asked. She had evidently seen the scratches and scrapes across Liz's face and forearms, evidence of her scuffle with the New York banshee.

"Just dandy."

"How was the banshee?" Kate asked.

"Old, ugly, and pissed," Hellboy said. "And smelly."

Kate frowned, Tom walked in, and Liz took a seat beside Hellboy. He leaned toward her and sniffed, then smiled. "But you'll be pleased to know that its scent doesn't linger."

"London," Tom said. "You sure that's what it was saying?"

Hellboy looked steadily at Tom. "Well, it had my fist down its throat at the time, but yeah, I think that's what it said."

"Sorry," Tom said, shaking his head. "Look at these." He slid some photographs across the table to Liz and Hellboy and sat back with his hands on his head and his eyes closed. Hellboy thought he looked exhausted. There was only so much stress a man could take.

"So what new delights do we have here?" Hellboy said. He separated the pictures on the table and leaned over them. "Oh, nice."

The first picture showed a sea of bodies bobbing against a boat's hull. They were broken, ruptured, and leaking. Hellboy guessed there were more than a hundred dead people there, bloated and pathetic. "Another kraken?"

"Sea serpent, off the coast of Gibraltar," Kate said. "A

sergeant from the Gibraltar police contacted us, but we've had to put him on standby. He's not happy. The serpent has sunk several pleasure boats and a police launch. It seems to kill people for pleasure, no reports of any eating yet."

"Charming," Liz said. She was scanning the picture closely, as if looking for someone familiar. Hellboy knew she took this all so seriously, making herself a part of each tragedy instead of just coming in from the outside. She claimed that being able to empathize gave her an edge. He thought that sometimes it just gave her a head full of grief.

"It capsizes boats and thrashes around until all the passengers are dead, either drowned or . . ."

"Torn up," Tom said. He leaned across the table. "This one was taken in the Egyptian desert: fire dogs, scorching everything they come across. Dozens dead so far, but the death toll's probably a lot higher because of all the Bedouin settlements that haven't been reached yet."

"Fire dogs," Hellboy said. "Damn!"

"There's lots more," Kate said. She nodded at the pictures. "Lots more cryptids, so many more dead people. Hundreds. Thousands. You can look at them all if you want, but it all amounts to the same thing."

"We're under attack," Hellboy said.

The room fell silent. Liz was still studying the photographs, but Hellboy knew she was still listening, waiting for someone to speak.

"What?" Hellboy said. "You don't agree with me?"

"I'm not sure what I think," Kate said. "We've been asked for help from more than forty places across the globe, and most of them we've put on hold. The military of several countries have had contact with cryptids, and mostly they've come out worse. Jets weren't designed to fight dragons; machine guns can't harm wraiths. This is technology versus mythology, and the unknown has always been stronger."

"Well, dammit, let's go! Liz and I can leave right now, and I'm in the mood for a fight. That banshee pissed me off."

"London," Tom said. "Don't you want to hear about that?"

"So what's tearing up London?"

"Nothing." Tom flicked through the papers he still clasped in his hand. "Nothing yet. But there's a meeting being held there day after tomorrow, a conference of world leaders spending a week talking about environmental issues. The plan is, at the end of the week they'd have come up with an action plan to save our planet." He smiled grimly.

"Yeah, right," Hellboy said. "So long as it doesn't cost too much, eh?"

Tom shrugged. "Not our problem right now. What is our problem is that if the banshee was right and Blake is targeting London, it could be he's planning to take them out."

Hellboy frowned. "So . . . everything else is a distraction?"

"That could be why London has escaped thus far."

"World leaders, you say?"

"Some of the biggest."

"Hmm. So we leave these monsters all over the world to get on with their killing and murdering, and we fly off to London—where nothing has happened so far—to baby-sit some soft-assed, smooth-skinned politicians?"

"Hellboy . . . we're not trusted. You and I aren't trusted, the BPRD is a shadow organization to many people, and what we do here is often questioned at the highest levels.

We make our own choices because we're allied to no one. Do you think I'm going to come off the phone this afternoon having convinced NATO that they need to mobilize their armed forces? Protect London? What do I say when they ask for proof of this theory?"

"Tell them I beat the truth out of a banshee in Central Park."

"Precisely."

"Abe," Liz said. "Abby!"

"I was going to come to that," Kate said.

"What?" Hellboy asked.

"Abby killed a werewolf in Baltimore," Kate said. "And Abby *is* a werewolf. She disappears just as the cryptids pop up . . . and maybe I'm adding two and two to make five again. Or maybe I'm not."

"Hang on," Hellboy said. "You're suggesting that Abby is one of Blake's?"

"I don't know," Kate said. "Dammit, we know *nothing*! But it just seems to be strange timing, and I wouldn't be surprised if what's happening now is relevant somehow to Abby. Why else choose now, when shit the size of Nova Scotia is hitting the fan, to do a runner?"

Hellboy stood. "This is all too much," he said. "Too clear and convenient, and too woolly. Where do these things come from? The Memory? What *is* that? Somewhere described by a book that probably doesn't exist? How can Blake—if *he* even exists—pull them through? You say he'd be over ninety. That's old for a magical criminal mastermind. Where is he hiding? What are his reasons? Where are the other things he's created out of mythology and legend? Where, what, how, why, who, and why am I so damn *pissed* that I can't put any of this together?"

"Way I see it," Liz said, "is that none of that matters." She stood and walked over to Hellboy. He was resting his forehead against the window, scraping the glass with his right hand as if trying to score his way through. "What matters is this, HB." She showed him a picture of a dead child, throat ripped out by a monster. And then a photograph of a building smashed to pieces by something big. Another one, a tank on its side with its crew spilled out like soft red innards. They were all dead, and black things with membranous wings were eating them.

He turned and pushed past her, going back to the table. "Let Abe know," he said. "And tell him about London. If there's any truth in all this, Abby may somehow know where Blake's going. And for whatever reasons she may have, she could be going there to meet him."

"Hellboy, I don't think Abby—"

"We just can't tell," he said. "Dammit, Abe." He shook his head and wished more than anything that he could take off after his friend. But Liz was right. She had shown him what mattered. Conjecture aside, there were certain truths that could not be denied. BPRD could not fight this whole new world of chaos, but if there was the slightest chance that they could tackle its cause, its core, then that was where he should be.

"London?" Liz said.

Hellboy nodded. "London. Let's see if we can talk some sense into those Brits."

Yorkshire Moors, England—1988

"It was a long time ago," Richard said. "Almost five hundred years. Around that time there were few records being made of the world, few histories written down for future generations. But our friend Zahid de Lainree has those histories, and they're as certain in his book as any I've ever read."

"So what does he say about the werewolf?" Galileo Blake asked.

"Nothing too obvious," Richard said. "That wasn't his way." He was tired and angry, and having to hike across the moors in the dark had set him on edge. He had been to many strange places—underground tombs, forgotten temples, graveyards to myth and memory—but these misty, mysterious plains really got to the heart of him. Perhaps because everything was so of the here and now, yet they could have been walking across a landscape ten thousand years old. The fears of the moors were timeless. And that was why he and Gal were here.

"But he says something that led us here, now, to this pissing place? Yes?" Gal was obviously tired and edgy as well.

Richard smiled at his brother, but perhaps the moonlight distorted it into a grimace. "It's obscure," he said.

"Isn't it always?"

Richard closed his eyes and let the coolness of the moor wash over him. He felt the breeze whispering secrets, felt the age of the land beneath his feet, sensed the mysteries it contained if only he were prepared to dig. He *would* be digging, but not here and now. Later. This evening probably, the following morning at the latest. And if the *Book of Ways* turned out to be as accurate and trustworthy as they had found it over the years, by tomorrow lunchtime his brother would be sending a trace of werewolf back to their father.

His brother. Galileo had aged over the past few years. His hair had thinned, its remnants turning gray, and his face had taken on the contour lines of a map of sad places. His eyes still showed the heart of him, the pain there, the anger, consuming and as rich as the day they had found their mother's body in the burning house. But there was something else there that Richard had grown to fear. He had suspected it for several years . . . but this was his brother, his own flesh and blood, and the last thing he wanted to believe was that Gal was mad.

"Well?" Gal said.

"It tells a tale and draws a map," Richard said. "I can follow both, given time."

"Good." Gal groaned and pulled his coat around his shoulders, trying to shield himself from the breeze.

"Gal, are you sure you're ready for another sending?"

"Never ready," Gal muttered.

"Maybe we should wait?"

Gal shook his head but did not answer. In the stark moonlight, as the mist thickened and settled on their clothes like rain, Richard thought he looked like a walking corpse.

"They chased it," Richard said. He had cast a spell of course and was hunched over the book, reading by moonlight. It gave the words a particularly sharp edge. "It had taken a child, a farmer's baby, and the father was killed trying to fight it off. But they thought it was wounded. Its familiar call was higher and more frequent. They saw a shadow as they ran—the creature with the child in its mouth. Out of the village and across the moor toward the rock like a pointing finger. There." Richard nodded at a distant hillside, where a single weathered rock pointed skyward. He set off, and Gal followed.

Richard kept the *Book of Ways* open before him, staring down and trusting instinct not to walk him into a hole. The spell of course was still rich and potent, and he could still see the truth threaded between Zahid de Lainree's words and diagrams. The book's stories were as hidden as the creatures it talked about.

"How did they wound it?" Gal asked.

Richard stared at the book and shook his head. "It doesn't say. I suppose even a werewolf will develop an itch with a pitchfork in its throat."

"Father will use this well," Gal said, quieter than before. "It'll be one of his secret weapons. It can sit among people forever until he needs it to do his bidding. No tentacles or fire breathing, you see."

Richard heard no jest behind his brother's words. "If you want me to go on, then keep quiet. This isn't easy." He stopped and looked down at the book again, half closing his eyes so that the true path of the words could shine through. "Here," he said. "This is where it made its first stand. Dropped the child. Hid behind a rock—that one there— and pounced as the pursuers reached where we are now." Richard looked at the huge rock, half expecting the werewolf to appear from within its shadow again. But the moor was as silent and secretive as ever.

"*First* stand?"

"Yes." Richard squatted and looked again at the book. "It

killed two men and a woman here, and took more wounds. But each cut made it more ferocious. It tore one of the men apart while others were spearing it. And then it picked up the child . . ."

"And?" Gal said after a pause. "Which way did it go then?"

"It picked up the child and killed it in front of everyone. It wasn't hungry anymore. Just wanted to make a point." Richard stood and started walking again, conscious of Gal following him. *Is this really us?* he thought. *Do we really want something that'll do such a thing? There are wonders in the Memory, but monsters too. Have we been doing this for so long that we've forgotten how to differentiate?*

Gal walked past him, still hunched into his coat. "This way?" he said, pointing. "That way? Which way, Rich?"

Richard closed his eyes and pointed. "There. Down into the valley. It was running faster now, and the people were terrified at what they'd seen. But there were two who followed hard on its heels: the child's mother, eager for revenge, and the werewolf's wife."

The brothers walked down the hillside into the shallow valley. Richard led the way, the *Book of Ways* held open before him, and Gal held back. The mist was heavier here, and soon they were enveloped, its coolness like a moist breath on their exposed skin. Shapes floated here and there, parting the mist, and they could have been wraiths. Richard ignored them, knowing that they would not trouble the two brothers.

"Here," Richard said. His brother stood by his side and waited. "This is where it made its second stand. There were still a few villagers keeping up with the child's mother and the creature's wife, and this is where it stopped to dispatch them. There, on that rock. There were scratches and cracks on the stone surface, and by the time the battle was over, they ran full of blood. They gave a message . . . but no one ever knew what it said."

"I'll bet we would," Gal said, jumping onto the rock and striding across its surface. He looked down, kicking at moss here and there, trying to uncover the faults and scores talked of in the book. "This is much older than everything else around here, you can just feel it. And it's been used for . . . things."

Richard moved on. "Gal. Whatever was written there has been changed since the werewolf. Too much time has gone by, too much weathering, and it isn't used anymore."

"But it will be," Gal said. "When Father's time comes, places like this will come back into the land. And we'll be there to see it happen!"

Sacrifice and murder, Richard thought. *Werewolves killing children and adults becoming monsters. Father never told me it would be like this.* He had never stated his burgeoning doubt to his brother, and he hoped that Gal could not sense it. Richard had no idea what his brother's madness could make him capable of.

"After that," Richard said, "there was only the wife left. The child's mother lay dead on the flat rock."

"So how did she kill it?" Gal asked. "I assume the wife killed the werewolf, otherwise why would we be here?"

Richard shrugged. "It wouldn't be the first time de Lainree's text has led us astray."

"No," Gal said. "No, the wolf died here. I can feel it. Can't you? Can't you smell its final breath on the mist, see its final visions flitting through the shadows?"

Richard kept walking, but he knew what Gal meant.

They had entered a haunted place, and the haunting was not merely human. It was something else and something more. "A marsh," Richard said. He looked down at the book and turned a page, and the mist parted to allow the moonlight access. Like blood running across the flat rock, moonlight illuminated the paths of truth between and under de Lainree's writings.

Richard stopped and pointed. "There. The werewolf fell into a marsh . . . the wife saw it struggling, sinking, howling . . . and when it went under, she sowed the marsh with her and her husband's lifetime savings: a handful of silver coins."

"How poetic," Gal said, but he sounded hungry.

"I'm tired," Richard said. He sat on the damp ground and dipped his head, closing the book at last. The spell of course faded quickly, and he felt the usual sense of relief at its passing. Magic had never been easy for him. "I'm exhausted. I need to rest, and you . . . you . . ."

Gal placed his coat around his brother's shoulders. "I'll dig," he said.

The werewolf had been preserved by the peaty ground. Much of it had reverted to the man upon death, but here and there patches of fur remained, and its lower jaw still sprouted fearsome teeth that were chipped with use. Gal had a whole body to choose from.

When he finally had the small sample to send, he drew shapes in the damp ground with his shovel and placed the werewolf's finger inside. And then he cast his spells, started chanting, and submitted himself to the Memory once again.

———

Both brothers woke up at daybreak. The mist was gone, the sun was up. And the moor felt just as haunted and alien as ever.

Baltimore, Maryland—1997

Kate Corrigan called Abe and filled him in on Blake, London, and the possibility of Abby Paris being more of a mystery than they thought. Abe listened and responded at all the appropriate places, but when Kate severed the connection, he sat staring at his satellite phone, blinking slowly and trying to digest what he had just heard. He had pulled off the freeway to answer the phone, and he watched the cars going by, taking people from here to there, the past to the future, and none of them really knowing anything about the world around them. He often envied them that.

He threw the phone onto the passenger seat and shook his head. The more he thought about what Kate had said, the more worried he became. He knew Abby better than anyone, yet still she was an enigma, and some of what Kate said could well be true. Perhaps that was part of what drew him to her so powerfully: she was as mysterious as he. Now that she was missing, and this stuff about a mad old scientist and magician had surfaced, he was more worried about her than ever.

Especially as she had killed her own kind. He had no concept of how that would make her feel.

But Abe was unconvinced by the Benedict Blake idea. It all seemed too easily explained and logical, whereas what was happening in the world right now was the return of mystery.

He sat by the freeway and thought things through, but whichever way he went he came up against a wall. Abby's disappearance did not surprise him—he had always thought that she would run one day—but its timing did. While not as involved as Abe or the others, she had seemed committed to the BPRD and the cause it furthered. To abandon it in what might well be its hour of need . . . that did not seem like Abby. It did not seem *right.*

But am I *abandoning it as well?* Abe thought. *Leaving Hellboy and Liz and the others to face these things on their own?* It was an uncomfortable thought, and yet it did not trouble him as much as it should. Because somewhere, beneath the surface action and reaction that had ruled his day, he could perceive a deeper truth: Abby was still involved, and by following her he would be playing a significant role in events. All he had to do was work out how, and why.

As it stood he had no idea where Abby was going. He had suspected Paris, and Kate had mentioned London as a possible target for some sort of attack. Those two cities weren't a million miles apart, so at least he had the larger destination of northern Europe in mind. Once he was there, the situation might have advanced enough for him to pin down her location much more easily.

But first he had a dead werewolf to view.

"Take it easy, Abby," he said, pulling out onto the freeway. "Just take it easy. I'll be with you as soon as I can."

In the morgue of the Baltimore Medical Center, several policemen stood in a close huddle while Abe waited for the mortician to wheel out the body. They stared at Abe, whispering behind gloved hands, but he ignored them. He was used to the attention. If they got too annoying, he'd flare his gills. Give them something to tell their grandkids. The world today was full of bedtime stories in the making.

"Nothing weird, nothing wacky," the mortician said, pushing the trolley into the room ahead of her. Her name was Mary, and Abe had spoken to her before on several occasions. She had worked at the hospital for more than thirty years, and by her own admission she had seen many strange things, and a few beyond strange. "Just a dead guy with half his head blown away."

"I guess you see that all the time," Abe said.

Mary shrugged. "Enough to make it normal." She flipped back the sheet.

Abe glanced at the dead man's face. Witness statements said that Abby had pushed the pistol into his eye and pulled the trigger. Abe could believe that. The top of the guy's head had disappeared, and a flow of brain matter stained the gurney.

"Still traces of the silver bullet in his skull," Mary said. "That *was* strange. Cops said a few of the witnesses reckon he was the supposed werewolf that's been stalking Baltimore."

"Do you believe in werewolves?" Abe asked. Mary looked at him with such a strange expression that Abe went back to examining the corpse.

Even dead, the man seemed to have a smile on his face. If he'd died with Abby straddling his chest, Abe could maybe understand. He closed his eyes and shook his head, wished Hellboy were here to offer a wisecrack. Then when he looked again, he saw something.

"What's this?"

"Where?"

Abe pointed to a part of the spilled brain that looked as though it had been heated with a blowtorch.

"Powder burns is my guess," Mary said.

"Powder burns inside a head?"

"I'm thinking she pulled the trigger twice in quick succession. First bullet blew out the skull and left bits of itself embedded in the bones. Second one splashed the guy's brains all over the road. Ballistics are still down there, scooping out the gutters to find the second bullet."

Abe shook his head. "It's the effects of silver. Melted the guy's brains as it opened up his head."

"Right," Mary said. It would have been difficult to inject more sarcasm into her answer, so Abe did not look up again.

He moved down the body, pushing the sheet to its feet. The postmortem wounds were roughly sewn. The man's chest was hairy but not unnaturally so. His nails were well manicured, his toes the correct length, and while he was well muscled, there was nothing here that could not be worked on in a gym.

But Abe saw what he was looking for straight away, and he could not believe what Mary had missed.

"Thanks, Mary," he said. He turned to leave, and the mortician called after him.

"Is that it? So what did you find?"

"Something not there," Abe said. The cops parted and let him walk between them. "Guys," he said. The morgue doors closed with a secretive whisper, and Abe made his way quickly from the building. It was dark and raining outside. He stood with his head up and his mouth open, refreshed.

He has no navel, he thought. *The werewolf was never born.*

In the single, confused, intimate moment he and Abby had shared, the first thing that had struck him about her—beyond her beauty and grace—had been her lack of a belly button.

Abe sat in his car and spent a long time wondering what this meant.

Somewhere below the North Sea—1997

The serpent blinked the rush of tainted salt water from its eyes, felt the sea's acidity working at its scales, snorted out the stench of unnatural filth and rot that permeated the ocean, and yet still it reveled in this wonderful new existence. Where it had come from the floating had been of a different kind, and the simple pleasure of life had been absent for so long. Existence had been of a moment, a space between heartbeats, a point of potential rather than the endless sea of sensation it was now experiencing. It had no memory of that place other than a long, blank eternity, and each instant that passed by now was the richest it had ever known. It swooped deep and startled a school of small fish; it rose up and felt the alien heat of the sun on its slick spine. It had been back for years, yet life was as exquisite as ever.

There were other things with it down here in the ocean. It had sensed the huge shadows deep down, and occasionally it sank lower to feel their weight. Deeper than light could go, they floated in ocean currents of their own making, great masses of life that seemed to carry their own gravity with them. The serpent saw and understood, sensed their common source, and yet still it feared these things. They went beyond the scope of its senses. They were as big as the world, and the one thing the serpent's father had communicated before setting it free was that the world was something to fear. The serpent knew that the world would poison it, eat it, kill it, and forget it. Scared by these thoughts—angered as well—it was happy that the vast shadows were doing their own thing. Its father had created them as well; they were on its side.

Something bade it rise. It cut through the water and broke surface to sunlight. It swam that way for a while, dipping in and out of the waves and playing with them. To its side swam other things, with tentacles and suckers and faces it had never known before. To its other side . . . Father. He stood on the huge ship and stared down at his creations, smiling, talking, setting the air aflame with words that lit on the serpent's skin and burned their way inside. It was a gentle sensation, as if something warm were pressing itself in through its scales, and as it sank below the waves again, it began to make sense of what its father was saying.

And it prepared.

The shape closed in later that day.

The serpent sensed it from a great distance. It was a solid, dark presence in the ocean, something unnatural and clumsy that hacked at the sea instead of stroking it, slashed it apart to move instead of shifting with the water. This thing traveled with a confidence that was unfounded. It sent probing tendrils of sounds ahead, and the serpent and other shadows swallowed them up. It exuded other signs as well, scents and signals that marked it as something definitely not of the ocean but rather something here to destroy.

Unclean, the serpent's father had said. *Poison . . . filth . . . rancid . . .*

When the visitor's sounding struck the father's ship and became confused—echoes, spiraling back and forth and casting the sea in a less friendly tune—the serpent knew that it was time to act.

It rose to the surface and leaped, arching through the air and landing back with a huge splash. It thrashed its tail, flexed its body, and twisted and turned, creating a great disturbance in the ocean that it hoped its father would see. And then it dove deep and swam hard.

The water parted silently around the serpent's head. The creature sliced the ocean as if it were only a shadow, and it set fish and other sea life spinning in its wake, confused and startled at what had just passed by yet ignorant of its shape. It felt the distance growing between it and its father's ship, and that was uncomfortable. But its course was plainly set. The serpent was here because of its father, it was here for a reason, and today it would express its gratitude in one of the greatest ways.

The soundings from the invader came strong and hard, parting around the serpent and being swallowed. The closer it came, the more it hurt the serpent's innards every time one of these echoes sounded. Anger grew, rage wallowed in the creature's guts, and by the time it reached the huge metal invader, it was alight with violence.

Too late, the invader noted its presence. With a pathetic cough it unleashed a defense against the serpent. The creature twisted and evaded the torpedo, then darted in at the vessel's hull. The submarine—home to the killers of memory, the serpent's father had said—roared on through the depths, but now there were sounds coming from it that the serpent relished. Breaking sounds, creaking, moaning.

It took the submarine deeper.

Another torpedo fired, and the ocean caught fire.

Stunned, confused, the serpent parted from the submarine and sank quickly, trying to escape the pounding impact of the explosion that had ripped its skin and shattered its insides. But above, the invader was also in trouble. The metallic creaks and groans had increased into a drawn-out squeal, and another, smaller explosion sent a wave of heat through the water. The serpent halted its descent and rose again, pained but exhilarated.

The submarine had all but stopped moving, and it now hung still in the water. Great streams of bubbles rose from its nose, and in those streams were other things that smelled bad, felt worse. Even in death, this thing was dirtying the sea.

Enemies of memory, the serpent's father had said.

Killers of wonder.

Enraged, the serpent rose quickly and struck the submarine again.

And then—sensing a great shadow rising from below, feeling the rush of displaced water, hearing the thumping impacts of the thing's mind as it turned over those same words from Father—the serpent darted away, happy to let another forgotten memory finish the task it had begun.

Soon it was in free water again, untouched by the noises and impacts of the submarine's demise. It swam back to the ship, ignorant of its wounds. The main thought in its mind was, *Killers of memory, memories themselves.*

In the serpent's mind, Father smiled.

Baltimore International Airport—1997

Abby Paris sat at a coffee shop table in BWI, absently stroking her smooth stomach as she noted and doodled in a writing pad. Her mug of coffee had grown cold on the table before her, and the bustle of passengers lining up to pass through security had faded away to a background murmur. All her concentration was on her pen, the paper in front of her, and the shapes that were appearing there. Her hand moved, but she was not doing the drawing. She was remembering the Memory and the voice of the thing that had spoken to her in there. She was certain it had given her information. No matter how old it claimed to be, how awful, how faded and alone now that Blake had passed it by, she thought it had given her *something* of value before she withdrew. Trouble was, she had no idea what.

She closed her eyes, hoping that complete disassociation would aid her automatic drawing.

"Hey, nice picture."

Abby opened her eyes. A young man was sitting across the table, smiling at her as he sipped from a cup of coffee. He was fit, attractive, and evidently untroubled by deeper things.

"Get lost," Abby said.

"Hey now, no need to be like that!" He leaned forward, glancing left and right as if about to impart a secret. "How about we get lost together?"

Abby dropped the pencil, leaned across the table, and hissed. She felt the power coming to the fore, the lack of control that gave her such dreadful freedom, and she tasted the tang of blood in her mouth. Whatever the boy saw or smelled scared the hell out of him. He stood, knocked his coffee across the table, and ran. He didn't make a sound.

Abby sat back and snatched up her writing pad before the coffee could stain it. Her heart had not skipped a beat. But inside, where nobody ever saw, she could feel the change coming over her. *Why the hell did I run two days before a full moon?* she thought. But it had been an impulse, and there was no way she could have controlled what happened. Perhaps she *had* no control. The birthing at the hands of Blake, escape from the *New Ark,* being rescued by Abe, the BPRD, killing that werewolf in Baltimore . . . her whole life had the feel of being preordained, and the more she fought against it, the more she felt steered by something way beyond her ken.

"Shit." She opened her eyes, glanced down at the pad, and saw yet another signature of fate.

Growling at the boy had split her gums, and blood had sprayed across the table and pattered down onto her writing pad. It was smudged now, already drying, and it had smeared into a pattern she recognized.

A *place* she recognized.

How can something from the Memory make that happen? she thought. *That wasn't me, not my hand, not my subconscious. That was . . .*

But it would not do to think about this too much.

She tore off the sheet of paper and screwed it up. She had seen enough maps of Great Britain to recognize this impromptu bloody sketch. And the one place where her dripped blood had remained in a raised bubble instead of being smeared into coastlines was London.

Abby went to buy a ticket, hoping that she would not see the boy on her flight. She had caught a whiff of his blood, and it smelled good.

Private airfield, Bridgeport, Connecticut—1997

Liz sat in the driver's seat of the Humvee and watched Hellboy inspect the Lear jet. He'd told her to sit and wait while he gave it the once-over. *Don't want any little green men ripping the engine apart when we're at twenty thousand feet.* Said he'd be using a particularly probing talisman, and her presence could mess up the balance. *Got this from a demon in Marrakech, and it's not a girl-friendly spell.* Liz had smiled at him and nodded, and she sat watching him stride around the aircraft. Maybe he just wanted to impress her. She didn't know. Lots of stuff about Hellboy impressed her, and lots of stuff was still a mystery as well. For someone so open and unencumbered by ego, sometimes he wasn't only a closed book, he was a book yet to be written.

Maybe his real time's still to come, Liz thought. It was an idea she'd had a few times before: that Hellboy was here for some specific purpose, and all this BPRD demon-chasing, ghost-hunting, paranormal-investigating stuff was just practice for the real job to come. And that troubled her more than anything. Because she knew that Hellboy was far from normal, and his eventual fate would be far from normal as well. She dreaded that. He was the best friend she'd ever had, and she never wanted to lose him.

———————

Hellboy was nervous. The Lear sat proud and magnificent on the concrete, waiting for the crew to board and wind her up, waiting to jet him and Liz off to London, and it was all so damn normal and easy and convenient that he couldn't help but feel jumpy about the whole thing. Usually he preferred the simple explanation—and a lot of times he'd found it to be the correct one—but this time the simple explanation left a lot unsaid.

Then there was Kate's little lecture about Zahid de Lainree and the Memory. That had really set Hellboy's teeth on edge. The Memory sounded too much like places he'd been to before. And this de Lainree character, though dead a long time, must have known far too much for his own good.

Arcane knowledge sometimes scared Hellboy, because there was so much he didn't know. About himself, for instance, and where he'd come from, and why he was here. He could gloss over those questions as much as he liked, avoid their implications, but they still needed to be answered.

He walked around the aircraft, peering into the two jets, stooping to go underneath and check out the landing gear, running his fingers around the window rims, checking that the flaps were clear and the fueling points were shut and locked. He fished around in his belt while he went, fingers brushing against talismans and wards, precious stones and dust from distant deserts, until he found what he wanted. In fact, it found him, pricking his finger and drawing blood.

"Ouch!" He pulled out the demon's hair and held it at arm's length, narrowing one eye and making sure its tip was clear of blood. He didn't know whether that would affect any readings, but demons were devious creatures, and any excuse would do.

The hair clear, he rested it in the palm of his huge right hand and gently blew on it. It spun like a compass needle and nestled along a crease in his hand, like a line of dirt ground into his lifeline. "OK, here we go. Ready, demon?" There was no answer, but the hair twitched slightly. "Now, what were those damn words . . . ?" Hellboy closed his eyes, concentrating on his time in Marrakech back in '71. He pictured the scene with the demon and the tea shop, the rancid pipe smoke filling the room and outlining the fiend as an invisible space of clear air. Ironic, as that demon had been as dirty as they come. The imp and Hellboy had cut a deal, and the payment was a single hair from the creature's head. Unable to lie—most couldn't with Hellboy's fist down their throats—the demon had nodded a promise, and when Hellboy let it go, it made good on its vow. Strange behavior for a demon, but he guessed he'd scared it. "Those damn words!" he muttered, frowning hard in concentration. And then a small breeze blew across the airport concrete and set the hair tickling his palm, and the words came back to him.

"*Ystrad bwlch, penperlleni mynach fwnynw.*" The hair rose above his palm and spun in the air, a compass gone mad. "Ahh, my memory's not as bad as I thought." Hellboy smiled, the hair flopped back into his hand, and the smile slipped from his face. "Damn."

"What's up with you?" Liz called. Obviously bored with sitting in the Humvee, she'd come to investigate. He could hardly be angry with her.

"Nothing really," he said. He shook the demon hair, threw it into the air, and caught it again. It did nothing of its own volition. "The reading says the jet's all clear."

"Then why is that bad?"

"It's not, it's just that I don't trust it."

"Then why use whatever it is you're holding there in the first place?"

"Er . . ." Hellboy shrugged, slipped the hair back into a belt pocket, and started inspecting the aircraft again.

Liz tapped his shoulder. "What are we looking for, exactly?"

Hellboy turned. His shoulders slumped as tension lifted—a little—and Liz's dry smile lit him up. Hellboy had a lot of friends, but they were mainly people he could call on when he needed help. Liz was someone who knew to call on him. "Well," he said, "anything that doesn't belong on a plane. Or anything that does belong but looks like it doesn't. Or something that should but looks like it shouldn't."

Liz frowned. "Oh, my God," she said. "Look! Hellboy, there!" She pointed over his shoulder.

He spun around, fisting both hands and squinting against a possible impact. "What? Where?"

"It's a *wing*!"

He lowered his head. Yeah, Liz was a good friend, and she knew she could get away with more than most. Hellboy turned quickly and slung her over his shoulder.

"Damn ape!" she said. "Unhand me! Let go! You're a Neanderthal!"

"I'm just looking after you while I check the plane over," he said, and he did. Liz struggled and kicked for a couple of minutes, then just lay there having a rest while Hellboy did another circuit of the aircraft. He tried to hold in the laughter that was brewing. At first he passed it off as a burp, much to Liz's disgust. Then another rumble he put down to hunger. And then, just as his laugh burst out to deny explanation, Liz started laughing as well.

They boarded the Lear jet, holding on to each other as they climbed the steps.

"So we're going to London," Liz said.

"Yep. Back to good old Britain. Been there a lot, you know. Ireland, Scotland, Wales . . . the place is steeped in history. Rich in mythology."

"Dripping with ghosts," Liz said.

"Awash with apparitions."

The Lear's jets roared, they accelerated down the runway, and Liz grasped his hand. "Swarming with specters," she mumbled.

The jet lifted clear of the runway, and Hellboy looked out the window. As always he was amazed at how quickly the ground fell away. Dawn was just rising out of the Atlantic, and down below, the freeways were starting to clog with rush-hour traffic. The low sunlight cast long shadows of houses and woods, and he wondered what hid within those shadows today. It seemed the world had changed a lot over the past twenty-four hours. For Hellboy it had never been a safe place—he had seen too much to believe that—but there had always been a balance, a natural equilibrium that had seemed to right wrongs, calm chaos, and set normality back in its place. Admittedly he often had a hand in that, but he was not arrogant enough to believe that he alone was responsible. Today, watching the land fall away below and not knowing what was to come, he felt more unsettled than he ever had before.

"Hey, HB," Liz said. "Dinner's served."

They sat and ate in companionable silence, swapping bits of food that one or the other did not like. Hellboy had a beer, and Liz took advantage of the well-stocked single-malts cabinet on the Lear. They both knew that the journey would take a few hours, so there was time to relax a little, drink a little, and reflect on what the next few days might bring.

Swirling her drink, ice clinking, Liz broke the silence at last. "It's all happened so suddenly," she said.

Hellboy nodded. "I was just thinking the same thing." He finished his beer, smacked his lips, and found himself looking forward to real British ale. Assuming he'd have time to sample it, of course.

"I hope Abe finds Abby soon."

"Yeah, he's sweet on her."

Liz continued swirling. The ice had almost melted. "She's strange."

Hellboy looked at Liz until she glanced up to meet his eyes. "You're not?" he said.

"You know what I mean, HB. There's something about her. Something hidden. She's never fully submitted herself to the BPRD, not like you, or even me. Hell, you're strange enough, but at least you admit it, you know it, and you'd happily do your best to make that less so."

"You really think so?" Hellboy said. "I thought the ladies liked an enigma."

"Well, some do."

"Then I'll retain my air of mystery, thank you very much. I'm actually an accountant from New York who collects beer mats and stamps in his spare time. I just paint myself red. It's all the rage nowadays."

"Yeah. Right." Liz finished her drink, reclined the chair, and sighed. "So . . . Benedict Blake."

"I dunno, Liz. Kate's rarely wrong, and she has a mind

like a damn encyclopedia. But if this is all about revenge, it seems a bit—"

"Extreme?"

"Well, yeah. If his wife really was killed in a state-sanctioned hit, why's he suddenly killing thousands of innocent people?"

"Maybe he isn't. Maybe he brought these things up out of the Memory for his own reasons, and now they've escaped and are causing all their own chaos. He could have had a base somewhere—South America, in the jungles—and the mythological animals broke out, and now they're going to change the world, and he can't do anything about it."

Hellboy stared out the window at clouds catching the sun. The ground had disappeared from view, and they could have been anywhere. Below them, hidden, the world was continuing on its own way for now. They were removed from it for the next few hours, and he was glad for that, but he was also nervous. When they broke through the clouds again on their way to land, he had no idea how much the world below would have changed. "This is just so big," he said.

"So visible," Liz said.

"Yeah. I'm used to fighting monsters in subterranean caverns or old tumbled-down places of worship. I'm never on the TV. Now my ass kicking by a dragon is probably prime-time the world over. That's not good."

"It's almost as if it's intentional."

Hellboy nodded. Intentional. That's what he had been thinking. Fate, he'd been thinking a lot on that too. And what were they doing now, if not dancing to the tune of everything that had happened? That was another reason for him to feel nervous, and why he'd checked the aircraft so thoroughly before they took off. "I guess events this big just can't be controlled, and you're rolled along with them," he said.

"Like Abby," Liz said. She took out a cigarette and flicked a flame from her thumb. The smoke curled up and set off a subtle, polite alarm somewhere in the cockpit. A heavy curtain was pulled aside, a man peered through and disappeared again, and the alarm was turned off. "Look at that," Liz said, drawing deeply on her cigarette. "They're used to dealing with freaks."

"Don't be so hard on yourself, Liz," Hellboy said. "At least people don't think you wear goggles on your forehead."

Liz laughed, and Hellboy liked the way that made him feel. Sometimes he thought if she were more level-headed, he'd maybe care for her less, but that was an uncomfortable idea, so he shoved it away. It was Liz the woman he loved as a friend, not Liz the firestarter. That was just a small part of the larger package.

He sat back and closed his eyes, but sleep, as ever, would not come. Instead he started turning over the facts in his mind, searching as hard as he could for the aspect of all that was happening that made him the most uncomfortable.

He'd been beaten by the dragon. That was hard, but it was hardly the first time. He had scars and aches to display other times something had got the better of him . . . but he'd always won out in the end. Maybe that was it; maybe he felt unsettled by unfinished business. Wherever the dragon was now, it had an appointment with his fist.

His defeat had been shown on TV. That was bad, and unusual, and it opened up a whole can of worms for the BPRD. But although it had set him on edge, he was pretty sure it wasn't what was upsetting him right now. There were things going on in the world that were demanding much more attention, and it would be arrogant of him to believe that the sight of the dragon kicking his ass had any real significance at the moment. The film of the ocean liner had proved that.

So Hellboy swung back to fate yet again, and control, and the fact that he felt as though he'd been steered into this course of action. They all had. Even Kate Corrigan's recollection of Benedict Blake and his mad ideas had seemed so inevitable, so well timed, that Hellboy could not help but wonder just how involved Blake might be with all this. Was he the kingpin? Or just another backer? Did the mad old guy even know what he was doing?

Hellboy drifted, but he did not sleep. Every few minutes he woke up and glanced out the window, expecting to see little green men working on the wing joints with wrenches, or great beasts flying out of myth and memory to bring the jet down. Beside him Liz slept fitfully, frowning and mumbling her way through unknowable dreams. At one point light blue flames played across her eyelashes like Saint Elmo's fire, and Hellboy held his hand above her face and smoothed the flames away.

Later Hellboy slept, and he dreamed of the Lear jet's crew turning into ghosts and melting away, leaving him and Liz to wait until the fuel ran out. He dreamed of Liz erupting into flames beside him, a long-feared self-immolation that seared away everything he knew and loved and left her reborn, more of a mystery than ever. He dreamed of Abe, off on his own and so vulnerable, and Abby Paris, a werewolf the BPRD had tried to tame but who was untamable. He woke up and opened his eyes, and his right hand had twisted itself into something unknown, blood-red and ready to fulfill whatever destiny Hellboy knew he must have been born for. But then he woke again and sat up, startling the copilot, who had come back from the cabin to say that they were beginning their descent. Hellboy nodded his thanks, turned to Liz, and watched her sleep. She seemed more at peace now—no flames on her face, no twitching and mumbling—and as the Lear dropped slowly out of the sky, Hellboy wondered whether anyone ever truly woke up.

They broke through the cloud cover over southern England and began their approach into Heathrow, and Tom called to tell Hellboy the world was at war.

PART TWO

New Memories

Statement broadcast by major TV and radio networks across the globe—1997

"My name is Professor Benedict Blake.

"I am a man whom many will grow to hate, but everything I do and have done is out of love. I want to tell you that now, because for the next few days that may be difficult to believe. Years down the road perceptions may change, but now . . . all I can say is that love is harsh, and it consumes. And more than anything, it demands sacrifice.

"The love I feel will be familiar to many: love for my dead wife; love for my sons, for whom all I want is a better world; and an endless love for the world I live in. Its multifarious wildlife, its varied geography, the smell of a rainforest after a storm, and the feel of desert sand between my toes. Many people love our world, and as individuals they worship it and call it home. But as groups—as a species—that love is beaten down by money and a desire for betterment. Call me cynical if you may; I've been called worse.

"You may feel that I have been bent out of shape—that what I have started here is madness—but sometimes harsh measures are necessary to protect those you love. I have been planning this for a long, long time.

"I am a scientist and a magician. Many of you will laugh at that or fail to understand, either because you do not believe that the two can be one or because you do not believe in magic. That does not concern me, as what I am doing requires no faith but my own. I do not ask for your faith. I do not ask for your understanding or even your blessing. Consider this an education.

"Twenty-five years ago I was wronged by people I trusted, shunned by fellow scientists, and my family was destroyed by murderers sent by my own government. My wife was killed, our home burned down, and my sons and I were forced to flee for our lives. I was blamed for their deaths, and in my absence—and without my being able to defend myself—my name was made dirt. My wife was buried without my being there, and only once have I visited her grave. She is a memory now, nothing more, though the memory is a rich and vibrant place indeed. My sons and I have been in hiding ever since. I suspect most people believed that I was dead as well. More fools they.

"Few recognized the warnings I gave, and yet now many have come true. Humankind is destroying the world. I predicted this, I foresaw the dirtying of the atmosphere and the poisoning of the seas, the death of crops and the spread of disease. Nobody appreciated the powers I had fashioned within myself—born of a melding of pure science and pure magic, the unsullied potential of nature realized at last—and yet the fear I instilled in people is still there.

"It is time for that fear to be turned back upon the world. It is time for me to take action, where governments have not.

"In recent days the world has seen its purest and most natural inhabitants return to their rightful homes. I brought them here, and soon I will introduce more. The world is about to change. I am proud to be the originator of the glorious new age that will arise, an age where myth again becomes reality, and the earth itself will be renewed and refreshed by its new inhabitants and rulers. These are creatures that love their home. A dragon will not dump toxic waste in deep caves. A troll will never rape the land of oil and minerals. A rukh will respect the air, not pollute it.

"I demand nothing, because justice will arise as a natural consequence of my actions. I do not want for anything, because I have the whole new world at my fingertips. This is simply a warning and a plea. The warning is that these creatures, newly returned from Memory and angry at their timeless incarceration, will be untamable and invincible. It is a wild, wild world that the sun will rise on tomorrow, but one that will last forever. Today the earth started getting better. The plea is simply this: let me finish what I have started. Fighting against me will lengthen the process of transition, and each day that fight continues will cost the lives of many more. People will die, and that is a sad truth of today's destiny, but it is all for the good. Throw away your guns, deny your governments, and this war will be brief and targeted. Some of those who die will deserve it; others may not. But I hope that the casualties will be light in comparison with what my victory will give: a new world that can breathe; a place where your children can live in hope, not fear; and, eventually, a humanity that stops eating itself and the planet it calls home.

"This is not revenge. I am not mad. I am simply saving the world. I don't ask for or expect your thanks, but I hope that in the future you will see that I was right.

"If governments had acted on my advice twenty-five years ago—instead of murdering my wife, sending me into hiding, and shattering any hopes my experiments may have raised—this violent transition would not have been necessary.

"Whatever happens over the next few days is not my fault."

Heathrow Airport, London, England—1997

"It's getting worse," Tom Manning said. His voice crackling over the speakerphone was tired and jaded, and to Hellboy it sounded as though he'd already given up.

"What's happened?" Liz asked. "What have we missed?"

There was nothing for a while, and Liz glanced at Hellboy. He shrugged, smiled, tried to make light of something that was feeling heavier all the time. He had never felt so helpless. Every time he heard about another cryptid sighting, he wanted to jet off and sort it out, but he couldn't be everywhere at once. It was tearing him apart.

"Well, to start with, Kate was right. It *is* Benedict Blake. He issued a statement two hours ago, and it's set the media alight. Everyone wants to know who Benedict Blake is, and everyone wants to know whether his claims are true, and who's to blame, and what we're going to do about it."

" 'We' meaning . . . ?" Hellboy asked.

"The United States. He claims his wife was killed by the government, and there are a dozen countries—the U.K. included—demanding the truth."

"And the truth is?"

"Hellboy, Kate told you what she thought, and I'm with her. But right now blame will get us nowhere. While the governments fight it out, we have to find Blake and stop whatever it is he has planned."

"You said it was getting worse," Liz said. "I think the word you used was *War*."

The speakerphone crackled again, and Hellboy had a crazy image of his boss crumpling up a piece of paper in front of his microphone and saying, "You're breaking up, sorry . . . break . . . Then Tom coughed and sighed, and even electronically Hellboy could hear the director's weariness. "When you read Blake's statement, you'll see what I mean. It's like a declaration of war, reality against mythology. Several countries have already tried military attacks against these things. Spain and Portugal. Greece. North Korea."

"And what happened?" Hellboy asked, but he could guess the answer.

"Spain lost fifteen fighter aircraft against a swarm of harpies. More than a hundred Greek soldiers have drowned trying to deal with supposed mermaids, and our satellites tell us that the North Koreans lost an armored brigade."

"What were they fighting?" Liz asked.

"I don't know," Tom said. "But whatever it was, they're blaming South Korea and massing their forces along the borders."

"Oh, come on," Hellboy said. "Tom, can you send the Blake statement to us?"

"I faxed it a few minutes ago. Should be waiting for you with our people at the airport."

"Who's meeting us?"

"Two of our guys from the U.S. embassy. Don't worry, they're not diplomats or secret service. One of them is a sensitive from Boston, the other is a Brit ghost hunter we've worked with a couple of times before."

"What's his name?" Hellboy asked.

"Jim Sugg."

"Hey, I know Jim! I met him back in '84 when they had that trouble over in London."

"What was that?" Liz asked.

"They televised a supposedly dramatized haunting, turned out it was real. Double bluff. Nobody believed a word of it, of course."

"Triple bluff?"

"Er . . ."

"Hellboy," Tom said, "I want you and Liz to get straight to the embassy. They're already trying to set up a meeting with the British minister of defense. This is very sensitive. I don't want you just barging into London, not with everything that's going on around the world. The Brits are a bit jumpy right now, and it's no surprise. They're the only European country where nothing untoward has happened so far."

Hellboy looked from his window at the spread of housing, factories, shopping malls, road arteries, occasional clumps of green where planners had suddenly remembered what had been here before people. "I guess that's about to change," he said. His breath misted the window and obscured the scene, but it quickly cleared again, begging him to look.

"Tom," Liz said, "any news of Abe or Abby?"

"I called Abe and told him everything we know," Tom said. "And . . ." He broke off, but the connection was still open, crackling with potential.

"And what?" Hellboy asked.

"And he checked out the dead werewolf. Guys, Abe is certain that Abby is one of Blake's creations. He won't say why he thinks this is true, but—"

"I trust him with my life," Hellboy said. "If he says it's so, it's so."

"It's an added confusion," Tom said, "but it makes it even more important for Abe to find her. She's BPRD. We can't have her slaughtering a movie theater full of people come the full moon."

"Not to mention she's confused and hurting right now," Liz said.

Tom did not reply.

"We're about to land," Hellboy said. "Speak to you later, Tom."

"Best of luck," Tom said. "And Hellboy . . . Liz . . ."

"Yeah, we know, Tom," Liz said. "We'll do our best."

The satellite phone hissed off, Liz grabbed Hellboy's hand, and a few minutes later the Lear screeched down onto the tarmac at Heathrow Airport.

The jet taxied along a runway to a private arrivals building. Hellboy and Liz had time to freshen up before they came to a stop, the jets winding down and the aircraft structure creaking and clicking as it accustomed itself to solid ground again. The pilot came through from the cabin and glanced nervously at Hellboy.

"Customs will be along in a few minutes to escort you to the terminal," he said. "From there you'll be taken to the main Terminal Four in an airport bus, where the two guys from the embassy will be waiting for you."

"Thanks for a comfortable flight," Hellboy said.

"No problem." The pilot nodded at Hellboy and Liz, then disappeared quickly back into the cockpit.

"Feels like we've landed somewhere hot," Liz said. She had changed her blouse and trousers and tied up her hair, as if expecting summer.

"I know how you feel," Hellboy said. Seen from the window, the expanse of concrete seemed depressingly barren and empty. He wondered how much of this world would have changed by the next time he and Liz had cause to fly somewhere.

A few minutes later a small cart trundled across the concrete and parked beside the jet. The driver regarded the aircraft with the bored stare of someone long used to celebrity and politician arrivals. Hellboy looked forward to exiting the plane and relieving the monotony of this guy's day.

He was glad to feel solid ground underfoot once more. He and Liz sat on the back of the cart while the suddenly nervous driver guided them left and right between buildings, parked aircraft, piles of luggage containers, and storage compounds.

"Ever want to get lost somewhere, come to an airport," Hellboy said.

"I'll remember that." Liz had an unlit cigarette in her mouth, ready to light it as soon as they entered the arrivals building.

At customs they were greeted with suspicion. Hellboy couldn't blame them, he supposed, but it still rankled when they asked him to empty his backpack. They checked through his clothes and toiletries, then the blank-faced customs guy nodded at his belt.

"Not that," Hellboy said.

"Sorry, sir, but I have to insist."

"Buddy, even I don't know everything that's in there."

"HB," Liz whispered. "That's probably not what they want to hear."

"Sir, there's a lot of trouble in the world today. I understand that's why you're here visiting the U.K., but I can't just let you stroll through without ensuring that you're not carrying anything—"

"Once you're finished with my belt, who's doing my internal?" Hellboy said. He reared up to his full height and swung his tail up behind him.

"Sir—"

"Just give me back my pistol and let me go kill some bad guys."

The customs man turned around to look at his colleagues, but there was no help there. He turned back, defeated. "Sign this."

Hellboy scribbled his name on a piece of paper, took the secured box containing his pistol, and went to unlock it.

"Please, sir," the man said. "Not in the airport."

Hellboy glared at him, then sighed and looked away. "Pal, you need to loosen up."

"Mr. Boy, I'm only doing my job."

"It's Hellboy," Hellboy growled. He walked away with Liz, finding guilty pleasure at the sight of tears in the customs guy's eyes.

"That was uncalled for," Liz said, but he could hear the laughter distorting her voice.

"Hey, it's been a long flight."

"Notice they didn't search me at all? You must look suspicious."

"Ha!" They exited the building, ready to board the bus that would take them to Terminal Four, when they heard the first shouts from behind them.

"Now what?" Hellboy said. He was becoming really annoyed now. But when he turned, no fingers were aimed at him.

They were all pointing up.

Hellboy looked. "Oh crap."

"Hellboy—"

"I know, Liz. You ever get the feeling trouble follows us?"

"What the *hell*?"

"Dragons. I hate dragons." He plucked quickly at the clasps on the pistol box, but already the immensity of what he was seeing had hit home. It would take more than a big gun to stop these things. It would take more than a whole damn army of big guns.

What they needed right now was a miracle.

There were five dragons, all of them concentrating on one jet. From this distance Hellboy couldn't tell which airline it was, but it did not matter. It was maybe a mile out, a few hundred feet above the ground and coming in for landing, when the first of the dragons strafed its port wing with fire.

The pilot had obviously seen the huge lizards buzzing the aircraft, but he had kept his aircraft straight up to now. To do anything else would be to put everyone onboard even more at risk; an aircraft of that size could not be swerved or swayed from side to side, and if he could not avoid the dragons, he would fly right through them.

That changed when the first dragon attacked. The jet juddered and tipped to one side, the pilot obviously panicking, and the port wing tip narrowly missed colliding with the attacking dragons. The great lizards twisted and danced in the air, their grace and natural abilities putting the aircraft's maneuvrability to shame. The jet swung the other way, the pilot trying to come back on line with the runway, and two more dragons dove in. One of them jetted flames at the tail, the other attacked mid-fuselage. Perhaps speed aided the pilot, because ferocious though they were, the flames seemed unable to catch hold. They left black smears on the white paintwork, great smudges of soot that followed the airflow around the aircraft, and then fluttered out in the wake from the jet's passing. The dragons swooped in again—three of them this time—and they grabbed on to the fuselage, securing themselves with claws or tails, concentrating their fire at one place, letting go and lifting back into the air as an explosion of pressurized air and gushing fuel jetted up out of one wing.

"No!" Liz said. "What's the point, why the hell—"

"Let's get to the terminal," Hellboy said. He grabbed Liz's hand and ran, looking back over his shoulder at the stricken airliner. The five dragons were still buzzing it, swooping in and attacking the main fuselage again, holding fast with their claws and coughing out flames like giant blowtorches.

The pilot shook the plane—left and right, wings visibly vibrating up and down under the sudden movement—and the dragons let go, one of them spinning out and down as it was struck by one of the wings. It recovered quickly, hanging motionless in the air and shaking its head. Splashes of flame flew like saliva. It flapped its wings and in an instant joined the fray once again.

"Run!" Hellboy said. "Liz, don't look back, just run!" He knew that if she saw what was about to happen, she would want to stay and help. Helpless though she would be, her instinct would allow for nothing else, and he did not want to have to carry her away from something like this. She'd never forgive him, and he'd never forgive himself. But right now there was nothing to be done . . . and his main concern was where the dragons would come next.

He had to get to the terminal. If he could be of help anywhere, it was there.

At the last instant Hellboy actually thought the pilot would get the jet down. The dragons came in again and again, taking turns clamping themselves to the fuselage and wings and directing searing jets of flame onto and into the aircraft. There was a fire inside—he could see it spewing from burst windows—and he could not bear to imagine what it was like for those poor passengers. But the plane kept level, its rate of descent seemed good, and when it was a hundred feet from the ground, Hellboy believed it would make it down in one piece.

Then one of the dragons crawled forward along the jet's back, claws digging in, tail waving, and when it reached the cockpit, it twisted its head around and down and vomited a burst of fire. The cockpit glass melted and burst inward, the front of the jet erupted and split apart under the onslaught, and it struck the ground and flipped over onto its side. It would have rolled, had it not come apart. Already weakened by several holes and doomed by the fires that had been consuming its insides, it burst and exploded across the runway. Flames engulfed the tumbling mass, plane and dragons alike, and the ground shook under Hellboy's feet as he ran, threatening to topple him. The crash was half a mile away, but it shattered windows all across the airport. Wrecked metal screeching along the concrete sounded like five hundred people screaming as one.

The five dragons rose from the conflagration, shook

themselves free of debris and flames, and spiraled upward to hover above the airport.

"They haven't finished yet," Hellboy said. "Damn them, they haven't finished."

He and Liz stopped running, unable to do anything but stand and stare at the burning wreck of what had once been a plane containing hundreds of people. Hellboy felt something on his cheeks and wondered if it was tears. Liz was crying freely. *At least it was quick,* he thought, but it had been almost a minute between the first attack and the crash, and in that time . . . he hated to think about it.

"It was quick, at least," Liz echoing his thought, but she too sobbed as she realized the truth.

Hellboy had unclipped his pistol and thrown aside the box. He made sure the chambers were loaded, aimed up at the dragons, and fired.

"You won't hit them at that height!" Liz said.

"But it makes me feel better." He emptied every chamber, seeing no evidence of the dragons' even noticing him all the way down here. But he was wrong. It did not make him feel better. If anything, he only felt more useless, so he nodded at the huge terminal building and started running again.

"Why are they doing this?" Liz said beside him. "It's a concerted attack, not random. Five of them, and they know what they're doing."

"Knocking out the airport?" Hellboy suggested. "You heard what Tom said . . . we're at war."

The constant roar of aircraft surrounding the airport had changed in tone. Planes that had been circling or lining up to land powered up to pull away, veering left and right away from the runway and climbing over London, seeking new heights and fresh, safe airports. Hellboy only hoped they would get away in time. The dragons were still circling Heathrow in a tight spiral, and now they had started screaming.

Around Terminal Four there was panic. Emergency vehicles were tearing across the concrete, most of their crews looking up instead of across at the burning wreckage. Passengers from a couple of smaller aircraft had rushed down the steps and were now running for the building, casting fearful glances over their shoulders, faces white and eyes wide. Old people stumbled, children cried, and Hellboy and Liz stopped to help people to their feet. A woman stared at Hellboy and screamed, saw the pistol in his hand, and screamed again. Someone else shouted his name, but Hellboy could not tell who had recognized him. He looked up at the building and saw faces and hands pressed against the glass wall, bearing silent witness to the atrocity.

"Hellboy, this can't be over," Liz said.

"It isn't." He grabbed Liz's arm and pulled her to one side of an entrance to the terminal. "Look." The dragons had stopped circling and were now hovering in place, infrequent wing beats apparently enough to hold them aloft. They were turning their heads, scanning the ground below and the air around them, looking for a new target. When they found one, they screamed and converged quickly on the helicopter.

"What the hell are those idiots doing?" Liz said, aghast. The helicopter was flying toward the dragons, not away from them.

"Press? Politicians?" Hellboy shrugged his shoulders and thought, *At least it'll give all these people time to get inside.* "Liz, let's get inside," he said. "Uh-oh, here comes the cavalry."

Several policemen in body armor burst out of the terminal, machine guns in both hands. They skidded to a halt on the concrete, staring up at the dragons. The lizards were converging on the lonely helicopter, circling it, casting brief bursts of fire against its fuselage. Playing with it. One of them drifted in and swiped the helicopter with its tail, sending it into a dangerous spin. The pilot recovered, only to be knocked again from the other side. Then all five dragons spat fire, and the helicopter exploded. The policemen opened fire.

"Now they'll come down here," Hellboy said. He pushed Liz inside and followed.

From outside came the sounds of machine-gun fire, and Hellboy had a sense of being closed in from all sides; it felt as though the heavens were falling, and when he glanced from the next available window, he saw that was true. He could hardly see any sky. All he saw were dragons' wings, and all he heard were the cries of dying men. The gunfire lessened, then stopped, and all fell silent.

"Go!" Hellboy said. He was pushing people ahead of him up the staircase, desperate to reach the first level, where they could go deeper into the building. Here they were protected only by a thin layer of blockwork and metal siding, and the more walls there were between these people and the dragons, the better he'd feel.

The sense of being enclosed lessened. He glanced at Liz, and she said, "They're moving away." Hellboy nodded grimly. Good news for them, bad for someone else.

They made it up into the departures concourse. The crowd hurried through toward the huge departure lounge, but Hellboy and Liz held back, waiting by the wide spread of windows and looking out over the airport. The downed aircraft was belching clouds of rolling black smoke at the sky, forced aloft by towering flames. Hellboy tried not to think about what was feeding that fire and giving the smoke a definite oily texture; he could smell the conflagration from here, and that was bad enough. There were several emergency crews vainly pumping foam, many of them scanning the skies as they did so.

Of the dragons there was no sign.

"Those bastards!" Liz said. "That's plain murder. Damn Blake. Whatever his mad gripes, there's no justification for something like this."

"None at all," Hellboy said quietly. The anger was building in him. He needed to hit something, and soon.

"We can't just leave this," Liz said. "We can't just go." The huge fire outside was reflected in her eyes, and Hellboy thought he saw the ice blue of her own personal inferno in there as well.

"We won't," he said. "I fought one of these things—though that one looked bigger than these damn worms—and got my butt kicked. But five . . . that's another thing altogether."

"Yeah, but now you've got me," Liz said. "And you've got that new cannon."

Hellboy held up his pistol and rested it in his big right hand. "Isn't she a beauty?" he said. "This'll put a hole in a tank."

"And a dragon?"

He nodded. "Oh, I *really* want to see what this'll do to a dragon."

Liz took a deep breath and turned away from the window, and when she looked at Hellboy, her eyes were still aflame. "Then let's go," she said.

But they did not have to go. The fight came to them.

Even above the screaming, they heard the roar of fire belching from a dragon's mouth.

"That's coming from inside!" Liz said.

"Departure lounge," Hellboy said. Then he ran. He pounded onto the moving walkways, nudging people aside and apologizing as he went. He heard Liz behind him doing the same. The pistol was a reassuring weight in his left hand, and he made sure he had a perfect grip. They were getting closer.

Another roar, and something exploded at the heart of the terminal, setting ceiling tiles vibrating and advertisement frames falling from walls. Hellboy vaulted the handrail of the moving walkway and ran for a fire exit, shouldering his way through and crashing across the corridor into another door. It had been a guess, and a good one. He burst through and stumbled into a display of perfume and moisturizing cream, dropping to his knees, smashing the shelving away from his face, and bringing the gun up in one smooth movement. Someone screamed—a sales clerk, he guessed—but he ignored her, standing and forcing his way through the shop and out onto the concourse. People were running left to right. Some of them looked fearfully over their shoulders, most simply ran, terrified and determined. Children screamed as parents squeezed their arms. *Hold tighter*, Hellboy thought. *These kids need to grow up to tell the story.* He turned left and ran against the flow. Most people moved out of his way.

"You there, Liz?" he yelled.

"Right behind you."

"I thought I'd lose you in the perfume shop."

"Sexist ape."

Skidding around a corner, Hellboy saw what had caused the explosion. There was a dragon thrashing and twisting amid the ruins of a car display stand. The car itself—once a polished and curvaceous totem of materialism—had been kicked aside into a tie shop, and was now a burning wreck. Several bodies were scattered around its broken chassis. They too were burning.

"Son of a *bitch*!" Hellboy yelled. The dragon stopped its orgy of destruction and turned to face him. It grew quiet for a moment, perhaps confused at this big red man. Then it growled. "Oh yeah," Hellboy said. "Your cousin was an ugly mother too."

The dragon darted forward, surprisingly nimble despite its size. It coughed fire at the same time, and Hellboy and Liz rolled to the side. They ended up in a coffee shop— spilled coffee sheening the floor, discarded bags and magazines pushed against walls like snowdrifts—and they had to duck again when the dragon drew level and let out another gush of flames. The fire consumed the air around them and stole their breath, blazing across the counter and bursting bags and cans. As it receded the pleasing smell of roasted coffee filled the air.

"Now I'm getting very pissed," Hellboy said. "Liz?"

"I'll give you first shot," she said, smiling.

"So considerate." Hellboy stood, brought the gun up, and fired. The dragon seemed to dodge, flexing its neck and body as if it knew where the bullet was aimed. Then it lunged with its heavy front claws, dashing him aside, dragging him out, holding him down so that it could twist its body and stand on his chest. Hellboy aimed again and fired, but the bullet glanced from the thing's skull and took out the display window of a sports shop. Sneakers and footballs tumbled out, and the dragon snapped its head to one side and fried them.

Hellboy squirmed against the weight of the beast, taking in a huge breath and smashing at its foot with his right hand. The dragon screeched and lifted its foot . . . and then brought it down again, hard. Hellboy's breath was forced from his lungs, and he felt the tiles beneath him shatter from the impact. He kept hold of his gun.

From his left he felt the livid simmering of a different fire.

The dragon turned its foot left and right, crunching Hellboy down into the floor. The sharp edges of broken tiles scraped his skin, the beast's claws bit into his chest and abdomen, and Hellboy looked up and saw a security camera turn toward him, flashing red. *Great,* he thought. *Ass kicked on film for the second time.* He turned the gun, pressed the barrel against the dragon's foot, and pulled the trigger. Blood exploded in his face, and the dragon fell to one side, howling like a puppy left on its own.

Hellboy rolled toward Liz, and as he knelt and brought the pistol up, he felt the hairs on the back of his neck singed. A roar of flame curved over his head and struck the dragon on the face.

"Burn," Liz said. Her voice sent a shiver through Hellboy. He would trust Liz to death and beyond, but hell, she had hidden depths.

The dragon reared up and flapped its huge wings. They scraped walls, smashed doors, and scored the tiled floor. When it opened its mouth to inhale Liz's fire, Hellboy knew they were in trouble.

He aimed the pistol. "One good shot," he said. "That's all I ask. One . . . good . . . shot." He pulled the trigger and suddenly believed in the power of prayer. The bullet hit home in the dragon's throat.

The giant lizard froze, stiffened, let out a small squeal. The hole in its throat spewed something colorless that distorted Hellboy's view of the monster's head—gas or heat, he could not tell—and then its eyes rolled up in its head.

"Oh, Liz," Hellboy said, "this is going to be—"

The dragon exploded. It gave a wet, dull thud that thumped through the ground into Hellboy's legs and set his eardrums pounding. Its neck was pushed apart by a ball of fire. Blood, flesh, and bone spattered the walls and powered in through the coffee shop entrance. Hellboy barely brought up his hands before he was hit by a slab of meat almost half his size. It was warm and stinking, and it rolled him to the floor and slid against the back wall with him. He tried to push it away but found that it was burning, pockets of gas in its flesh popping and sparking and dribbling fire down across his face and neck. It fused the meat to him, and he started to smell like a bad steak.

"Dammit!" He kicked up and out, shoving aside the still-melting chunk of meat, and then Liz was there adding her weight. The piece of dragon parted from Hellboy with a sucking sound, and he kicked it away. "Now, that is grim."

"The dragon's still burning," Liz said. She was covered in blood, and a shiny, oily scale was stuck to her forehead. Hellboy plucked it away and held it up to the fires cast by the monster.

"Looks almost pretty," he said.

"You've got time to collect trophies later," Liz said. "One down, four to go."

"Yeah, and if they're all that easy to kill—"

"You call that easy?"

"Comparatively."

"Compared to what?"

He shrugged. "Give me a minute, I'll think of something."

Liz smiled, and a hail of bullets slammed into Hellboy.

Liz stumbled back, tripped over a discarded rucksack, and fell. Hellboy had pushed her. Maybe he'd seen the policemen out of the corner of his eye, or perhaps he'd sensed the danger. Bullets stitched his chest and threw him against the wall. He slid to the floor muttering something, but Liz could not make out the words.

"Stay still!" someone shouted. Liz, lying on her back, put her hands in the air. She was breathing hard. Blue flames licked her fingernails. She raised her head and looked at Hellboy, and he stared back with a look of almost comical surprise on his face.

"Keep your hands still!" the same voice shouted.

"They're up where you can see them, asshole!" Liz said.

"She's American, guv."

"Hey, that's no dragon. That's *Hellboy*."

"I swear," Hellboy whispered, "anyone calls me a dragon again . . ." Then his eyes closed, and his chin dipped to his chest.

Liz stood. "If you're going to shoot me, do it, but make the first bullet count." She did not even look at the policemen. In two strides she was at Hellboy's side, kneeling down and gasping at the sight of the blood seeping from his wounds.

"Holy shit, I shot Hellboy . . ." a voice said.

Another voice, this one whispering. "You better hope he stays down a while."

"HB?" Liz said. She leaned in close, angry, terrified, flames lighting the undersides of her fingernails. "HB, open your eyes at least?"

His mouth twitched. Only slightly but enough to make Liz hold her breath. He whispered something, but she had to lean in closer to get the sense of it. ". . . spoil a good rest?"

Liz bit her lip, stood, and spun around. "He said he's going to insert his right hand into the one who shot him," she said. There were three policemen there, each of them nursing a machine gun, all of them looking as though they'd just fallen into hell and been dragged out the other side. One of them had burns on his right arm, and his eyebrows had been singed away. She suddenly felt sorry for them and tried to put herself in their position: one day minding the airport concourse, the next fighting dragons and shooting big red men. She almost smiled. Almost.

"He . . . I didn't know who he was," the burned policeman said. "It's chaos out there. There's a plane down, didn't you know? And dragons! And I come in here, see you and him, and how was I supposed to know who the hell he was?"

"Stop gibbering," one of the other officers said. "Miss, the airport ambulances are busy as hell, and I'm not sure—"

"I'll live," said a voice, gruff and pained. Liz sensed him standing behind her. And from the looks of the policemen's faces, he was a sight to behold.

She turned around, smiled, and cried. Hellboy was touching the three holes across his torso, swaying on his feet, and rubbing the blood between his fingers.

"Been stabbed," he said. "Been slashed with an ancient sword. Been bitten and thrashed with giant tentacles. Never been shot." He reached into his belt, and the knife he brought out and flicked open was long and thin. It reflected fire from the burning dragon. He never even glanced up before slipping the blade into the first of the wounds.

Liz grimaced, but she could not look away.

Hellboy hissed as he eased out the first bullet. The second had gone deeper, and he really had to work at this one, the spent slug finally flicking out and shattering a glass on the shop counter. The third bullet had barely penetrated his hide. Hellboy pulled this one out with his fingernails.

"Holy shit," the burned policemen said. He turned and ran past the dead dragon, departing the departure lounge at speed.

The sergeant started to go after him but then turned back to Liz. "Miss, if possible, I'd like to ask you both to accompany me."

"Accompany you where?" Liz said.

"We're evacuating the airport. The things that brought down the aircraft are setting about the buildings now, and the parked jets, and just about anything that moves. The military is on its way, so the best we can do for now is get away."

"Oh, great," Hellboy said. "The military."

"They're better trained to deal—"

"With dragons?" Liz asked.

The sergeant looked away, unnerved and confused. He glanced at the dead dragon, its head and neck a ruined mess, flames still licking across its ruptured body and igniting the fat with a bluish fire.

"Sergeant," Liz said, "we need to get to the arrivals exit

quickly. We're meeting someone there, and it's vital that we make it."

"Miss, with all due respect, I don't have time for that. My job is to protect the airport, now more than ever before."

"And I respect that." Liz smiled at him; she knew how disarming her best smile could be. He was a tall man, fit, proud, and this was a day that he'd never forget. He had seen people killed—probably some friends among them—and the killing was obviously not yet over. But sometimes there were difficult choices to make. "We're here to try to prevent more like this happening. Haven't you seen the news lately, from all around the world?"

"Yes," he said, unable to meet her eyes. "Around the world. Not here."

"You thought Britain was immune? Look at that." She pointed at the burning dragon. It was twitching now, fleshy ripples passing across its corpse as small pockets of gas burst deep inside. She was worried there might be another explosion.

"You say you're here to stop more?"

Liz nodded. "We can't know for sure, but this could be just the beginning."

A distant explosion reverberated through the terminal, the floor jumped beneath their feet, and from somewhere came the sound of shattering glass. "Oh, God," the sergeant said. "I think that was another plane."

Liz closed her eyes, hoping he was wrong, sensing he was not.

"We need to go," Hellboy said. He was still scratching at the wounds on his chest, slowly flexing his upper torso as if to work out the pain. "Tell your guys to aim for the necks. That's where they have their gas sacs. Or whatever." He cringed and rubbed one of the bullet holes. "Damn, this'll be sore in the morning."

"Er . . . I'm sorry I shot you," the sergeant said.

Hellboy shrugged. "Good shooting. I can't hit the side of a barn."

The sergeant raised an eyebrow and looked at the dead dragon.

"Third shot," Hellboy said. "And look at the size of that thing."

The four of them walked past the burning beast and headed toward the vast check-in hall. The sergeant's radio crackled once or twice—shouts, panicked mumbling, shooting—and he walked quickly, glancing back at Hellboy and Liz every few steps.

"What's happening?" he said at last. "Why us? Why here?"

"Reaping what we've sown," Hellboy said.

"I'm sorry?"

Liz nudged Hellboy and shook her head. "He's delirious," she said. The sergeant obviously doubted her, but he was not about to argue.

They walked past a vast panoramic window that looked out over the runways and other buildings, and the scene that greeted them stunned them to a halt. The airport was a war zone. The first crashed passenger jet was burning as fiercely as ever, but now there was an even greater conflagration a mile away across the concrete. It looked as though several parked aircraft and a hangar had been set alight, and the flames reached for the sky like the souls of the doomed jets. A dragon was buzzing the flames, drifting in and out as if reveling in the heat splashing across its body.

Closer by, several emergency vehicles had been attacked,

and they lay scattered across a runway like a child's discarded toys. At least one had exploded, the force of the blast having extinguished whatever fire caused it.

"Look," the sergeant said. "Terminal Three." He spoke without emotion, because really there was little that could be said. Terminal Three, a mile away across the airport, was under attack by the other three dragons. One of them perched on the roof and coughed fire down between its feet, apparently trying to burn through like a blowtorch. Flames and gases erupted about its head, but it shook them away and gushed fire again. The other two lizards hovered at windows and holes in the walls, pouring flames into the building, moving back as part of a wall blew out. People fled the building in every direction, from this distance resembling little more than colored ants desperately trying to escape a cruel child with a magnifying glass.

One dragon took off, strafed the fleeing crowds with fire, then went back to its attack on the building.

"Bastard!" the sergeant yelled. He stepped back and fired at the window before them, shielding his face as the glass shattered outward and fell to the concrete thirty feet below. Then he braced the machine gun against his shoulder, aimed, and cried out in frustration when he realized how foolish his gesture had been.

His cry turned from anger to triumph when several war planes passed overhead.

"Oh, tell me they're not . . ." Liz said, but she did not have time to finish. The missiles flew, the dragons moved out of their way almost lazily, and the west façade of Terminal Three erupted outward in a ball of smoke and flame.

"Get me the hell out of here," Hellboy said. "Liz, we need to make contact with the embassy, and fast. I want to stay here, but we'll be more help talking to someone who can affect this."

"That way, five hundred yards, turn right," the sergeant said. Then he and the other officer ran for a staircase that led down to the runway level.

Liz wanted to shout after them, tell them not to be so stupid, but she knew they would not listen. Not today, when madness had come and taken them away. They were hardly themselves anymore; angry, yes, raging at the dragons, but barely themselves. They were people in their own dreams, fighting the stuff of nightmares.

"Will this ever end?" Liz said.

"Yes," Hellboy said. "One way or another, it'll end."

That should have been something of a comfort, Liz knew. But the tone of Hellboy's voice brought no peace at all.

They moved away from the window and set off at a run. Hellboy seemed to have shrugged off his terrible wounds—sometimes, love him as she did, he terrified Liz—but he was frowning, disconnected, distracted. She glanced at him several times as they ran, and the last time she saw something in his face that she recognized from a hundred times before.

"Oh now, HB," she said, "come on. Come *on!*"

"Liz, I can't just run away from this," he said. "Those turds in suits from the embassy can wait." Thoughts vocalized, he suddenly seemed more sure of himself. He scratched at his bullet holes and smiled at her. "I've got a plan."

Liz closed her eyes and sighed. But inside, where anger always simmered, she felt her own desire for vengeance heating up.

———————

"Guys!" Hellboy shouted. A breeze came through the bullet-shattered window and kissed the blood on his chest. The wounds were healing already, but the three holes had left deep, heavy aches in his flesh, like fists of stone melded with his body. They itched. "*Guys!*"

The two policemen running away from the terminal turned around. Hellboy waved at them, gesturing them back. The sergeant shook his head and carried on, but then he paused again and shouted back. "Tell me you have a plan!"

Hellboy glanced at Liz and smiled. "He may have shot me, but I think I like this guy."

Liz shook her head. "Male bonding. Always did go way over my head."

The policemen ran back to the building and waited below the smashed window. Hellboy held on to the frame and leaned out, looking left and right, trying to make out the lay of the land. He glanced across at Terminal Three. It was a ruin now, fire belching from the shattered east wall, the three dragons still dipping in and out to add to the conflagration. The Tornado jets roared by overhead, but they did not fire any more missiles. Packing state-of-the-art firepower, faster than a bullet, they were all but helpless against their flesh-and-blood foe. Hellboy was glad their pilots did not have itchy trigger fingers.

"Wait there!" he shouted down. He ducked back in and turned to Liz. She was twisting her hands in front of her as if nervous, but her eyes were as cool as cut steel. "Liz, I've got an idea. It's crazy, and it'll probably get us all killed. But I'm not doing much else today. What do you say?"

"I say tell me the idea."

"Right. OK." He looked around: up at the ceiling, back

at the burning mess of the dead dragon, out the broken window at the ruins of the jets and airport buildings. The Tornados roared overhead again, as if an angry noise would scare the dragons away. "Liz, I want to fight fire with fire."

"How do you mean? They duck in and out of fire without a touch. Just like me. I can't do much against them—"

"But you can *distract* them!" The idea was rolling now, and Hellboy liked the way it was going. It was simple, that was the key. Simple . . . though dangerous as dragon shit after a spicy chili.

"You want me to act as bait for four dragons."

"Yes!" *She won't mind,* Hellboy thought. *She'll do it. This is Liz. She'll do it.*

"Did one of those bullets get you in the brain?" she asked, aghast.

"Hellboy!" the sergeant called.

"Wait up!" Hellboy roared, and several loosened ceiling tiles tumbled from their grid. The policemen fell silent, waiting out of sight.

"You're mad."

"I'm red." He raised his eyebrows. "And cute."

"You are not cute. Intriguing, interesting, distracting, but never cute. A bunny rabbit is cute. A pussy cat is cute."

"Yeah, but they're not as suave as me."

"Are you trying to wisecrack me into submission?"

"Has it worked yet?"

"No."

"Right. OK. I'll tell those guys to run to their deaths, then."

Liz growled. *Just like a tiger having its tail pulled,* Hellboy thought. Not that he'd ever pulled a tiger's tail.

"That's not fair!" she said.

"Liz, listen to me. No more joking. No more gallows humor. We've seen a lot of people die today, and if we leave this to the military, a lot more will die. We've dealt with crap like this before, and we won't let amazement or disbelief cloud our judgment, not like them. So here's what I thought: you call up some fire and send it out; the dragons see it, and they're intrigued; they come; those two cops and I kill their scaly asses."

"You think that'll work? It's too easy."

"That's *why* it'll work."

"You're a terrible shot."

Hellboy shrugged, glanced along the concourse at the smoldering lizard. "I'll concentrate."

Liz bit her lip and looked from the window. She walked to the opening and looked down at the policemen below, smiled, turned back to Hellboy. "Where do you want me?" she said.

Hellboy smiled. "That's my girl."

How did I let him talk me into this? Liz thought. *This is insane. This is suicide.* But at the same time she thought of the phoenix in Zakynthos, and the way it had reacted to her display of fire making. At first it had appeared bewitched, as if fascinated or enamored of someone with its own talents. That had all changed later. But perhaps the dragons would act the same to begin with, long enough for Hellboy and the policemen to get off a few clear shots.

Failing that, she'd just curl up into a ball and jump.

Liz was standing on top of a mobile staircase, staring out over the airport. The crashed aircraft burned on the runway, emergency vehicles still gushed flames here and there, and scattered across the wide flat expanse were smaller shapes, some colorful, mostly just black and scorched. Each shape had a million stories attached to it and dozens of people who would spend the rest of their lives grieving. Liz saw each one as a dead person, and the tears that came unbeckoned were for every one of them. She imagined people at home listening to the radio or watching events unfold on TV—there were certainly press cameras focused on this from many distant angles—and she could not conceive of the worry and heartache being felt across the country right now. Mothers would be watching for missing sons, husbands for absent wives, and children would be huddled against babysitters and wondering whether Mummy and Daddy would be coming home tonight.

Liz closed her eyes, and the tears that squeezed out were hot.

The sound of another explosion came from across the airport, and she saw a dragon setting upon a parked jumbo jet. The worm slithered under the body of the aircraft, unleashed a burst of fire against a wing, and was engulfed in another, more massive explosion as the fuel tanks erupted. The tail flew backward, the wings thumped across the concrete, and wreckage rose high and wide on the expanding ball of flame. The fire roared skyward into a mushroom cloud, edges folding down and drifting back to the ground as ash and smoke.

"I hope that was empty," Liz whispered. All this fire . . . all this destruction . . . if she closed her eyes she was somewhere a long time ago and a long way away. She hated to think on that, yet she concentrated her thoughts and wallowed in those terrible memories. They fed the rage. They fueled the thing inside her, the fire that was cool to her but so deadly to others. And when she opened her eyes again, she viewed everything through a wavering curtain of heat.

She held her arms straight out from her sides, breathed deeply, and then forced her breath out like a rampaging dragon. A burst of fire poured from her, and she caught it in both hands, working it, twisting the ball of flame, and making it bigger with every touch. *Go,* she thought. *Go higher, grow bigger. Call the bastards in.*

With a sound like a jet taking off, a mass of fire engulfed Liz and poured skyward. *So rich,* she thought. *So pure. If this keeps going, it'll part the clouds!*

She looked across the airport and was shocked to see how close the dragons already were.

The first lizard was flying just above ground level, looking like a bottom feeder in clear water. It was using its claws to guide its way across the concrete, while still beating its wings to keep it truly afloat. Its mouth trailed streamers of meat, clothing, and skin. Its eyes were black. Just as it reached the wheeled steps Liz was standing on, it skirted sideways, performing a full circle around her, its head tilted up and its black eyes reflecting her flames.

The other two dragons from Terminal Three followed close behind. One flew in high, the other copied the first, flying clockwise around Liz instead of counterclockwise. All three of them stared at her and her fire, perhaps impressed, perhaps hypnotized by this alien creature that could perform their own incredible trick.

But Liz knew it would not last for long.

Come on, Hellboy, she thought. *Don't screw around. Shoot the damn things!*

One dragon roared a mouthful of flame at Liz. Her own fire consumed it and cast it skyward. The dragon paused and roared again, but this time only the sound came out. It looked up at the tower of flame, back down at Liz, and as it opened its mouth for the third time, several holes appeared in its neck, and its head flicked sideways.

Liz could not help staring. *This is when it—*

The dragon's neck exploded, sending its severed head spinning thirty feet into the air. Blood and flickering flames trailed behind it. Its body slumped to the ground. Dead, it was no longer immune to fire.

The other two dragons screeched, and Hellboy and the policemen moved out from cover to open fire. Hellboy had been hiding up on the terminal roof, and Liz saw him from the corner of her eye. His big cannon was blasting holes in the air, but not every bullet was finding its mark. The policemen emerged from a line of loaded luggage carts, and their marksmanship left no questions. Bullets raked the beasts' flanks, wings, and stomachs, and when a slew of slugs hit the second dragon's neck, it screeched like a wounded baby, spun down to the ground, and clawed at its throat. It was still hissing when a chunk of its head was blown off by gases erupting from its torn hide. It crawled across the ground, aimless in death, and flames began to eat it from the inside out.

"Crap!" Liz heard Hellboy snap open his pistol and lock in another load, but it was as if the third dragon had instantly sensed his weakness. It darted past Liz and aimed for Hellboy.

She turned and threw a punch at the dragon. Even though it was twenty feet away, it took the blow hard in the side, Liz's bluish flames knocking it out of the sky. They did not burn the beast, but the flames of her wrath obviously carried weight. Startled, winded, the dragon was an easy target for the policemen. While his colleague was reloading, the sergeant stepped forward and emptied a magazine into the thing's neck. He ducked back as the lizard burst open and caught fire.

Liz threw a ball of fire at the gaping wound and smiled in satisfaction as she saw it settle into the creature's still-leaking flesh.

"Still one more!" the sergeant yelled, scanning the skies. His colleague, wide-eyed and stunned, finished reloading with shaking hands.

Liz looked up at Hellboy. He stood smiling on the roof's edge, hands on hips as if surveying a job well done, and as he opened his mouth to say something, a shadow fell over him. The dragon powered in from behind, plucked Hellboy from the parapet, and rose quickly into the sky.

Liz threw a ball of flame after it, but the dragon was rising too quickly, and the fire spluttered out after a hundred feet.

Hellboy twisted in the monster's claws, looked down at Liz, and she saw him raise his gun. She did not hear what he said next, but she could imagine it: *This is going to hurt . . .*

Shocked for a few seconds, by the time he gathered his wits, Hellboy had been hauled several hundred feet into the air. The dragon drove upward, trying to escape the field of fire from the policemen below and probably never believing that the man in its claws would usher in its own demise.

But Hellboy was more than a man, and more determined than that. He was also very, very pissed; this was the second time he'd been carried off by a dragon. But now that he knew their weakness, he had no intention of letting this one get away with it as well. It stank, for a start, like a car exhaust stuffed with dead fish. And its claws were slick with the remains of fresh kills.

Hellboy looked down at Liz receding below him, blue flames still dancing about her like frolicking ghosts. "This," he said, "is gonna hurt." Then he aimed the gun and fired six shots in quick succession.

The dragon veered across the sky, hissing, wings flapping faster as if trying to maintain altitude. Flames flitted past Hellboy, ejected like blood from the fresh wounds on the dragon's neck, and then a heavy thud was followed by a gush of fire, enveloping Hellboy and accompanying him on his long journey down. He managed to turn so that he could see where he was going to fall . . . and his impact site did not look good. One of the dead dragons lay below him, opened up and burning out. Above him, still squealing even with only half a throat, his abductor followed him down.

He struck hot, wet flesh, and immediately the lights went out. To add insult to injury, there was another explosion as the dead dragons met, and Hellboy felt the sense knocked from him. For once, he welcomed the darkness as it took him away.

"There's no way he's alive in there!" the policeman said.

"Shut your trap," said the sergeant. He was looking at Liz, not the mass of burning dragons.

"He's been through worse than that," Liz said, but she was trying to convince herself as much as the cops. *He has,* she thought. *Much worse. He's just been shot and got better. This won't touch him. Sore in the morning . . . that's all.*

The Tornados roared overhead once more, and looking

up, Liz could actually see their pilots staring down at the flaming mass of dead dragon meat. She felt a sudden, unaccountable sense of emptiness and sadness, and she thought, *Is this what we really do? Is this why I'm really here?* Myths lay dead at her feet, and in some way she was mourning the loss of mystery once again.

"Hellboy?" she called.

He stood, dripping with blood, fire erupting all around him, dragon meat sliding from his body, horn stumps glimmering with blood and flame, and he looked both magnificent and terrifying. Liz caught her breath and tried to look away, but she could not. Hellboy's eyes were dark pits in that firelit mess, and as he twisted his head to one side, she heard the distinct click of bones snapping together.

"Hellboy. You still with us?"

"Sure," he said. "Just enjoying the barbecue." He struggled out of the mess of dead dragon, kicking aside the burning fat and trying to wipe the stuff from him as he went.

I can see why they're scared of him, Liz thought. She had known Hellboy for so long that she looked at him as her friend, little else. She rarely saw him with a stranger's eyes. He was Hellboy to her, not some demon that had risen out of hell. *I can see very well.* She looked at the sergeant and his colleague, still nursing their machine guns with obvious intent.

"They're all dead now, Sergeant," Liz said. "Good shooting."

He grunted, glanced at Liz, looked back at Hellboy. His gun did not lower. He was scared and shell-shocked, and she would have to keep her eye on him.

And then Hellboy plucked the stub of an old cigarette from his coat pocket, flicked a bit of fluff from the end, and the sergeant stepped forward with a light. "Thanks," Hellboy said.

"Welcome."

And in that human gesture, any tension remaining evaporated.

"Hellboy," Liz said, "we need to meet the embassy guys. Now more than ever! We need—"

"We need a drink," Hellboy said. "My mouth tastes like a butcher's slop bucket."

"There'll be a drink at the embassy."

"You think?" He shrugged, turned around, and looked across the airport. "Damn, those bastards made short work of this place. Sergeant, I guess you and your buddy will be wanting to get off."

"I think so," the sergeant said. "I've got a lot of friends who work in Terminal Three, and . . ." He looked across at the wrecks of the passenger jets, unable to say any more. But nothing needed saying. Now was the time for clearing up and helping, not sitting down and weeping. The weeping would always come later. Right now, shock still had these men in its grasp, and it was the buffer they needed against the awful truth.

Hellboy and Liz went back through Terminal Four to the arrivals lounge. The place was almost deserted, except for a man lying across three seats, snoring. "There's always one," Liz said.

"Lucky guy."

Outside, police had sealed off the pickup area, but Liz spotted the embassy guys standing behind the makeshift barrier, waving a large red card as arranged.

"Hey," Hellboy said, "they're playing my song."

"Are you OK?" Liz asked.

"Sure. Why?"

"No reason." Liz looked at Hellboy, and he would not meet her gaze. His eyes were distant. His quips were automatic, and he kept wiping at the blood even now drying to a crisp across his skin. They walked on in silence.

"Hellboy," the taller of the two men said as they approached. He held out his hand. "It's been a long time."

"Jim, good to see you again. I had no idea you were working for our embassy out here now!"

"Just an adviser." He glanced at Liz and smiled, but she could see that he was a haunted man. He looked so tired, his eyes deep and brown, the skin of his face sallow and seemingly hanging from his bones. Even what had just happened to Heathrow Airport seemed not to have shocked him.

"Liz Sherman," she said, holding out her hand. Jim Sugg shook, his own hand cool and damp.

"Pleased to meet you, Miss Sherman."

"Call me Liz."

"This is Peter Fray. He works at the embassy." The man with Sugg smiled and nodded, but he did not offer his hand.

He's the sensitive, Liz thought. *Maybe he's scared of what he'd see if he touched us.* Fray was looking at Hellboy constantly, but he did not seem able to keep his attention on him for more than a couple of seconds without looking away again. Hellboy seemed not to notice.

"We need to get away from here," Sugg said. "Much as I hate to mess with the law, they'll be wanting to talk with you about all this, and once they've got you, they'll quiz you forever. And from what Tom Manning told me, there's a lot more to discuss."

"Oh yeah," Hellboy said, nodding. "So much more."

"We'll get to the embassy, you two can get cleaned up, then we'll do our best to organize a meeting with the minister of defense." Sugg's voice was a tired monotone. He actually sounded bored, but Liz knew it was a lot more than that. Either he was guarded and protective of his thoughts, or he had seen so much that nothing surprised him anymore.

"You're the ghost hunter," she said. The words came out without her thinking. She supposed she was testing him.

Sugg looked at her, and for the first time she saw the flicker of amusement in his eyes. It suited him, and she was glad. "That's a term I prefer not to use, but yes. I look for ghosts."

"Why?"

"To prevent them from coming to look for me. Shall we go?" Sugg turned and walked quickly toward a big black Mercedes, Fray following.

Liz glanced at Hellboy and raised an eyebrow. Hellboy only shrugged. They walked to the car together, sat in the back, and were glad when Sugg's security card seemed to get them past the dozens of police roadblocks already set up in the area.

"Get attacked by dragons, set up roadblocks," Liz muttered.

"Hey, kid, what else are they going to do? It's not something they're used to dealing with every day."

"I guess not." Liz closed her eyes and surprised herself by dozing.

Manchester Airport, England—1997

"Something about a disturbance at Heathrow," the man said. "They've had to divert us to Manchester. Bloody idiots, I don't know, they can't do anything right nowadays, always something causing problems, leaves on the runway or bloody air traffic controllers on strike. Don't know their arses from their elbows. I've got a meeting to go to, you know?"

Me too, Abby thought. She had just woken from a deep slumber to find the guy next to her blathering on. "What sort of disturbance?" she asked.

"I don't know, maybe a luggage cart broke down or something. Please excuse my Britishness, young lady. We're the country where everything grinds to a halt at the slightest provocation. An inch of snow in winter? Close the schools, panic, buy bread and milk, barricade yourself in your house. Really, you'd think we were under siege by the rest of the world."

Maybe you will be soon, she thought, but saying it would have achieved little. "I'm sure they have their reasons."

"Whatever." The man had turned on his mobile phone, and his annoyance found new direction when a flight attendant requested that he turn it off until they landed.

Abby turned and looked out the small window at her side. She had a view of the wing and the green landscape down below, fluffy clouds passing by here and there, roads and rivers meandering across the surface of this country she was coming to for the very first time. *I'm not that far from Paris,* she thought. *Maybe that's where Abe will think I'm going.* The thought of her friend was depressing, because she was betraying all the faith and hope he had developed in her over the years. But at the same time there were reasons, there was rhyme. When the time eventually came for him to discover the truth, she hoped he would understand. "Understand," she said. Her breath misted the window and then faded away.

A dream came back to her, sudden and hard. She was alone in the dark, except that the darkness itself was not barren and neutral as it should have been. But neither was it alive. It watched her without eyes, listened without ears, and spoke without breath, and though she could not recall the words that had been whispered to her, she knew that they were all bad.

Awake now, an unbearable sense of unease had settled over her. She looked out at the aircraft's wing and hoped it would not break off. She looked down to the ground a mile below and hoped the landing gear would lock down correctly. Her dreams had always affected her intensely, and mostly she put it down to having been born of a memory herself. She supposed dreaming was her way of thinking back to the time before Blake had brought her into this world, her own memory of the Memory. Her recent brief foray back there had revealed that great, conscious darkness to her once more.

But this dream was different. It had felt intentional, not random, as if something had come into her mind to present it, instead of her mind presenting itself. She shivered and closed her eyes.

Full moon tonight, she thought. *I've set myself free to murder.* She hated thinking about what would happen when she changed. She had all but ignored it since fleeing Baltimore, dismissed the thought with some vague idea of locking herself away or being able to hunt animals, not people. But she could sense the blood flowing around her, smell the meat, and even through the staleness of the confined atmosphere, the smells were good. Her mouth watered. She hated that, but she could not control it.

"Stupid bitch," the man next to her said, staring after the flight attendant. He flipped out his phone again and switched it on.

"That can interfere with communications," Abby said.

The man looked at her, smiled, and pressed the phone to his ear.

Abby narrowed her eyes. She saw a vein pulsing at the man's throat, a tic in his left eye, and she could smell his wet flesh beneath his rank body odor. She thought he would probably taste tough and insipid—a lifetime of discontent would do that to a person—but still she grinned, and growled, and the man turned away and slipped his phone back into his pocket.

Abby closed her eyes. Her bones and muscles were beginning to ache. *Just let me find him before I change,* she thought. *After that . . . I don't care. Blake needed stopping years ago, and I failed in that. This time I'll do the right thing.*

The plane touched down and eventually disgorged its disgruntled passengers. Abby immediately noticed the way the ground crew kept looking away from the passengers, out the tunnel windows, and up at the sky. They were nervous. No, they were terrified. They were trying to hide it, but everything about the way they stood, silent and twitchy, told her that they really did not wish to be here. At the junction of the tunnel and the arrivals terminal she paused and looked out the window. The sky was clear, the afternoon sun shining down on the busy airport . . . and there were army vehicles flitting between buildings, disgorging soldiers who carried heavy machine guns and rocket launchers.

Abby walked into the arrivals terminal. It was silent. Hundreds of people stood clumped around TV monitors, and those who had just arrived soon joined the silent throng. It spooked her seeing so many people doing nothing, saying nothing, simply watching the screen. But even from a distance she could see flames smeared yellow and orange across one of the screens, and immediately she thought, *Heathrow.*

"What is it?" she asked a young man, his eyes wide, face slack with disbelief.

"Dragons just destroyed Heathrow," he said without stopping. He was walking from TV to TV, as if viewing different channels could alter the truth.

Abby did not stay long. She had seen one of the dragons in the *New Ark,* and she had no wish to watch them raining fire and destruction down on innocent people. "You bastard," she muttered as she left the terminal. *Whatever cause Blake claims as his own, there's no justification for this.*

She had to get there. Hire a car, drive to London, because the hints she had received from that awful, ancient entity in the infinity of the Memory had seemed to be right. London was where things were beginning to happen, and she knew that Blake would be there soon.

She would meet him. Father and daughter reunited. But this child had nothing but hate in her heart for her father. Hate and fear and a growing desire to kill him and eat of his flesh.

———————

Abby breathed a sigh of relief as she pulled out from the Avis parking lot and found her way onto England's motorways. She supposed the world had far greater problems to contend with right now, but she had still been expecting the BPRD to put out information about her, telling airport authorities that she was . . . what? A monster? A runaway werewolf? A danger to herself and everyone around her, come full moon?

She smiled, shook her head, turned on the radio. "Bad Moon Rising." Great.

Jerusalem—1990

"Gal, this is madness. Father would never want us to do what you're talking about doing. It could destroy everything we've done over the past fifteen years!"

"Zahid de Lainree doesn't agree, you said that yourself."

"Yes, but he was obviously mad."

"Mad," Gal said, and he smiled. His cigarette lit his face in the darkness of the sultry night, a pale yellow glow that set his skin aflame. "One man's mad is another man's sad."

"You know how things are, Gal." Richard loved his brother so much, and yet lately he had grown to fear him as well. He was afraid that Gal was dying—the sending weakened him more every time, and his recovery periods between instances were starting to overlap—but he was more afraid that his brother was going slowly, comprehensively mad. Whether madness or death would take Gal first, Richard was terrified at the thought of either.

"Yes, I know. I know I'm more than just a son to our father. I'm a way for him to better his plans."

"He told us what to get, and we've been getting just that."

"And is there no room in that plan for betterment?" Gal said. He leaned forward in the chair and stared at Richard, his face illuminated by vague light from a balcony farther along the side of the hotel. "Do you run through your life simply doing what you're told, instead of trying to find better ways to do the same thing?"

"This is not a better way, it's a different way," Richard said. Gal's eyes were deep black pits, and he could not look straight at them. So he looked out over the city instead, amazed as ever by the lack of light reflecting from the low clouds. "We have no idea what may happen if we find this thing. What if it speaks to us? What if it's never been asleep and gone, just lying there dormant, waiting for someone to come and speak the right words to give it life again?"

"That's just what we are going to do. You'll lead us to it from de Lainree's book, we'll find it together, then I'll send whatever I can to Father, wherever the *Ark* is right now. And after that . . . the choice is his."

"No," Richard said. "If we do this tomorrow and find something, we're taking all choice away from Father and putting it in the hands of something else."

"We're giving him power."

"He has that already. Can you imagine the *New Ark* now, Gal? Can you picture what he has on there and what he has yet to bring through? If only we could see . . . if only we could go to him."

Gal sighed and lit another cigarette. His face was gaunt and weak, skin yellow and saggy in the match's flare. He drew in the smoke and leaned back in his chair. "It's a beautiful night," he said. "So warm, peaceful. So filled with potential."

Is he really thinking this? Richard thought. *Can he really believe we'd be doing any good?* "Potential for chaos," he said.

"And isn't that what we've been working toward for years? Chaos?"

"No," Richard said, and he was certain of that. He'd asked himself the same question every time they went in search of something else from de Lainree's book, and each time he watched Gal perform the sending spell, his answer was the same. "No, not chaos. Order. We're helping Father bring order back into the world. We're saving the planet."

Gal laughed, loud and surprisingly bitter. "Richard, for someone so old you still hang on to your cute childish conceits."

"I'm not embittered by what we're doing," Richard said, regretting it instantly. The sending was killing Gal, and they both knew it.

Gal sighed again. "Well, it's your choice come sunup."

But it was not Richard's choice, and it never had been. They both knew that, both acknowledged it, and yet they had these conversations and pretended that their outcome could make a difference. Gal—in pain, weak, feeble, and quite probably mad—was the stronger of the two by far. His will steered their lives. Richard, protesting and hesitant, followed along every time.

Next morning Richard woke early and found Gal poring over the book. He was sitting in the same chair out on the balcony of their hotel room, and Richard wondered whether his brother had even gone to bed. He often seemed not to sleep at all.

The streets around their hotel had come to life with the dawn, and Richard was relieved that the silence of the previous night was no more. People talked and shouted, cars growled and hooted, motorbikes roared, traders called, and children chattered in the street two stories below their balcony, and the mouthwatering aromas of street cooking wafted up to them on pale smoke. He liked the feeling of the world around them being alive, yet at the same time Richard knew that he and Gal were apart from this world. They had removed themselves the day they fled their burning home with their father. Ever since, they had been hiding beneath the skin of reality, digging deeper into the petrified flesh of history. Anyone who happened to look up would see two middle-aged men on a hotel balcony, one staring intently at a big old book, the other standing at the rear of the balcony, looking out over Jerusalem with an expression of confusion that would be familiar to the observer. Many foreign tourists came here, but few ever truly understood the city.

Richard looked down into the crowd below. None of them could have any idea of what he and Gal were considering doing this day.

"How can you read this?" Gal said. His voice was croaky from too many cigarettes and too long sitting on his own, not talking, just thinking. "There's no sense here at all, no meaning. It's all distortion."

"That's because it's what you perceived the very first day Father showed us the book."

"And you saw clearly what it said?"

"No, I saw what it meant. I knew page one, and every page since has been open to me, with a little concentration."

Gal shook his head, closed the book, and smoothed its time-worn leather cover. "I'm glad I have you with me, Rich," he said. "I truly am."

Richard's heart missed a beat at the unaccustomed softness of his brother's voice. The brash man of last night had gone, burned away perhaps by the morning sun, and in his place there was his brother. Vulnerable, wasted, tortured by many things from many times, yet still his brother. They were from the same father and mother. However different their personalities, Richard liked to remember that.

"Are you ready to go?" Gal said quietly.

"I suppose so. But I think I need something to eat first."

Gal stood, twisted his body this way and that, easing out the stiffness. "We can pick something up on the way." As he passed Richard on his way back into the room, Gal put a hand on his brother's shoulder. "You know this is the right thing, don't you? It's in de Lainree's book, it's part of the Memory, and Father will only thank us." Gal went inside to get ready.

I hope so, Richard thought.

It took them most of the day to find the entrance to the tomb.

They walked through the streets of Jerusalem, ignoring street traders, avoiding police and army patrols, pausing every half hour at a street café, drinking strong coffee while Richard strengthened his spell of course and tried to make sense of that most esoteric chapter of the *Book of Ways*. He was doing his best. Whatever doubts he felt about what they were doing, never did he feign confusion. The words and text and strange drawings merged in his mind, steering him this way and that, until late in the afternoon, as they sat in bright white plastic chairs outside a building a thousand years old, two symbols bled into each other and showed Richard the way.

He sighed, slumped in the chair, picked up his coffee, and downed it in one gulp. "I have it," he said.

"Good." Gal leaned across and touched Richard's shoulder. "I knew you would."

They remained in the café for a while and ate, Richard to regain the strength he had lost through that long day of spell casting and concentration, Gal to fortify himself against the sending yet to come. The sun dipped toward the western hills, and they both decided at the same time that they should not remain aboveground to watch the sunset. Much better to be on their way by then. They had flashlights, folded digging tools, and a crowbar packed into their rucksacks. They were used to breaking and entering, finding buried history. Richard sometimes felt that all the relevant moments of their lives had been spent underground.

He led them to a deep drainage ditch beside a park, filled now with discarded bicycles, clothing, cardboard boxes, and other refuse.

"Down there?" Gal said.

"Down there."

They began to dig through the rubbish, heaving it behind them and forging a path down to the base of the ditch. Richard cut himself on an old rusted baby carriage, Gal scraped his hand along the ragged mouth of a broken bottle, and they both gave blood to the land. Nobody came to see what they were doing. Whether they went unseen or people thought it best to keep to themselves, Richard was relieved.

"Here we are," he said at last, panting and sweating.

"There should be a stone slab in the base of the ditch. It'll be well fitted, might need to break it instead of lift it."

Gal set about prodding through the hardened silt along the bottom of the ditch with the crowbar, and right at the edge of the patch they had cleared, he uncovered a straight stone edge.

Fear and awe prevented Richard from saying anything. *What in the name of hell are we doing?* he thought, but it was too late for that now. Perhaps it had already been too late fourteen years ago, when they had uncovered the phoenix feather in Egypt. He often wondered when their lives had changed, and sometimes he marked a moment in case he thought the same way ten years down the line. *Now,* he thought. *This could be the most important moment of my life.* He looked up at the sinking sun and hoped he would remember.

It took Gal half an hour to expose enough of the stone slab for them to see what was written on it. "That's old Hebrew," Richard said. " 'Here lies chaos.' "

"Comforting," Gal said. He hefted the lump hammer from his rucksack and started knocking the crowbar down beside the slab.

The sun was setting by the time Gal broke the stone. Richard had sat on the sloping side of the ditch, looking up now and then to see whether the noise of their efforts had finally attracted attention. All he saw was sky, birds, clouds smeared red by the setting sun. He thought it grew suddenly cooler, and then Gal gasped and said, "I'm through."

The slab fell away into the darkness below, a darkness untouched by light for many centuries. There was a heavy, long sigh as air pressures equalized—it seemed that a breath came out of the chamber rather than going in—and then

Gal looked up and smiled. "Almost there," he said. "Rich, don't be scared. Father will be thrilled."

"I hope so," Richard said. Together, he and his brother descended into the long-forgotten tomb of a demon.

It's name was Leh. Zahid de Lainree called it "the sham Voice of God," an exhalation from hell made flesh. It had been put down by Jesus Christ himself, its remains left belowground, smoldering in a fire that would never go out. It was destined to be forgotten forever, cast from the minds of humankind just as the story of its defeat at Christ's hand was purged from any history of his time on earth. De Lainree had written of the words that would guide the searcher to Leh's underground prison and the chant that would serve to extinguish its restraining fire. Richard had never wanted to believe everything he read, but all other prophecies in the *Book of Ways* had proven to be true, and he had no real reason to doubt this one.

"I smell burning," Gal said. They were walking along a narrow tunnel, their route lit by the wavering light of Gal's powerful flashlight. This was a prison, carved for one purpose only, and there were no warnings scratched into the walls, no barriers across their way. This was always meant to be a forgotten place that would never be touched by light again.

And yes, Richard could smell the burning as well. "Maybe its an old smell," he said. Admitting that this was the tang of smoke . . . that would be saying that all this was true. That there was a demon down here, once flesh and blood but now just a memory. And memories were what they had been chasing for years.

"It's new," Gal said. "It's the endless fire, keeping Leh down. You know that." He was whispering, his words returning from the dark as sibilant echoes.

"Gal, let's get out of here," Richard said. "This isn't right. It doesn't *belong*! We've brought back things of myth and legend, and things that once were, but never anything like this. This thing was *never* natural! Who knows what it'll do if Father brings it back?"

"I send it to Father, and the choice is his," Gal said. "You trust him, don't you?"

"Of course," Richard said. *I haven't even seen him for fifteen years.*

"And you know why we're doing this? For Mother and what they did to her?"

"Yes." *He may have changed, he may be nothing like our father anymore. We really have no idea what he's going to do.*

"Then let's go." Gal moved on, expecting no reply.

Richard followed, sniffing, smelling the fire, and after a couple of minutes a glow seeped into the tunnel ahead of them. A minute later the walls opened up, the floor sloped down, and they were in a circular room twenty feet across. Theirs was the only way in and out. Again there were no signs of decoration of any sort. The only thing contained in the room was a hollowed pit at its center, within which lay something black and burning.

"Oh, shit," Richard whispered.

"I second that," Gal said.

The flames were pure white. They rose only a few inches from the black mass in the pit, flitting here and there, dying down and rising somewhere else. They looked cold. Smooth plumes of smoke rose above them, swirling in the disturbed air of the underground cavern and painting ghosts in the torchlight. Shining his flashlight up, Richard could see how the ceiling of the chamber had been blackened by centuries of smoke. Directly above the smoldering demon, the ceiling was so black that it looked like a hole in reality itself. *Maybe that's where Leh went,* Richard thought. *Perhaps that's how it fled into the Memory, even though its body is still here.*

"I'm going to look," Gal said. He moved forward. Richard raised his hand but did not touch his brother. He suddenly felt very much alone down here, less involved, more a product of his own thoughts and experiences than ever before. For a long time he and Gal had been one unit; now he was a man on his own.

Someone who could make his own choices.

"Rich, come and see this," Gal said. He only whispered, but the cavern caught his voice, bending it into echoes that stayed there for several seconds.

Richard walked forward and stood next to his brother. He looked down. The demon was blackened by two millennia of flames, yet its form was still apparent, curled into a fetal position within the pit, head covered by its long-fingered hands, legs drawn up, feet curled inward and folded over each other.

Richard let out a held breath, and dizziness faded away.

"That's a demon," he said. "We've found a demon."

"Leh."

He spoke its name! Richard thought. But nothing happened. The white flames died down on the demon's shoulder and sprang up again on its arm and hip, flickering across its leathery skin like rapidly growing frost.

"Are you ready?" Gal said.

No. Not ready. I'm not ready to do this.

"Rich? Ready? Open the book. Read those words."

"I'm not sure I want to."

"That doesn't matter."

"Whose fires am I putting out if I utter these words?" Richard said. "Leh was put down by Christ himself. Whose flames will I be extinguishing?"

"If the fire can be extinguished, then surely there's a reason for that?" Gal said.

Richard did not know. Slowly, without taking his eyes from the demon, he slipped the rucksack from his shoulder and pulled out the *Book of Ways*. He closed his eyes for a few seconds and cast a spell of course, dizzied with the effort. Then he opened his eyes again and started reading de Lainree's words.

The flames flickered, touched with a breath for the first time in almost two thousand years.

Richard fell back exhausted, and Gal took over. He used his pocketknife to chip off a portion of the carbonized demon, hissing as he burned himself. He blew on his fingers and stared at them for a few seconds, as if expecting something to sprout from his skin.

Richard held his breath, then sighed again as his brother continued.

He knelt close to the firepit—a firepit no longer—and drew the required shapes on the ground with a lump of chalk from his rucksack. He glanced back at Richard, expression unreadable, and then started a quiet chanting. The echoes of his words stumbled over each other.

The air in the chamber began to move, and Richard

hoped it was because of an evening breeze in the Jerusalem streets above them.

Gal's chanting grew louder, and he swayed on his knees, leaning down to the left, the right, then forward over the chunk of burned demon he was trying to send. His clothes, loose on his thin frame, shivered as his muscles tensed and untensed, and Richard could see sweat dripping from his brother's nose and chin.

"It's going," Gal said.

Richard crawled back against the wall of the circular chamber. He heard a sigh—his brother, or a breeze coming along the tunnel from the drainage ditch, or something else entirely. A wavering white flame sprang up on Gal's right shoulder, smoke rising from his jacket as the fire ate into it, and Richard almost shouted a warning to his brother. Almost. Because then the shape Gal was hunkered within was scoured from the floor of the chamber by a blast of air, and the blackened shard of demon disappeared.

"It's gone," Gal said, and he fell onto his face.

Richard stood and hurried to his brother, terrified of what he would see, certain that the white flame would have found a new home in Gal's fresh flesh and that he would lie there burning for a thousand years. But the flame had disappeared, and though Gal's eyes had closed, he was still breathing, fast but regular.

A blackened patch on the floor was all that remained of the portion of Leh which Gal had sent through to their father.

"I hope you know what you're doing," Richard said, talking to the man he had not seen for fifteen years. "I really hope you know."

They stayed down there until morning, and then Richard helped Gal hobble up out of the tunnel. The Jerusalem sun felt good. On Gal's shoulder, beneath his singed jacket, was a wound that would never heal.

American Embassy, London—1997

"Hey, Jim. A beer would be really good about now."

"I happen to have a few bottles of Abbot Ale in my office. You two wait here, and I'll be right back. Liz? Drink?"

"Whiskey?"

Sugg smiled. "Glenlivet." He left the room, and the door swung shut behind him. Fray had already gone to try to set up a meeting with the British minister of defense.

Hellboy ached. His muscles were sore, and his bones felt abused. He wished this were the end of something, not just the beginning. He could not remember the last time his stamina had been pushed so far. "Got to say it about the Brits," he said. "They do know a good drink when they see one."

"God bless them and all who sail in them," Liz murmured. She was lying on a leather sofa, while Hellboy had taken a huge floor cushion. He was not quite sure what to call the room—entertainment suite?—but it was tastefully furnished and pleasing to the senses. He could stay here, given half the chance.

Jim came back within a couple of minutes with their drinks, and the three of them shared a few silent moments. But that was all. Hellboy knew it was coming, and he knew that Jim knew, so it was no surprise when their peace was broken.

"They're scared of you," Jim said.

"Who?"

"The British government. They don't know what to think of you. You're . . . strange. Out of the ordinary. They can't trust that, especially now, today, when all this shit is going on and Heathrow has just taken a battering."

Hellboy frowned. "Any casualty figures yet?"

Jim shook his head. "Too early. It'll be four figures, for sure."

"Damn." Hellboy closed his eyes, but his mind was full of flames. It was too hot in there. He looked at Liz and smiled, wondering how she could live with what she had.

"Don't they realize we might have an answer?" Liz asked.

Jim nodded. "Of course they do. Tom Manning has been on the phone for the past couple of hours trying to find someone who'll listen. So far as I can tell, he's been promised that a couple of helicopters will scout the approaches to London on land and sea, see what they find."

"A couple of helicopters?" Hellboy said. "London is hosting a huge gathering of international leaders, its main airport is fried by dragons, and they can spare the BPRD a couple of helicopters?"

"They're scared, Hellboy. Petrified. They don't know what the hell is going on, or who's doing it, or why. And think of the responsibility . . . a major disaster here could leave half the countries on the globe without a leader!"

"Yeah," Hellboy said.

"We don't have time for this," Liz said. "We—"

"Why's he killing so many people?" Hellboy said.

"What?"

"You read the message from that psycho Blake, Liz. His stated aim is to put the world to rights. Give it back to those who should really rule. Cleanse the planet. Not your average psycho raison d'être, granted . . . but think about what he's doing here. A thousand dead at Heathrow? The kraken that took that cruise ship? What possible good is all this doing him?"

Liz frowned, bit her bottom lip. "None."

"None," Hellboy said. "Maybe he's losing control of his little pets."

"They're a diversion," Liz said. "This stuff has been happening all over the world for the past few days as a diversion away from his main attack, here and now. The environmental conference. Wipe out a load of world leaders, cause chaos and anarchy, giving the world's rightful owners their chance to take control."

"Dragons and kraken?" Jim asked.

"And more," Hellboy said. "Plenty more."

"But now they've launched their first attack in Britain," Liz said, "and soon he'll go for the conference. He doesn't need the diversion anymore."

"So why do the airport?" Hellboy said.

Liz shrugged. "As you said, in a war you take out enemy airports. Jim, any reports of other attacks in the British Isles yet?"

Jim shook his head. "None that I'm aware of. Could mean that the military has been hit, but that's not something they'd release quickly."

"Nah, it's not that," Hellboy said. "From the beginning he's been relying on surprise and disbelief. Now that the dragons have hit Heathrow, he's lost his surprise—"

"Has he really?" Liz said. "Even after that, Tom still can't get the Brits to do anything more than commit a couple of choppers."

Hellboy nodded. "That's where the disbelief kicks in." He took a swig of beer and sighed. There were three more bottles lined up on the table, but he knew he'd never get to touch them. Those bottles would be opened when all this was over. Who would drink the beer inside? That depended so much on the next few hours.

"Jim," Hellboy said, "can you give us a rundown of the situation here? Conference arrangements, defenses?"

"The British are being very tight-lipped about it all. Understandable. But then we do have Fray." He smiled, poured himself a drink, and sat down. "The conference is being held at a new hotel in the London Docklands, the Anderson. Huge place. There's a heliport there, a train link from central London, and there's easy access by water. I've been there once, a year ago when they were building it. Visited in a professional capacity." He swirled his whiskey, staring into the amber fluid.

"Find anything?" Hellboy asked.

"The docks are old. Ships from all over the world have docked there. Of course I did." Jim glanced up from his drink, looked at Hellboy and Liz, smiled thinly. "But that's for another time."

"We've all got stories to share," Hellboy said. "So defense and security. What have they got?"

"Officially the largest police posting in London's history, armed units on all the surrounding rooftops, security checks throughout the land and sea approaches, heavy security at all air and sea ports."

"And unofficially?"

"Unofficially the British are taking the conference even

more seriously than they're letting on. There are two dozen SAS and SBS units in and around London. The army was quietly put in place weeks ago. There are fast-response units housed in old abandoned warehouses scattered across Dock-lands—tanks, helicopters, hundreds of troops. Their pres-ence isn't exactly secret, but it's been heavily played down. The Royal Navy has upped its patrols in the English Chan-nel and the North Sea, and the Royal Air Force has a squadron of Tornados on standby."

"Yeah, we've met those guys already," Hellboy said. "About as effective as a fart in a hurricane."

"They're ready," Jim said. "Remember, the Brits had the Irish Troubles for the past thirty years, and they're very good at this sort of thing. They're ready . . . but they don't know what for. Dragons? Kraken? A bunch of terrorists sail up the Thames, and they'll be blown from the water before they smell London. But things like you're describing . . . well, they don't *exist.*"

"Didn't," Liz corrected.

Hellboy stood and drained his beer. "Look, Jim, we know who's been the cause of this crap over the last few days, and so do the Brits. All we have to do is convince them of the seriousness of the threat. And if they're not talk-ing sensibly to Tom, even after Heathrow, then we've got some work to do."

Jim looked pained. He finished his drink and went to pour some more, then stopped. "It's not even that easy," he said. "British Intelligence thinks the message from Blake was a hoax."

"What?"

"They don't believe it. Fray met with one of them yester-day, had a drink, read him . . . all he found there was confusion and indecision. No plan, no acknowledgment, no understanding of what's going on."

"So the diversions *have* worked," Liz said.

Hellboy grunted. "Guess so. And here I was thinking some of them were for us."

"That had crossed my mind too," Liz said. "Spread BPRD thin across the ground. But then why the statement? There were enough hints in there that he's targeting the conference, why flag that up?"

"Maybe because he knew how the governments of the world would react." Hellboy sighed. "They don't believe. Most people don't believe. Down in Rio, as soon as that damn dragon flew away, everything went back to normal. Maybe it was shellshock, but it was also a deep-rooted disbelief in things beyond the norm. That's where Blake has his advantage, and will for some time. Whatever happens in the next day, it'll take the world some time to come to terms with recent events."

"But what if we—"

"Ah, crap, Liz." Hellboy strode to a wall and slammed his left hand against it, palm flat. "I just want to hit something! Jim, can you take us to the minister of defense?"

"We've been trying to set up—"

"And you'll try forever. But can you *take* us to him, *now*? Do you know where he is? If I have to break a few heads to get in there, maybe that's better. Get the asshole's attention."

Jim raised his eyebrows and smiled. "I'd forgotten how unique it was working with you, Hellboy."

"Hey, I'm here to please." Hellboy fisted his right hand, heavy knuckles crunching, and the pain from his various wounds seemed to fade even more. The bullet holes on his chest were little more than bruises now. Dangerous. Sometimes he thought of himself as invincible, but in calmer, more reflective moments he knew that there was an end waiting for him somewhere out there. What hurt the most was that he guessed it would not be gentle and kind.

The door burst open, and Fray came in. "Jim, the British have lost a submarine."

"Where?"

"North Sea."

"Who did you pick that up from?" Hellboy said.

Fray smiled. "Telephone. I have a friend at the Admiralty."

"Nuclear sub?"

"Yes, but it wasn't armed. Out on maneuvers after being refitted. The core's stable, and they've already launched a salvage operation."

"What happened to it?"

"It's confused. But my contact says the final transmission from the sub talked of something attacking it."

Hellboy nodded. "He'll be coming in by sea."

"How can you know that?" Jim asked.

"It's the only logical way. He's been out there for years, somewhere, creating these things. Pulling them out of the Memory. Whatever. Where would he be safe doing that? A South American jungle base? No mobility. Easier to move around by sea." Hellboy turned to Fray, who immediately averted his eyes. "Thanks," he said. "And hey, you can look at me. I don't bite."

"One day you will," Fray said. Then he hurried from the room and slammed the door, suddenly keen to be elsewhere.

Hellboy, Liz, and Jim Sugg were silent for a few seconds, deep in their own thoughts. Then Hellboy punched the wall once, hard, and the patter of shattered plaster ended the moment and moved them on to the next.

"Jim," he said, "the minister. Now."

"Meet me in the lobby," Jim said. "I'll sort out a car."

Manchester Airport—1997

Abe Sapien waited until Abby had pulled out of the Avis parking lot before following her. The Jeep was big and comfortable, the wheel chunky enough for his webbed hands to grab, but it was hardly discreet. He only hoped she was not looking out for pursuit.

He could have stopped her any time since she'd disembarked. His own flight—chartered using the BPRD account, although if Tom were being picky, he'd probably class Abe as AWOL right now—had been diverted to Manchester after the trouble at Heathrow. He had landed and passed through private customs, and he'd been thinking about where to go next when he heard Abby's flight announced. Baltimore. Perhaps it had been a hunch, or maybe just a long shot, but he'd stood in arrivals, hidden away behind a pillar, and watched as the passengers came out of baggage claim. And there she was, Abby Paris, the girl he'd rescued from her own suicide and who was now running away.

Or perhaps she was running *toward* something.

And that thought had prevented him from approaching. Kate Corrigan had called to fill him in on Blake and Hellboy's discovery of London as a possible target. Abe had called back later to tell them of his suspicions about Abby. And suddenly her disappearance had meaning. If she really was a product of Blake's peculiar blend of science and magic—and all evidence suggested that was the case—then her fleeing at this moment could surely not be coincidence. For whatever reasons, Abe believed that she was going back to Blake.

The thought of betrayal crossed his mind, and that made him uncomfortable. But then he kept thinking back to the dead werewolf, brains leaking onto a morgue trolley, and that was not the action of someone keen to be going home.

She knows, he thought. *Somehow she knows where he is, and she's going to him.* Tempted as he was to stop Abby and question her, he had decided that allowing her to pursue her own course could be the best tactic. If she led him to Blake, he could contact Hellboy, call in the cavalry. If not, then he could still pick her up. Either way, Abe was determined not to lose her.

Abby drove fast. Abe glanced at his dashboard clock. It was almost two in the afternoon. London was maybe three hours from here, and this evening there would be a full moon.

Full moon . . .

The idea of what Abby would become sent a shiver down Abe's spine. The potential for what she could do come moonrise was another reason he should be picking her up right now. He was taking a huge risk. She was a sweet girl, Abby. But she was also a monster.

He had seen her changing many times. There was a room at BPRD Headquarters that they had used several times before to contain . . . things. When they first suspected what Abby might be—that first full moon, when her shape began to change and her mind turned to violence and blood—he and Hellboy had locked her in that room and observed what happened. The change was very fast and very thorough. One minute she was Abby, a young girl still scarred by whatever had happened to her, still shadowing Abe as though he had saved her from a fate worse than death, not just death itself. The next minute she was a wolf. A big wolf, fur patchy and exposed skin pale, but a wolf for sure. Scraps of her clothing had hung on the beast's shoulders and thighs. Blood had pooled on the floor beneath it, leaking from every orifice. And in its face, as it turned to the reinforced window they watched through, Abe had seen Abby's tortured eyes.

It had thrashed around the room, breaking bones and scraping long gouges in the walls, until Hellboy opened the door and shot it with a heavy tranquilizer.

She had been in there for three days.

Their mistake during her first change was not to feed her. As the full moon waned she had transformed back, the reversion much slower than the initial change. She was much thinner and weaker than she had been before the change and had lost far more weight than should have been possible in three days. It was as if her werewolf incarnation consumed much faster, swallowing her own body when there was no fresh meat to be had, and that had almost killed her.

Next time the change approached, she went in voluntarily. They watched the transformation and immediately introduced several small deer into the room.

For a few minutes the werewolf had glared at the terrified creatures as if transfixed. They were huddled in one corner, hardly moving, staring anywhere but at the creature Abby had become. Abe had started to think that it would refuse the food. But then it had lunged, and blood splashed the window from the inside, and when it finished an hour later, there were only scraps of fur and bones spread across the blood-slicked room.

They got through a herd of twenty deer in those three long nights.

Coming out again, Abby was strong and powerful, her naked skin gleaming with health, unabashed at her nudity. Dried blood was crusted beneath her fingernails, and her chin was black with it. Her eyes glimmered with satisfaction, and when she looked at Abe and Hellboy, she smiled.

That had been the pattern for the next several years. Abby had cost BPRD a fortune in cattle, but Abe insisted that they were saving her. She grew stronger, and the Abby he knew between full moons developed more of a personality, a confidence, and even a history. She was making her own life hour by hour, day by day, and he and the others at BPRD were doing their very best to help her.

And yet . . .

And yet there was a hunger in her that had never been sated. He could sense that every time he talked to her, and on occasion he walked into a room and found her staring out the window, musing on something he could not know. She never admitted it in so many words, but he knew that she was unfulfilled. Abe started to grow nervous before each full moon, and Abby grew more and more fidgety. He had always suspected that she would flee one of these days, free herself to find the true food she had always craved, and the potential of that had terrified him. He had always thought that there was a fine line between those who worked at

BPRD and the things they hunted. He did not want Abby to be the first one to cross that line.

He had never asked her what she had eaten before he found her in Paris, and she never volunteered the information.

Now she had gone, and the full moon was bearing down. Whatever had instigated her flight, however tied up it all was with Blake's sudden resurfacing, Abe's one great fear was that Abby would, at last, find that which had eluded her for so long.

So he kept on her tail and watched the sky. And he promised himself that should the situation arise, he would kill her before she stained her soul by killing someone else.

Ministry of Defense, London—1997

"We have . . . the situation . . . under control," the minister said. She was a tall, charming brunette, but her eyes were hard.

"With respect, ma'am, you don't." Hellboy stared at the minister, impressed that she was able to return his gaze. She was nervous, he could see that, but she was also very much in control. Confident of her control, at least. His job was to blow that confidence out of the water and get some action, not words.

"Heathrow was a disaster, I'll admit that, and I'd like to offer our government's official thanks for your help."

"It was nothing."

"But I assure you, the conference *will* go ahead. I can't go into details, but the security arrangements for it are *very* stringent."

"Those police marksmen on the rooftops?" Hellboy asked.

"Yes, those," the minister said. She took a drink from her cup of tea, averting her eyes for the first time.

"Hmm. Pretty good. And the army guys hiding out in warehouses across Docklands? Tanks, helicopters . . . that *does* sound stringent."

The minister raised her eyebrows, but she was not naive enough to ask how Hellboy had come by his information.

"And those SAS guys? Now, *they're* good. Dealt with them once back in the seventies. Impressed the hell out of me. No pun intended."

"I won't ask how you know the more refined details of our security arrangements, Hellboy. It doesn't surprise me. You're not . . . normal. No offense."

"None taken." Hellboy pursed his lips and sat up straighter. His tail whipped at the floor and pulled threads from the minister's expensive carpet. *What's normal?* he thought. *You see normal when you look in the mirror every morning, Minister?*

"But this is *our* security operation. We're acting in close liaison with several foreign governments, including your own, and everyone's happy with our arrangements."

"Have you polled them again since your largest airport was almost wiped out by dragons?"

The minister glared at Hellboy. Again, he was impressed. *She's hard. Or maybe just stubborn. Sometimes the two get mixed up, and they mean very different things.*

"What do you want from me?" she said.

"I want you to admit the possibility that you're not as well prepared as you thought."

The minister snorted, and Liz cut in. "Your Tornados got to Heathrow very quickly," she said. "I'm impressed. They were obviously on standby for any trouble."

"And?"

"The missiles they did manage to fire missed the dragons and destroyed Terminal Three. How many of the hundreds dead are a result of that? Friendly fire, I think they call it."

The minister stood and walked to the window. *Hell, she is big,* Hellboy thought. *Six-two if she's an inch.*

"I've heard about you, Miss Sherman," she said. "I don't trust you. You killed your family."

Hellboy raised his eyebrows and glanced at Liz, sensing the heat of rage simmering beneath her surface veneer of calm anger.

The minister turned to Hellboy. "And I don't trust you either."

"And what's my special reason?" he asked, voice as cold as an Arctic night.

"You're from hell."

The room fell silent. The minister and her bodyguard stood behind the desk, waiting for Hellboy and Liz to leave. Hellboy stared at the minister. A clock ticked, and somewhere ice chinked in a glass. *She never offered us a drink,* Hellboy thought.

He stood. The bodyguard moved slightly, bracing himself, hand already disappearing inside his jacket. Hellboy smiled at him, and the guy's face paled. "Ma'am," he said, "I understand your doubt, and I'm used to not being trusted. But if you don't get your head out of your butt, very soon you'll all know what hell is like." He strode from the room, feeling Liz burning with anger behind him.

They met Jim outside. He was leaning against a wall smoking, watching the cars crawling past in the never-ending London gridlock.

"No joy?" Jim asked.

"What do you think?" Hellboy said. He lit a cigarette and stood next to Jim.

"People just can't get beyond the norm," Jim said. "They see the surface of things, and if that's acceptable, they have no inclination to go deeper. Too much trouble. Too much thinking involved. And too much fear."

"Fear of the unknown?"

Jim shrugged, then shook his head. "Fear of knowing too much," he said. "Most people want a simple life. Look, over there. See that bus stop? Young woman waiting there, short skirt, leather boots, presenting a nice image?"

"Yeah," Hellboy said. "Cute." He glanced at Liz, and she rolled her eyes.

"There's a ghost standing behind her," Jim said. "Just standing there. No expression on its face. Arms down by its sides. It's looking at her, as though it can make itself felt if it really concentrates. Probably someone from her past, family or friend, but she'll never see it, never give it peace. She doesn't know how. Most people don't, and it's because they're scared of knowing too much. They'll happily buy a tabloid newspaper and think that's it, that's the news, that's what's happening. This celebrity's marrying that one, and all is good in the world tonight."

"I can't see a ghost," Hellboy said. He looked hard,

glancing left and right to give his peripheral vision a chance. But she was just a young woman waiting for a bus.

"Maybe you're too optimistic," Jim said.

"I see it," Liz said. "The instant you told me it was there, I saw it."

Jim smiled sadly. "Then you're someone not scared of knowledge."

Hellboy threw down his cigarette and crushed it out. "Jim, we need your help. We have to get close to the Anderson Hotel, and we need to be able to move fast when the time comes."

"What do you think will happen now?"

"War," Liz said. "Fast and bloody. Blake is ready to start a war for what he believes in, and it's obvious from Miss Minister up there that she's ready to lose."

"We have to spend more time here," Jim said. "We have to try harder to make her understand."

"We go in there again, and they'll throw us in the deepest dungeons they can find," Hellboy said. "At least, they'll try. And whether they believe what we're telling them or not, the time will come very soon when their forces are forced to face what we're warning them about. Forewarned is forearmed, but at least we know they have *some* protection down there."

"We need to be ready to go after Blake," Liz said.

"Exactly." Hellboy rearranged his coat over his shoulders and delved into the pockets for another cigarette. Stumps. That's all he had. One day he'd have to buy some new ones. "And that's why you need to find us a helicopter, Jim."

Jim Sugg raised his eyebrows.

Hellboy smiled at him. And he kept smiling until Jim looked away, shaking his head.

"There are some favors I can call in," the ghost hunter said. "Damn, Hellboy, this is getting messy."

"Getting? Wait till this time tomorrow. I hate to say it, but by then this city will know what messy means."

Jim led them back to the embassy car, and within minutes they were fighting their way through the London traffic. It was almost two in the afternoon. The environmental conference had begun at midday. Somewhere a clock was ticking down, and Hellboy thought it might be only hours before the alarm started to sound.

North Sea—1997

The rukh drifted half a mile above the ocean, keeping watch. It was unnerved at being this far from its father and home, but it also knew that the time was close for it to launch out from the *New Ark* one last time, and then home would be a different place entirely. It experienced freedom every minute of every day. Now, its father had said, it would have the opportunity to experience life as it should be lived.

Below, the *New Ark* had been slowing down for more than an hour. Its wake stretched behind it like a scar on the ocean, and occasionally the wake itself was disturbed by things breaking the surface. Its bow pointed toward land— the first land it had seen for some time—and every one of the heavy hold doors along its deck was swinging open. Several large boats were being lowered along both sides of the ship, and the rukh could see shapes scurrying, walking, or sliding across the deck, filling the boats and readying to depart.

Several flying things rose from the *New Ark*'s holds, spiraling skyward and heading off to the west. The rukh knew its kin, and it also recognized the other things that took wing: the dragons, the phoenix, the griffin. Shapes that it did not recognize rose from another hold; too small to identify from this distance, there were so many of them that they seemed to form a cloud, drifting across the surface of the ocean.

And below the ocean there were shadows. From this high up the rukh could make out several areas where they were concentrated, a couple on either side of the ship and more farther away, ahead, heading toward land. It had seen the things breaking the surface sometimes, sliding out and back into the water as if testing an alien environment for just a few moments. There were hooks and claws, teeth and suckers, horns and other appendages that could kill, and the rukh was astonished at the variety of deadly weapons the things of the sea possessed. It made it grateful that it was of the sky, not the ocean, and that its own defenses were the beak and the claw. It had only ever used them for the hunt.

But now Father said there would be fighting and war. And it was ready.

The rukh performed a long, wide circle around the *New Ark,* and when it faced west again, it saw a spot on the horizon that did not belong there. The spot grew quickly, manifesting itself into a machine that had no right to be in the sky. The rukh could smell it from miles away, stinking up the air and slashing at it with spinning slices of metal. The giant bird rose into the clouds, drifted for a while, and then came back down, falling onto the noisy machine and smashing it from the heavens. It came apart as it fell, disgorging several waving shapes that screamed as they tumbled into the sea. The rukh watched them fall down, saw the splashes as they hit the surface, then the larger eruptions as things rose to feed.

The boats had left the sides of the *New Ark* and were powering toward land. There were six in total, containing all manner of its father's creations, all ready to serve and fulfill the purpose they had been given. "Find life," Father had told them all as he rescued them from Memory. "Find life, but first there will be death to mete out."

More shapes rose from the *Ark* and took flight. More shadows swam from underneath. It was as if the ship were bleeding itself into the water and the air, and by venting life it was giving it as well.

The rukh called out loudly, thrilled and excited and proud, and when the last shadow had left and the ship was still in the water, it turned westward and followed its cousins toward land. It had its own mission that Father had whispered in its mind that morning.

It could see its proud father on the bow of the ship. It knew that it was leaving him behind. But it knew also that it would see him again.

They were leaving their home, and the memory of the Memory, to find a new home out in the world. Their father had promised them this, and now the time had come. His thoughts followed them all, and in each alien mind he was saying something slightly different. But the messages amounted to the same thing: *Now is your time.*

Motorway approaching London—1997

It was only as she neared London that Abby began to worry about Blake sending something to stop her.

She had touched something there in the Memory, or been touched, and if she could do that, then so could he. She had hurt him on the day she escaped, both physically and mentally. The physical hurt would heal, but the mental hurt—the betrayal he must have felt—would be paining him still.

The thing that had given her the hints that led her here was unknowable. She could not trust it, appreciate it, understand it, and yet she was following its lead, rushing headlong into something about which she had no idea. She did not know what to expect, and she had foolishly believed that the thing had spoken only to her. But what if it had spoken to Blake as well? What if that thing had motives more convoluted and obscure than she could possibly imagine? Blake had deserted it there in the Memory, so it said, but perhaps it wanted Blake for its own. Maybe it would haul him into the Memory as well, thereby finding its own way out.

Maybe, perhaps, who knew . . . there was too much going on in her head for her to insulate one problem from the next. She had been driving hard and was running out of fuel—one problem. She had no idea how she would get back onto the *New Ark* and confront Blake—another problem. And it was full moon tonight—there was another problem, the biggest of them all, and the one she would likely have to confront first.

She swerved back into the outside lane and overtook a

line of buses. She kept speeding without realizing, glancing in her mirror to make sure the police weren't chasing her. She was driving against the clock, she knew that, and as the minutes ticked by, she was beginning to realize that there was less and less chance of her actually making it to London in time. And even if she did, she had no idea where the *New Ark* was or exactly what Blake had planned. It was hopeless. This whole journey was hopeless, desperate, and by fleeing the BPRD she had exposed herself to a danger that had been kept down for so long.

But I'm sick of the taste of deer!

Abby hissed and shook her head, trying to clear the thought from her mind.

That bastard I killed in Baltimore, so mocking, so full of life.

"Dammit, just drive. Drive!"

Maybe it's because of what he eats.

Sometime back in the darkness of her past, after the Memory but before her real life began with the BPRD, there were the years she had spent on the ship. She had consciously cast them from her mind the moment Abe found her and dragged her kicking and screaming out of the Seine. Something had changed for her that day. To begin with, she thought it was recognizing the strangeness of Abe's existence and realizing that people—*things*—like him could exist without having any link to Benedict Blake. But she had eventually come to understand that it was nothing to do with Blake, or what he meant, or what he had done. It was Abe, and the look of concern in his eyes. People could care for her, she had realized then. The world was much larger than she had ever believed.

But still alive in her dreams of that time onboard the

New Ark—and always there as a memory after every full moon, whatever she had been fed, however satisfied she convinced herself she was with the deer and other cattle— was that tangy taste of warm flesh and rich blood, so peculiar, so distinctive of human meat.

Abby glanced across at the driver of a car she was passing. He looked at her and smiled, and she smiled back. As she passed he must have accelerated, because he remained alongside her for a few more seconds. Abby did not look again.

I could lead him off the road, climb into the back of his car, tear out his throat—

"No!" she screamed. She pressed down on the horn, leaning hard on the center of the steering wheel and lifting herself from the seat. Her car swerved across the motorway, cutting in front of the man and passing several feet from the nose of a bus filled with schoolchildren. Other horns blared, and she wanted to stop, run them off the road, watch the bloody red mess of the accidents—

"Oh, Abe," she said. "Abe, I'm sorry, I'm so damn sorry . . ."

Abby drove on, trying to ignore the thoughts instead of cutting them out altogether, but they were there always, like the echo of a meal waiting to be tasted again.

And there was something else. Intruding into her thoughts, then out again. Touching her from somewhere much farther back than she was prepared to go ever again. Intruding from the Memory, marking her and then withdrawing once more.

"Get out of my head," she said. In the distance came a rumble like distant thunder, or laughter.

———

Abe Sapien followed Abby's car. He watched it swerve across the highway and then straighten again. At one point he drew close enough behind to see her thumping the steering wheel, shaking her head, and shouting at herself in the mirror, as if her reflection were someone else. Several times he almost flashed and tried to pull her over, but he was afraid that to do so would only make her go faster, increase the chance of her crashing and burning away.

And besides, she obviously had a destination in mind. Unless something terrible happened, the best he could do was follow.

London Docklands—1997

They flew above London, sun slanting in from the southwest and warming their skin. They were losing altitude, heading down toward the conference hotel, and they had yet to be challenged.

"Thought you said security was tight," Hellboy shouted above the roar of the rotors.

"This is an official chopper," Jim replied.

"On unofficial business." Liz was smoking her third cigarette of the journey. She was doing her best not to look out the windows, but the sun came in and made interesting shapes of her exhalations. She stirred them with her hand and tried to make sense of them. She wondered whether this was the sort of thing Jim had seen to begin with, before he could see ghosts for real.

Liz kept thinking about the ghost standing behind that

woman at the bus stop. She had not wanted to see it, but she had, and she was not grateful to Jim Sugg for that experience. Not grateful at all.

"We're about a mile away now," the pilot said in their headphones.

Hellboy nudged Liz. "You OK?"

She nodded, then smiled at him for added reassurance. His expression said that he could read her smile so well. OK? Yeah, sure, apart from the fact that she'd just seen a ghost, they were hanging above a city in a machine that should never fly, approaching what could become the most momentous and important battle this country had ever seen. Yeah, fine, just dandy.

"They're only animals," Hellboy said.

"Say that to the people melted into the tarmac at Heathrow."

"Liz, they're only animals. I shot those dragons, and they didn't rise again."

"You didn't see the phoenix."

"Animal. Not understood as real anymore, but it's a creature. It's not something from beyond death, a demon or a monster conjured up by Rasputin. We're dealing with animals that've been brought back from a place they should have been left. We've fought their like before, but only singly. They've never ganged up on us before. And they were in the Memory for a reason: they'd had their time. Their influence on this world was over, apart from appearing in stories and movies and tucked away in the backs of people's minds at night. Dreams, that's what they should have been, because dreams are important. But Blake has brought them back and made them mad, given them his own agenda. And that's what we've got to keep in mind. The supernatural in this is balanced by the science he used. He's a scientist who knows magic. The bringing back, that was magic. The things we're about to see, all science."

Liz looked up at her big red friend and smiled. "You out of breath now?"

"Huh?"

"I think that's the most I've ever heard you say in one go."

Hellboy frowned. "I'm nervous."

"Scared?"

He shrugged. "It's a living."

The helicopter started to dip and turn, slanting sun moving across the cabin, and then the pilot swore.

"What is it?" Jim asked.

"Something . . ."

Hellboy clicked open his harness. "Let's take a look."

Liz followed him, holding on to his belt as he swung the sliding side door of the Lynx wide open.

"Oh hell, oh Jesus, oh what in the name of . . . ?" the pilot mumbled. He had brought the helicopter to a halt, hovering, paused just as his heart must have paused at the sight below.

"Too late," Hellboy said.

Below them, London Docklands was spread out like slabs of shattered glass: spits of land, spreads of water, docks and canals, islands and quays. Buildings rose like shards, their windows catching the sun and glittering at the sky. Roads and railways snaked between buildings and waterways. And things were moving down there. At first Liz thought they were boats, but they were moving too quickly and erratically. When she looked closer she realized that they were flying things, dipping and diving, climbing and hovering. And between them buzzed smaller, less able shapes, some spitting fire, others exploding, spiraling down to splash into water or erupt into fire on land or buildings far below.

"Dogfight," Hellboy said.

Liz could hardly believe what she was seeing. Even after the past few days, the sight of this battle over London was beyond belief. And that was exactly why the dragons and griffins and other flying things were winning.

West of the battle, perhaps a mile distant, the Anderson Hotel thrust up from the ground, an edifice of steel and glass. As yet untouched, it was being buzzed by several army helicopters, and three jets roared overhead as if to lay claim to the building. They were too far away to make out activity on the ground, but the hotel was built on a long spit of land, and on either side the water was lined white with the wakes of fast boats. *Ours or theirs?* Liz thought. *Metal and wood or bone and flesh?*

"It's really happening," Jim said. "Jesus, it's really happening."

"History in the making," Hellboy said. "Look. On the river."

The Thames curved away to the east, passing below the helicopter. Leaning forward slightly and looking down, Liz could see the wakes of several large boats as they powered upriver. Shapes parted from the boats as they moved, some splashing into the water, others taking to the air and breaking left and right. One of the vessels slowed and nudged against a timber jetty, and dark shapes swarmed ashore, splitting up and disappearing along roads, between buildings, under covered ways.

"Is that more of them?" Liz said. "I can't make out."

"If not, they're soldiers with wings and aqualungs," Hell-boy said. He leaned out farther, hanging on to the heavy winch that hung above the door. "Oh crap, that's not all."

"What?" Liz continued looking down at the river. Two of the boats were still traveling, the others having moored and disgorged whatever strange cargo they carried. The streets down there must be swarming with the things already, though the only movement she could make out was cars screeching to a halt, crashing into lampposts, and people fleeing their vehicles as they saw . . . something. "What, HB?"

"Look," he said. "*Under* the river."

The shapes had been too large for her to notice without being shown. She had assumed that the shadings and color-ing of the water were a result of silt beneath the surface, plant growth, the angle at which the sun hit the water and reflected from surrounding buildings. But the shapes were moving . . . and silt did not do that.

"They're huge," she said.

"What are they?" Jim was lying on the floor of the Lynx, head out over the edge. He looked up, and his eyes were more haunted than ever. "What are they throwing at us now?"

"Kraken," Hellboy said. "Sea serpents. Things with ten-tacles. Damn, why does it always have to be tentacles?"

The shapes crept upriver, shadows beneath the water that changed in size and shape as they moved. One of them passed under a large motor cruiser, and the boat flipped up onto its side and broke in half. Something gray rose from the water, glinting oily in the sun, curled around the broken boat, and pulled the bow down beneath the disturbed surface. It passed on, leaving shapes splashing in the river behind it.

"Jim, are you in touch with anyone inside that hotel?" Liz asked.

"Not directly, but I can patch messages direct to the American embassy. They've got people inside."

"Do it. Tell them to get everyone down into the basement, if they can."

"If there is a basement," Hellboy said. "That thing's built right next to the river."

"There is a basement," Jim said. "That's where I spent some time when the thing was being built."

"Then they need to get down there," Liz said. "We can hope the army and police on the ground will realize that. Easier to defend, especially against those flying things."

"What the hell are the kraken going to do when they get there?" Hellboy said.

"The hotel's right next to the water," Liz said. "My guess is that they'll try to bring it down."

Jim started talking into his satellite phone, and Hellboy and Liz watched events unfolding below. There was a terrible sense of inevitability about the whole scene. The flying creatures circled the hotel, darting in now and then to take on a helicopter, dodge fire from the hotel itself, and veer away again, skimming the rooftops of surrounding buildings and battling the snipers positioned there. The things that walked—Liz could not identify them from this high up, and she was grateful for small mercies—approached the hotel, darting from cover to cover, and fresh firefights broke out south and east of the Anderson. Explosions erupted between buildings, gushing flame and smoke at the sky. Bodies fell in the streets, mutilated by things with long bodies and many legs.

Closer to the hotel there was a larger explosion as a helicopter went down. Something was wrapped around it as it fell, a creature being whipped and torn to shreds by the rotor blades. It crashed on a walkway beside the hotel, and both creature and aircraft were engulfed in flames. The smoke rose high, staining the sky.

Liz could see men running back and forth across the roof of the hotel. Machine guns spewed bullets into the sky, but they seemed to be firing wild. A dragon flew directly up the side of the building, tail smashing windows and scoring a scar in the edifice, and when it reached the roof it hung on to the parapet and poured flames at the men. Some ran, others were caught, thrashing briefly until the fire scorched them into stillness.

"They've patched me through to an SAS sergeant in the hotel," Jim said. "Seems the minister of defense has suddenly realized there's a problem, and as we're on the scene—"

"We won't be for long," Hellboy said.

"What do you mean?" Jim asked.

"They're all coming upriver," Liz said, "which means we'll be going downriver. There's not much we can do here, other than relay what we know to that SAS guy. We have to find Blake."

"What good will that do now that he's released these *things* on us?" Jim asked. For the first time Liz heard a note of panic in his voice.

"Stop him, and maybe we stop this," Liz said. "Hellboy?"

"It's worth a shot," he said. "He's got to be controlling things somehow, guiding this. As I said, these are animals. Where's their purpose? What's motivating them to destroy a hotel? They're puppets. We need to find the guy who's holding the strings."

Liz nodded. "And cut them. Here, let me talk to the SAS guy." Jim handed her the satellite phone, and she pressed it to her ear, covering her other ear to try to shut out the roar of the rotors. "Sergeant?" she said.

"Smith. Who's this?"

"I'm Liz Sherman from the Bureau of Paranormal Research and Defense."

"Hey, this must be just your cup of tea." Liz heard some shooting in the background, someone shouting, and then the gunfire was suddenly lessened by the slam of a door. "Excuse me if I talk while I'm on the move."

"No problem. Listen, Sergeant Smith—"

"Just Smith."

"OK, Smith, now listen. You have to get everyone down into the basement or whatever the lowest point is in that building. Understand?"

"I'm approaching the conference hall right now. If I can get anyone to listen I'll do my best. You in a chopper?"

"Yes."

"How does it look?"

Liz paused for a couple of seconds, looked down at the battle. There were more fires now, more explosions, and the sky was filling with smoke.

"That bad, eh?" Smith said.

"It's not good. You don't need me to tell you what's happening, what's assaulting you?"

"I've just been out onto the concourse. Two of my men were killed there by a lion with a man's head, and I emptied a mag into a giant bloody black dog before the damn thing even decided to sit."

"They're in the hotel already?"

"No, we're—" Smith broke off, and Liz held the phone away as the crackle of gunfire came again. "We're holding them off," he said. "So yeah, I've got a rough idea of what's happening. The world's come to us. That sound about right?"

"That's about right. Smith, there's worse to come. You're being harried at the moment, but there are things coming up the river—big things—and they'll be with you any time now."

"How big?"

"Well . . . don't bother with machine guns."

"Right. Basement, then."

"We're heading away, but I'll keep the channel open," Liz said. "Good luck."

"Luck's got nothing to do with it." Smith clicked off, and Liz stared at the mouthpiece for a second, thinking she should have said more. But what more was there to say? He was the man on the ground, he was the one facing these things, not just watching from a safe distance.

"We need to go," Hellboy said. "Hey, pilot, follow the river down to the sea. Stay at this height, and keep a look out for . . . things."

"Yeah, sure. Things," the pilot said in their headphones. His voice was flat, panic subdued by shock. "And my name's Hicks."

"Hicks, you got any guns in this thing?"

"Usually a door gun, but it's not mounted today."

"Great." Hellboy pulled his pistol, checked that it was loaded, and holstered it again. "Let's go."

The three of them remained at the door as the helicopter turned and headed east, watching the battle recede behind them, seeing a Tornado smash into the hotel, sending burning debris to the ground below. Something rose from the flames, itself blazing, but the fire soon died out as the flesh-and-blood creature from myth and legend spun around for another attack.

"This is bad," Liz said.

"Yeah, it's bad." Hellboy turned to face Liz.

That was when the pilot started screaming.

Motorway approaching London—1997

Abe Sapien saw the shape diving out of the sun, flashed his lights, stepped on the gas, closed the distance between him and Abby, saw her glance in her mirror with her eyes open in recognition, pointed up, shouted even though he knew she could not hear him, and by the time she'd understood his message, the giant bird had landed on her car and lifted it clear of the road.

Abe gave chase, amazed. Abby's car's wheels were still spinning—he looked down at his own speedometer and saw that he was doing more than eighty—yet still the bird moved ahead. It followed the course of the road for a few seconds, and Abe instantly saw why. Drivers terrified at the sight of the thing swerved across lanes, crashing into the sides of buses, spinning from the road, and tumbling a dozen times across fields and into ditches, and he had to use every ounce of concentration to negotiate his way through the accidents happening all around him. Someone broad-sided him, and he fought with the wheel, letting the Jeep swerve across two lanes before halting its drift and bringing it back on course. He dodged past a white van shaking from side to side, ducked in front of a little two-seater sports car, then put his foot down and cleared the jam of traffic. At last free of the accident, he looked up, only to see the huge bird—he thought it was a rukh—turn sharply to the left and head off across the countryside.

Abe steered onto the hard shoulder and slammed on the brakes, leaving a cloud of smoke in the air behind him. He scrambled across the front seats and jumped from the Jeep, staring after the rukh and the car and Abby trapped inside. He had never felt so helpless.

"Now what?" he shouted. "Now what do I do?"

He called Hellboy on his satellite phone, but the ring was not answered. Maybe the big red guy was busy.

Abe jumped back into the Jeep and, lacking any other course of action, headed for London.

London Docklands—1997

"Come around again!" Hellboy screamed. "Don't turn your back on it!" The pilot swerved the helicopter. Hellboy swung from the open door, and his fist crushed metal as he struggled to hold on. He reached the pivot point and swung back in, and the griffin filled his whole field of vision. Someone shouted behind him, but there was no time to turn and look. He raised the pistol and let off three shots, seeing at least one of them find its target. The griffin raised its head in pain, and the rotor blades took a slice of skin and feathers from the top of its head.

It screamed, went into a dive, and disappeared below the helicopter.

"Go up!" Hellboy shouted. The helicopter rose, and he leaned out again, looking below. All he could see were the streets and warehouses around Docklands and the Thames widening as it neared the sea. The griffin was gone. "Left side?" he asked.

"Yeah, it's there!" the pilot screamed, and the helicopter dipped suddenly, lifting Hellboy from his feet.

He looked at his right hand where it was fisted in the door jamb. It had crushed straight through the door, and metal was tearing with every twist and turn the pilot performed. He glanced back at Liz and Jim where they sat strapped into their seats. Jim was praying. Liz was trying to light a cigarette, but her finger kept going out in the breeze from the door.

"Liz!" he said. "Can you—"

"Not in this wind. I'll fry us all."

The pilot brought the helicopter under control again, flattened it out, and Hellboy could see the griffin circling them, maybe fifty feet above. He let go of the door—having to tear his hand away, ripping the metal even more—and ducked briefly back into the cabin.

"Hey, Hicks," Hellboy said. "You're doing great. But there's no way we can outrun this sucker, so I want you to chase it."

"Go *after* it?" Even through the intercom, Hicks's voice was terrified.

"Take the fight to it, rather than wait for it to knock us from the sky."

"I did *not* sign on for this," Jim said.

Hicks was silent for a few seconds, the only sound a crackle in their headphones. "OK," he said. "You know, one good slash of these rotors, and he'll be mincemeat."

"Will they withstand that?" Liz said. This time the pilot's silence was his only answer.

Hellboy looked at Liz and shrugged, then hefted his gun and moved to the doorway again. He held on tight while the pilot dipped, then brought the helicopter up in a tight climb, heading straight for the circling griffin. Liz shouted, grabbing hold of her seat, and Jim still had his eyes closed, muttering a prayer or a curse or both. Hellboy looked up at the surprised creature, then lifted his gun and fired at it through the rotors.

The bullet hit home in the griffin's stomach.

"Damn!" said Hellboy, surprised. "Bull's-eye!"

"It's coming right at us!" Hicks screamed in their ears, and then the whole aircraft shook, shuddered, spun in the air, the stench of burning suddenly overpowering, metal tearing and scraping, the fuselage buckling and springing the fixed seats away from the wall, a splash of blood spraying past the open door and washing Hellboy's face, a burst of feathers and skin and flesh following, and then the helicopter was falling much faster than it should.

Hellboy struggled to his feet, holstering his pistol and wiping a great swath of sticky blood from his face. He tried to counter the spin of the helicopter, moving toward the steps up into the cockpit, desperate to see what had become of the pilot. If the guy was dead, then so were they.

"Hey!" Hellboy called. "Hicks!"

Their headpieces crackled, then started whispering, "Holy shit holy shit holy shit . . ."

Hellboy pulled himself up the steps into the cockpit. It was red. One side of the windscreen had shattered, the copilot was dead, and the bloody remains of part of the griffin were splashed all over the instrument panel, the floor, and the pilot's flying suit. His face was as red as Hellboy's but for his stark, staring eyes.

"Hicks!" Hellboy said. "We're going to crash!"

Stuff slid down the window on the outside, a feathery, fleshy mess.

"Hicks!"

The rotors were making a strange sound.

"Dammit!" Hellboy leaned forward and tapped the pilot's helmet, knocking his head to the side.

Hicks turned and stared at Hellboy, eyes wide, mouth falling open. He glanced at his copilot, then turned back and started fighting with the controls.

Hellboy waited, watching, realizing that Hicks was now doing his best to right the helicopter and assess the damage. He gave him a full minute before he asked.

"Well," Hicks said, "I could beat around the bush and give you all the reasons, but I'd say we're buggered."

"How long before you have to put us down?"

"Well . . . now!"

"Not now," Hellboy said. "Keep us in the air as long as you can. Follow the river."

"A thing the size of my family's car has just been diced by our rotors," Hicks said. "I don't think it would be safe to just—"

"You think we'd be safer down there, on the ground, with all that we've seen?"

Hicks looked away, fought against the shuddering controls. "I'll keep us up as long as I can," he said.

Hellboy touched his arm. "Good man. And good flying. I thought we were screwed for sure."

Back in the cabin Jim still had his eyes closed, and Liz had succeeded in lighting a cigarette. Her hand shook so much that she could barely take a drag. "I am never, ever, ever going onboard an aircraft with you again," she said.

"Me?" Hellboy said. "You blame me?"

"Got to blame someone." She concentrated on the cigarette, got it between her lips, and left it there.

"Well, let's hope there's nothing else between us and Blake," Hellboy said.

Liz stared through a haze of smoke. "You think?"

Hellboy looked away, down, back the way they had come. In the distance he could see a swath of smoke rising above the London Docklands. He hoped he was not yet looking at the ashes of world leaders.

Thames Estuary—1997

To begin with, she opened the passenger door and thought about jumping.

The giant bird's claws had ripped through the car roof and were now curled against its underside, and Abby had to squeeze past them. The driver's door was buckled and bent, but the passenger-side door swung open easily enough. The car shuddered as it opened, and the bird carrying her looked down to see what its catch was doing.

This is from him, Abby thought. *He's sent it to get me. He knows I'm coming. I've lost the initiative, and now he's totally in control again. It won't harm me now. He'll leave that till later.*

She wished she had a gun to test that theory.

The bird had flown fast. London was below them now, an untidy map of streets and river, houses and tower blocks, parks and parking lots. They were a mile up, maybe more, and the air up here was freezing. She could jump, she supposed. But if Blake was that keen to have her, the bird would likely drop the car and pluck her from the sky. And she'd rather spend the journey in relative comfort than clasped in the creature's rough claws.

She almost went anyway, seeing the Thames far below and remembering how she'd tried to end things in a similar river in another city. But since then she had grown and developed, become a person, and with the help of Abe she had started to make a life for herself. She had made herself better than Blake had made her, and that counted for something. Terrified though she was at what the night was yet to bring, she would not let desperation defeat her.

And besides, with this bird's help she was going exactly where she had intended. She thought of the *New Ark* and its inhabitants, the dark places deep within its holds where things that should never be had been resurrected . . . and she was one of those things. She thought of the Voice locked in the room in the depths of the ship and Blake striding through his domain with the arrogance of a father believing himself perfect. She wished, more than anything, that she had stayed behind to kill him.

London soon passed away below them, and she realized that the bird was following the course of the river. Over the Docklands area they passed above a stain of smoke and fire, and she wondered whether it had anything to do with what was going on today. She thought so. The world was a changing place, and with change came chaos.

The river widened as it approached the sea. Abby glanced at her watch. It was almost four o'clock. The bird began to drop, spiraling down as if to disorient her, losing altitude at a startling rate. She tried to look out the windows but saw only sea and land, sea and land, juggling position as if the bird could not decide upon its final destination.

It was only as they were preparing to land that she saw the *New Ark*, dilapidated and rusting, adrift and seemingly empty. All holds were open, all doors ajar, and there was no activity at all on deck.

The great bird lowered the car into one of the open holds, and Abby was home.

"So what the hell is that?" Liz asked.

Hellboy looked where she was pointing. A huge bird was flying high overhead, a bulky shape suspended beneath it. "It's a rukh carrying a car," he said matter-of-factly.

"Oh, like I'm supposed to know that."

He watched the bird move downriver. It was going faster than them, following the Thames, as if it had a purpose. "Hey, Hicks, look up and to your right. See it?"

"Jesus."

"Follow that bird, Hicks."

Liz smiled. "Bet you've been waiting to say that all your life."

"Didn't think I'd ever get the chance."

"What are we going to do?" Jim asked.

Hellboy looked at him and frowned.

"I mean when we get there," the ghost hunter said. "Wherever there is. What are we going to do?"

"Kick some ass."

"But this Blake character, surely he'll be protected? We've seen some of the things he's let loose on the world . . . he won't have left himself open to attack, will he? If he's the puppet master you're suggesting, he'll want to ensure that he can continue holding the strings."

"Maybe, maybe not," Hellboy said. "Depends on how long he thinks all this will take."

"He's been building up to this for years," Liz said. "If what our adviser back at BPRD says is true, the guy's probably nine parts mad. There's no rationality in this, no single sane reason to do what he's doing."

"Dunno," Hellboy said.

"What?"

He shrugged. Sat down. The helicopter juddered briefly, shook to the sound of grinding metal, then flew on. It would soon be giving up the ghost.

"HB, what do you mean, 'dunno'?"

"Well . . ." He scratched his goatee and looked anywhere but at Liz. "The guy's wife was killed. His research was trashed, even though it seems it was way ahead of its time. He was accused of murder. He and his sons had to go on the run, hide, disappear from the world. He's trying to restore the earth to its natural order, stop mankind from going down the route it's taken, a route that *will* destroy the planet soon. Ask any scientist. It's just that Blake has magic as an ally. He has knowledge. He's a genius, and madness and genius sleep well together."

"You almost sound as if you support this maniac."

"Not at all. I'm going to kick his ass. But I can empathize."

"You're a big softie."

Hellboy glared at Liz for a second, then away again. *Anyone but you*, he thought, but then he shook his head. Things
were getting to him. He should loosen up. There was a fight
coming—a big one—and he had to be at his best.

"Hey," Liz said.

"Yeah." He smiled at her, aware that Jim Sugg had
looked away from their private moment. *I'm a lucky man*,
Hellboy thought. *I'm a very lucky man. I have friends, people
who care for me. Blake? He has revenge. With nothing but that
driving him, madness is inevitable.*

"Blake won't be far away," Liz said. "This is his moment.
Even if he can't see it, he'll want to be close."

"Not far away at all," Hellboy agreed. "Hey, Hicks, you
still see that bird carrying the car?"

"Er . . . yeah. But we won't be following it for very much
longer. That other giant bird thing we hit did something
nasty to the motor. It's overheating, and something's broken
in there. I can hear it grinding. I want to take us lower just
in case—"

"We fly on," Hellboy said. "I thought helicopters either
flew or crashed?"

"Yeah, no gliding in this baby."

"So what's the point in going lower? We fly."

"Whatever you say," Hicks said. He mumbled something
else, but Hellboy missed it. Probably a prayer.

Hicks nursed the Lynx onward, still keeping the bird and
the flying car in sight. Hellboy, Liz, and Jim sat in the back,

staring from the open door—Hellboy's fist had crushed the jamb so that it would no longer shut—and using the noise as an excuse not to talk. Just as Hellboy noticed he could no longer see land to the south, Hicks called through their headphones, "Oh, screw me."

"What is it?"

"Come see for yourself."

Hellboy climbed into the cockpit again, doing his best to ignore the worsening shuddering of the helicopter. They wouldn't be up for much longer, and—

And there it was. The ship. He'd guessed it would be a ship, but not one like this, not one as *big* as this.

"It's an old oil tanker," Hicks said. "I just saw that bird dip down into one of those open doors on its deck. Car and all."

I wonder why it took the car, Hellboy thought. *I wonder who's in it.* "Can you land us on that thing?"

"Are you out of your—?"

"Hicks." Hellboy stared at the pilot. He gave him the glare. He hated doing it, but sometimes kind words just weren't enough.

"I can land on it," Hicks said. "And yes, you scare me. But all you had to do was say please."

Hellboy laughed briefly and went back into the cabin. "This is it," he said. He clenched his fist, checked his pistol, and wondered why he suddenly felt far from ready.

They landed on the wide bow of the old tanker, wondering why they had been allowed to descend uninterrupted.

It was only as the rotors wound down and the things came at them from behind the splayed hold doors that they began to understand.

The *New Ark,* English Channel—1997

As soon as the car bumped onto the deck, Abby was out, running for the shadows, hating the stink and feel and sound of this familiar, terrible place, yet desperate to hide and escape as quickly as possible. Lost, at least she would stand a chance. And there was still one place where she thought she could find help.

"Always in a rush," a voice said. "Always so keen to leave, when there's unfinished business behind you."

Abby spun around, searching the hold for Blake. All she could see were the wrecked car and the bird, flapping its immense wings and trying to loosen its claws from the buckled metal. Elsewhere were only shadows, nudged by sunlight slanting through the open hold doors.

"You rushed away from me," Blake said. "But now you're back, and at the most opportune moment. What am I to you now, werewolf? Am I unfinished business?"

"I should have killed you that night I escaped," Abby said. "And I have a name: Abby. I'm not one of your monsters anymore."

"Of course you are," Blake said, and he stepped from the shadows. He looked ancient. Slight. Weary. And Abby had to blink, because for a second he was almost *not there.* "And you always will be." Blake looked up through the hold at the deep blue sky, marred here and there by loose, wispy clouds. "It'll be dusk soon . . . *Abby.* And then night, and the full moon will be out. Ready to taste flesh?" He darted closer, his coat stroking the air.

"Stay away!" she said.

"Ready to taste *human* flesh again?"

"I eat cattle," she said.

"Now maybe. But not always. Don't you remember the first one, the boy from Hawaii? The rukh brought him to you, and you tore him to shreds, ate his heart, drank blood from his tattered throat. And I treated you like royalty. A whole hold of your own."

Abby closed her eyes and shook her head, trying to deny the images that Blake's words conjured. They were circling her like memories, but she tried to shove them away, make them lies. She put them on a screen and called them a film. But she had never tasted a movie or felt its skin split beneath her teeth—

"You're next!" she said, lunging at Blake.

He stepped aside and laughed. Her hands, tattooed fingers already clawed, slid from his chest and throat as though coated in oil. She pounced again, and again Blake brushed her off. She hardly felt him.

"You must be starving," Blake said. "No true flesh for so long."

"I'm a *person,* Blake. I have a place in the world, memories, a life." She stood back from him, spooked by the way he had felt. She squinted. Could she really see through him? Or was that simply the weird light down here, strobed by the rukh's wings as it struggled to flap itself free of the car?

"You're something I brought back!" he said, and she heard wounded pride in his voice. Good. She could use that.

"Are you so proud of everything you brought back? What about *him*? Is he still locked away down there?"

Blake's smile did not falter, but the humor dropped from his face.

"He's going to have you," Abby said. "And you know

that, don't you? He was always going to have you in the end."

"Once the end is here, I'll no longer care," Blake said. "Not long now. They're probably dying already, those pompous bastards pumped up with their own self-importance. They have no idea what's important! Money, oil, status . . . their place in the scheme of things has gone. It'll be a cleaner world, werewolf, the second blood from the first of them touches the ground."

Abby looked for a way out. She could see movement in the shadows: drones. They were small and weak, but enough of them could easily subdue her, should Blake command them to do so.

"No way out," he said.

"Why did you bring me here?"

"To kill you," Blake said. "You're my failure. I'll grant you your last meal, though." He smiled, and behind that grin she saw his downfall.

Abby smiled as well. "So even after all this grand talk of morals and responsibility, you still let pride bring you down," she said.

Blake shrugged. "It's tidiness, not pride. You'd be a loose end."

There was the sudden sound of gunfire from somewhere far away. Blake glanced around—just for a second—and Abby took her chance. She screeched loudly, startling the rukh into agitated motion, and ran the opposite way, ducking into shadows and hoping she would find a wall with a door. Several drones blocked her path, and when Blake screamed they turned on her with their stunted arms raised. She kicked one aside, batted another from her face when it launched itself at her, and then she was through a door and around the corner, running, trusting to instinct rather than trying to plan a route. Her senses were already heightened by the impending full moon. She smelled her way down, deeper into the ship, and within a few minutes she could no longer hear Blake raging behind her.

She got lost. Corridors and doors, stairways and open rooms, shadows and light, old pens and cooling birthing vats. She shut doors behind her, opened those that were closed, backtracked here and there, covering her path in the hope that she would buy enough time to do what she had to do. There was somewhere to visit and one final door to open at last.

After that, the future would be in very different hands.

"What the hell are *they*?" Hicks shouted.

"You have a sidearm?" Hellboy asked.

"Of course, but—"

"Get ready to use it."

Hellboy and Liz knelt in the doorway of the Lynx's cabin, facing the things scampering across the deck. Jim, pale and shaking, sat behind them. There was little he could do to help. Hicks was still in his pilot's seat, side window opened, the muzzle of his pistol resting on the glass lip.

"Black dogs," Liz said.

"They're the size of cows!" Hellboy said.

"How many do you see? I count four. Hicks?"

"I can't see, they're too fast."

Hellboy growled. "Let them have it." His pistol roared, and a shower of sparks erupted from the deck before two of the running hounds. They did not even turn aside.

The black dogs were huge, heavily muscled, their long

claws clicking on the metal deck as they ran. They made no effort to hide themselves or creep up on the helicopter. They were too large for one thing, and the setting sun washed their shadows far across the deck. By the time the first dog reached the long shadow of the helicopter, its jaws were dripping pink foam, teeth glinting, eyes narrowed as the vicious growl distorted its face.

Hellboy fired again, and Hicks's pistol added its own voice. Bullets thudded into the lead dog, catching it in the shoulder and mouth, and it skidded across the deck, shaking its head. It glanced over its shoulder and quickly ran again, obviously keen to keep the lead.

"Shit," Hicks muttered. He fired again. Red spots erupted on the fur of the dog's face, but the bullets did not faze it.

"Liz?" Hellboy said. He squeezed off another couple of shots. The large-caliber bullets struck home in the creature's front legs, delaying it for a few precious seconds. "Liz, I need help here. There won't be a second chance."

"I know, I know!"

Hellboy glanced at Liz. Her eyes were squeezed shut, concentration creased her face, and her arms rose on either side as fire flickered between her fingers. He could feel the power brewing in her, so alien and strange because it seemed to come from nowhere. He could sense its heat, its wrath, and not for the first time he was glad to be her friend. Pretty tough he may be, but he'd hate to be on the receiving end of Liz's fury.

"Liz . . ."

The first dog was within leaping distance. Hellboy's pistol clicked empty. Hicks fired again, his own peashooter having little effect.

Liz screamed.

The dog's eyes reflected the fire that leaped from Liz's hands, mouth, and eyes. The hound launched itself from the deck, aimed at the open door of the helicopter, but it never made contact. The fire batted it aside, swarming across its foam-speckled face and burrowing into its fur. The stink of burning hair and flesh quickly permeated the inside of the Lynx, even as the second black dog barreled into the first, sending it rolling across the deck, claws screeching up curls of torn metal.

The burning dog's howl was like the whole day screaming in pain. It streaked back across the deck, leaving oily smoke in its wake. Flames slithered across its skin. It struck one of the open hold doors with a meaty thud, rolled onto its back, and fell out of sight into the bowels of the ship.

Hellboy had taken the opportunity to reload. He jumped from the chopper, stood with his legs braced, and fired at the other three dogs, one bullet each. He saw one take out a dog's eye, wasn't sure what happened to the other shots, and then the second hound pounced.

It stood as tall as him. Its mouth was the width of his head. Each tooth was the length of his pistol's barrel, and the eyes were featureless black pits, no soul there, no hope, only a pledge of pain and a promise of death. As it came at him, claws reaching, mouth wide open, bloody saliva streaking back from its teeth, Hellboy swung his right fist to connect with its snout.

The dog's howl turned into a whimper as it struck the deck and rolled onto its side.

"Play dead!" Hellboy shouted. He leaped after the black dog, fist crashing down onto one of its back legs. He felt the bone crumble. The dog howled, jerking its head back and gnashing its jaws at him. He pulled back, and the dog's teeth snapped shut an inch from his hand, its fleshy lips smacking around his arm. Hellboy stood and brushed the sticky mess of saliva and blood from his skin.

The dog tried to stand. Its leg crumpled, so it dragged itself forward instead, jaws working at the air as if it were chewing its way to Hellboy. He backed away slowly, teasing the dog, until the angle was right for Hicks to fill its head with lead.

Six rounds sent the monster back to the Memory.

"Two down," Hellboy said, and then Liz shouted, Hicks gasped, and the two remaining dogs landed on Hellboy's back.

He was forced to the deck, smashing his face into the salty metal. They knocked the breath from him, the impact dulled his senses, and if the dogs hadn't chosen that moment to snap at each other—fighting over their share of dinner, Hellboy guessed—things might have ended up much worse. As it was, their bickering gave him a precious few seconds to gather himself, tense his muscles, and push upward from the deck. One dog tumbled away toward the helicopter, the other stayed right there on his back, its claws curling through his coat and piercing his skin, scraping against bone, its slavering jaws closing on the back of his neck and grinding together. His own warm blood mixed with the disgusting flow of saliva and foam down his back.

"No you don't," Hellboy whispered. He rolled, pushing hard from the ship's deck and flipping his head around. The stumps of his horns struck the dog's bloody teeth and knocked one out, its shards pattering down onto Hellboy's face. The dog reared up on its hind legs, shaking its head at the sky, and for a second Hellboy could not help but be impressed at the brute strength of the thing.

But it was an old legend, a memory, not something that belonged here in the fading sunlight of what could be a very bad day.

"Hicks?" Hellboy said, inviting the pilot to put the thing down. There was no response. He glanced at the helicopter and discovered what had happened to the fourth dog.

It was buried face-first in the Lynx, back legs scrambling to push its body further inside, and suddenly there was screaming, blood spurted, somebody shouted in agony, and Hellboy tried to stand.

The dog fell back down on him, the jagged remnants of its shattered tooth connecting squarely with his face. Hellboy shouted, punched upward with both hands, but the dog had been driven into a rage. It seemed immune to pain. The harder he thumped it, the more it raked at his chest and throat with its front legs and the more it bit at his face. Hellboy shifted his head from side to side. That prevented the dog from gaining good purchase, but it meant that its teeth slashed his face, left to right and up and down.

Hellboy felt around for his pistol, but it had fallen somewhere beyond his reach.

"Liz!" he shouted, but the screams from the helicopter told him she had more than enough on her plate. *Fight fire with fire,* he thought. He waited until the dog reared up again, then he raised his head and buried his teeth in the hound's throat.

The dog howled. Hellboy shook his head, ripping into its skin, tasting the meat of it on his tongue. It was awful, the tang of raw meat, the trickle of blood down his throat . . . so basic and animalistic. He hated it, but he knew that this could be his last chance to gain the upper hand. He knew also that something very bad was happening in the helicopter, because the screaming had suddenly ceased.

He bit harder, shoving his whole head forward into the yawning wound in the dog's throat, and then he felt the rich gush of a major artery opening under his teeth.

The dog's howl turned to a whine, and Hellboy shoved it up and away. It flipped onto its back and landed with a thump that shook the deck, legs pawing at the air, head falling to the side as if keen to observe the pool of blood already spreading beneath it.

"Stay," Hellboy said. He spat, looked at the helicopter. The last dog was fully inside now, head turned to the right, chewing at something as Liz's flames began eating into it from behind. And there she was, crushed against the inside of the Lynx by the monster's huge body, eyes blazing and hands melting their way into the black dog's flanks. It seemed not to notice. Its head was out of sight, but Hellboy could see the swaths of blood that had splashed the inside of the pilot's cabin, and something in there was throwing red shadows as it thrashed.

He grabbed at one of the dog's rear legs and pulled. Nothing happened.

"Hellboy!" Liz said. When she spoke she breathed fire. "Jim's gone. He's just gone. It bit him in half."

"Hicks?"

Liz glanced toward the cabin then back at Hellboy, eyes aflame. She pursed her lips and battered harder at the dog, each impact scorching its skin and spreading more fire through its fur. It started to whine beneath the terrible chewing sounds. "I can see bits of him," she said.

"Crap! Liz, can you get out?"

"My legs are crushed against the fuselage."

Hellboy grabbed the dog's leg again, pulled it straight, and brought his fist down, crushing the bone. The leg went to jelly in his hands and flopped down. The dog squealed. It rocked the helicopter as it struggled to back up. Hellboy hauled on the broken leg and shifted the thing's body, just enough so that Liz could free herself and climb out. She was grimacing, hands dripping flames like lengths of colorful cloth. She crawled over the hound's body, and wherever she touched, its fur burst alight. The stink was terrible.

Liz tumbled to the deck, looking around at the twitching remains of the other two black dogs, and turned back to the helicopter. "Poor Jim," she said. "Poor Hicks."

"That's no way to go," Hellboy said. He held Liz's arm, and they retreated. A few more seconds, and the dog would work itself free of the chopper. Hellboy had no desire to see its bloody head decorated with the remains of his ghost-hunting friend and the helicopter pilot. "Fry it."

Liz breathed in deeply, but she did not need to prepare for long. Fire expanded out from her, igniting both the dog and the Lynx.

"Come on!" Hellboy grabbed Liz, and they ran along the deck, heading toward the imposing bridge superstructure at the other end of the massive ship. They passed the open hold door, glanced inside, saw nothing. Hellboy could smell the stench of animals, but he could also sense that the ship was all but empty. The things that had once called this place home were now laying siege to the Anderson Hotel in the London Docklands. There would almost certainly be more guards like the four black dogs, but now he felt energized by the fight and ready to move on. His skin was ruptured and leaking. His fist ached with the need to connect again. His blood was up.

"What now?" Liz said.

"Now we find that bastard Blake and kill him," Hellboy said.

"He could be anywhere. This ship is the size of a city!"

"He'll be close to where we saw that car dropped in. That was brought here for a reason. Trouble is—"

The helicopter exploded behind them, casting a huge ball of flame and smoke skyward. Debris scattered across the deck, metal clanging on metal, and a chunk of smoldering flesh thudded down twenty feet away. Hellboy did not look to see what color it was.

"Trouble is, we've lost our element of surprise."

"And our ride home," Liz said.

They paused and looked back at the flaming aircraft. "I always treat these as one-way deals," Hellboy said. "That way, getting home is a bonus."

As they turned back to the hold doors they had been aiming for, the rukh rose up, turned its giant head, and stared right at them.

Hellboy sighed. "Next."

Even in the depths of the *New Ark*, walking pathways so close to the Memory that she could feel its infinite draw, Abby felt the weight of the moon pressing down upon her. The hairs on the back of her neck were constantly on end, her jaws and teeth ached, the bones of her back seemed to be constantly shifting as if readying themselves for their change. Her hunger was up, a raging dryness at the back of her throat and a hollowness in her stomach. Blood flowed hot in her veins. She could see around corners and hear through walls, and Abby knew she had very little time left.

If she were to kill Blake, it would have to be within the next couple of hours. After that she would change, he would see, and Blake would claim his victory by killing her at last.

I wish I'd finished him instead of just running away, she thought for the thousandth time.

Lost, she suddenly felt found. She was taking action to deepen her new life, not sitting back and letting her friends at BPRD do it for her. Abe had been her angel—he still was—but now, here, she was carving her own future from the potential of the present, not letting others guide her through it. Through these corridors that all looked the same, through the huge rooms where birthing vats now hung cracked and dry and unused, through the stalls and rooms and tanks where other creations from the Memory had spent their new lives waiting to fulfill Blake's desires— all of these places in darkness, all unseen—Abby ran, searching for the one door she knew she would recognize. She listened for the Voice that would welcome her back like an old friend. The one aspect from her time here that she enjoyed remembering was her conversations with the Voice and her growing realization that he was imprisoned, a conjuring that Blake had lived to regret long ago.

Now, Abby hoped he would regret it some more. The Voice must have a body, and the body must have a desire to be free. She would give it that freedom. In return, all she would ask for was help.

She rounded a corner in the corridor, skidded to a stop, and stared at the thing facing her.

It blinked. Snorted. Stamped one cloven hoof, shook its head, the ring in its nose swinging. Its furry head seemed too huge for its body, but it was muscled and wiry, and its naked man's torso was sheened with sweat.

"You know the maze of this place," she whispered. "Tell me the way to the Voice." She wondered why the minotaur had not joined in with Blake's attack and thought that maybe it preferred to remain within this labyrinth. Perhaps it liked being lost. She looked into its eyes and saw little to recognize there—no empathy, no understanding. She hoped it could hear the animal power in her voice, projected out from the change that even now was starting within her.

The minotaur roared at her, breath steaming in the cool atmosphere, and then it turned and ran. There was no way she could keep up—it disappeared too quickly—but she heard its hoof steps echoing back at her for several moments.

Abby went down another flight of steps to a lower level. The stink of animal was richer down here, as was the smell of stagnant water and old oil. She felt closer than ever to the junction between worlds. She did not believe that the sun could be shining thirty feet above her, could not comprehend the nearness of the ocean just a few wall thicknesses away. If she closed her eyes, she could imagine the Memory lurking just beyond her outstretched fingers, its cool emptiness drawing her closer, closer . . . and in that emptiness the memory of that old dead thing, the sleeping god so ancient and awful that Blake had left it behind.

Abby's eyes snapped open, and she looked around, seeing only rusting metal and the familiar haunt of shadows. "That thing didn't help me," she said, but she knew that was a lie. "That thing has no part in my being here." But that was untrue, and she could almost hear its appalling chuckle in her mind as she ran on.

At last, she found somewhere she recognized. The corridor was like a hundred others, but the door spacing was right, a scratch along one wall, the way light from an unguarded bulb spread itself across the decaying metal. She paused and walked on, experiencing a chill of déjà vu as she trailed her fingers along one wall.

Running, panting, sweating, a certain aim in mind, the smell of shit wafting from some lower level, heat emanating from the wall to her right, and a voice, the Voice, calling her on with whispers that started as a tickle somewhere deep in her imagination.

"I'm here," she said, drawing close to a door that looked as though it had never, ever been opened.

"Have you returned with a name?" the Voice asked. It was gruff from lack of use.

"Abby."

"Abby . . ." The Voice faded away into a smile. "Abby, you escape and choose to return. If only there was time to sit and listen to your reasons."

"There's never been time," Abby said. "Blake has always been mad. You have to help me. There's one thing I have to do before . . . before . . ."

"Ahh, the change is coming," the Voice said. Abby wondered whether the humor had always been there, just below its words, and whether she could only recognize it now after so long in the real world.

"It won't be long," she said. "Blake endangers the world."

"The world has done little for me."

"But Blake has kept you locked away forever!"

"Forever? That's a long time, Abby. I've been here for less than the space between heartbeats. And yet . . . further heartbeats I crave."

"Does that mean you'll help me?"

"Open my door, Abby. It's barred to me, but you . . . you might be able to break the wards."

"First tell me your name," Abby said. "You were Voice, and you were a friend to me, and now I need a name."

"Call me Leh."

"Leh. A good name. Old."

"You have no idea."

"Stand back, Leh. I'm feeling strong. And this feels so right."

Abby braced herself against the wall opposite the door, levered herself forward with one foot, and drove her shoulder against the metal. Something sparkled in the sealed space between door and frame—static, electricity, something blinking out with the stench of singed hair. She shoved at the door again, growling, feeling the energy rising up in her and powering her muscles. Blood dripped from her mouth as larger teeth began to break through. The fine downy hairs on the backs of her hands grew darker, thicker. Her perception of things grew wider, and looking up she could see her way through metal, the dark blue sky already revealing the ghost of the full moon.

Abby growled louder, shoved the door again, and felt it give beneath her. She tumbled into the room. Hands fell on her shoulders, cold and wet and devoid of life, and something breathed a word into her face.

"Abby," it said.

And Abby thought, *Oh shit, Abe, what have I done?*

The rukh had lowered its head back into the hold, leaving Liz and Hellboy staring after it in confusion. One second they were expecting the thing to attack, the next it had turned away, seemingly unconcerned, and dipped back down where it had dropped the car.

The ship moved gently beneath them, smoke from the burning helicopter drifted along the deck, and seagulls buzzed around the bridge structure at the stern.

"So?" Liz said.

Hellboy shrugged. The wounds on his face were terrible, and Liz had to look away. They would heal, she knew, but for now they were not something she wanted to see. Not on the face of a friend, and not so soon after seeing Jim and Hicks taken apart by that dog.

"Well—"

Liz's satellite phone rang, startling both of them. She grabbed it from her pocket and answered. "Abe!"

"Hey, Liz. You guys OK? I tried calling Hellboy, but I got nothing."

"I think a dog ate his phone," Liz said.

"Right. Listen, I'm in London, I was following Abby, and her car was taken away—"

"By a giant bird," Liz finished for him. A lot suddenly became very clear. Hellboy raised his eyebrows, and she nodded at him. "Carried off by a rukh," Liz said. "It brought her to Blake's ship, the *New Ark*."

"How'd you know all that?"

"We're here right now."

"How are things?"

"About average."

"Oh." Abe's voice crackled. "Liz, will you find her for me? Look after her? I think she's got where she was going anyway, but I'm not sure why she's there."

"I'll do my best, Abe. But HB and I have a lot on our

plate right now. And . . ." She looked skyward at the deep blue of the fading afternoon. She could feel the touch of the setting sun on the back of her neck.

"I know," Abe said. "It may have happened already."

"Abe, the attack's started on the conference," Liz said. "We passed it in a chopper, and it wasn't looking good."

"Doesn't look good from here either. I reached the Docklands five minutes ago, and I don't think I'll be going much farther."

"Can you see the Anderson Hotel?"

"In the distance, yes. What's left of it. Lots of fire, and smoke, and things flying around. I'm not sure I can even get any closer, there are roadblocks and . . . things . . . stopping the . . ."

"Abe? You're breaking up." Hellboy reached out for the phone, but Liz shook her head. "Abe?"

Static.

"How's my favorite amphibian?" Hellboy asked.

"Worried about Abby. He's in London, close to the Anderson. It sounds bad. HB, we need to find Blake as quickly as we can."

"Yeah."

Thames Estuary—1997

Abe dropped the satellite phone back into the car and set off on foot.

He was relieved that Hellboy and Liz now knew where Abby was, but that relief was countered by his frustration at not being able to reach her himself. The only thing he could do was head east . . . and hope that somewhere he would get lucky.

The road was a chaos of parked cars. Most people watched the confusion in the distance from the perceived safety of their vehicles, but a few sat on their car roofs. The police roadblock at the end of the street prevented them from going any farther. Abe's intention now was to find a way through.

The Anderson Hotel rose way above any surrounding buildings, yet it was all but obscured by smoke, buzzed by helicopters . . . and attacked by other things. Abe saw dark shapes dipping and weaving between the helicopters, playing with them the way a cat plays with a wounded bird. The sound of explosions and gunfire was muted by distance, and he had the distinct impression that the observers thought they were watching a movie being made. There was interest on their faces, not fear; excitement, not trepidation. If they were closer, maybe the explosions would scare them away. If they could see what was going on, understand its implications, perhaps the true seriousness of the situation would be brought home.

"You people need to wake up," Abe muttered.

And as if his wish had made it so, the wake-up call screamed down from the sky.

The helicopter was ablaze. Its rotors still spun, fanning the flames, and even through the smashed windscreen Abe could see the pilot's grim expression as he fought with the controls. But it was a losing battle. The aircraft lost height, spewing fire and oily black smoke behind it, and its rear rotor suddenly stalled and broke away from the tail, smashing into the fifth floor of an office block across the street from where Abe stood.

He backed into a doorway, watching a few other people do the same. And still some of them thought staying in their cars would help.

The pilot managed to steer the doomed aircraft away from the packed street and into a building just beyond the police roadblock. It struck the glass-sided office block and exploded, sending a million shards of glass glittering across the road, spinning through the air, reflecting the helicopter's demise, and forming a brief rainbow of fire as they fell.

Abe ducked into the doorway and covered his head with his hands. The sound of the crash went on and on, the helicopter's remains tumbling to the road and bringing half of the building's façade down with it. When he looked again, the whole street beyond the roadblock was aflame. It all but obscured the view of the Anderson.

"That was close," he muttered. And then the dragon came through the flames and brought the danger closer.

It was small—perhaps the size of a small hatchback car—but when it breathed flames they were white-hot. It swayed its head left to right across the roadblock, and the police cars erupted into flame, policemen scattering and falling beneath it. A gas tank went, then another, and the dragon hopped from one burning car to the next.

"Get out!" Abe yelled. People were still in their cars. Some of them were taking pictures with their mobile phones. "Get out, get away!"

The dragon hovered for a few seconds and landed on a Range Rover. It stared through the windscreen at the occupants. The driver leaned back in his seat, but the passenger stretched forward, now separated from the dragon's breath only by a sheet of safety glass.

Then the creature reared up and gushed flame straight

into the Range Rover, incinerating its interior in one fiery breath.

Abe ran. There was nothing he could do here. The chaos was spreading, and he was just one man. He found an alley, worked his way in between buildings—a service yard, a parking lot, a delivery area—and when he emerged again, he found himself on an empty street. To his left lay London, to his right, revealed in all its blazing glory, the Anderson Hotel. From here he could see the areas around the hotel, and what he saw was all bad.

Before him the river.

Miles away, Hellboy and Liz could well hold Abby's fate in their hands. He trusted them with his life—indeed, he had done so quite literally many times before—but at the same time he felt impotent here. This battle was much larger than him, and its real cause lay beyond the Thames Estuary.

Perhaps if he could reach the Anderson and persuade someone of that, the *New Ark* could yet be in his reach.

Abe slipped into the Thames and began to swim.

The *New Ark*, English Channel—1997

They moved together toward the open hold doors, expecting the rukh to spring up at any moment. A cool breeze smoothed the deck of the old tanker, hushing between the doors, whistling past taut wires and coiled chains.

"There'll be more than those dogs," Hellboy said.

"I'm sure."

"Liz . . . if we find Abby and she's changed . . ."

"Let's deal with that one if it happens," she said. "For now, Blake's our main priority. Abby has to look after herself."

Hellboy nodded. "She's a big girl."

Liz smiled, reached out, and touched his arm. He smiled back, past the blood and the hanging flaps of skin, past whatever was making him nervous. Liz knew him so well; something had got to him. He was tensed up, eyes shifting left to right, and even as the rukh finally powered from the hold and hovered before them, Hellboy's expression told Liz he had been expecting something else.

She looked at the monstrous bird and knew there was far worse to come.

"I spoke with you," Leh said. "Long ago when you were here, and more recently through the Memory. That place. That cold, dark place." Its words suggested fear, but Abby could not believe that Leh would be afraid of anything.

"That was you? You said he left you. You said Blake left you and ignored you, leaving you with the things too old and terrible to summon."

The demon sat in the corner of the room, arms around its knees. It had not stopped staring at the open door. It had the appearance of a person—tall, gaunt, thin. It looked like a man, but its eyes were deeper and darker than nothing. Darker than the Memory. And there was so much more to them. There was no way Abby should look at its eyes, and no way she could turn away.

"I'm a liar," Leh said. "And lies are simply truths yet to happen."

"He knew you," Abby said.

"He knew what his foolish sons had sent him, and he knew what he was bringing forth, and he knew to shut me in here with his magic and his invocations. Weak. Old." The demon trailed away, still staring at the shade of the open door. The weak artificial light from outside was filtering in, weaker than it should have been, as though struggling against shadows that should not be here.

"You mean Blake?"

"Me." Leh smiled, an open wound in its face. "Had my time. I was . . . *put down.*" It looked away from the door at last, shivering. Stared at its hands, steepled its fingers, looked inside. "And I want to kill him because he raised me again."

"I don't know you," Abby said. "You're a liar, you said yourself. I know the Voice, the friend I had. I don't know demons."

Leh shrugged and smiled, and when it looked at her, Abby could not turn away. She fell into its eyes and lost herself in there, adrift in the Memory, floating in so much nothingness that she thought its bulk would crush her soul right from her. She opened her mouth to scream, but she was only a mind. And in the distance, an eternity away, a form so large and old that it exacted a gravity on nothing. It was terrible, and more ancient than time, and so alone that she could almost see the universe it had built in its endless imagination. Alone, it had made itself everything.

Abby screamed and turned away, and when she next opened her eyes, she was looking at the floor of the cell, the stained metal rusted into magical words and sigils. And she realized that she was alone.

The light from the doorway faded as something passed the bulb outside, then brightened again.

"No!" Abby said. "He's not yours. He's mine!" She stood and walked toward the door, and for a terrible moment she sensed something of what Leh must have felt for so long: isolation, imprisonment, an awful elasticity to the air that prevented her from reaching the door. Then something sputtered out in the air around her, a mysterious charge dissipating in the presence of her animal heat, and she exited into the corridor.

"Leh!" she called, because she knew she could not pursue in secret. "Leh, he's mine. Blake's mine!"

"He'll always be mine in the end," the shadows said. Abby ran, but however fast she moved, Leh was far ahead.

One thing at least: the demon seemed to know where it was going.

Abby was happy to follow.

The rukh rose from the hold. Hellboy leaped, swiped its turning beak aside, grabbed the feathers of its neck, and fell back down with it. The hold swallowed them both, and shadows cooled his wounded skin. The bird screeched as Hellboy drove his fist into its throat, dipping its head to try and get at him with its beak. But Hellboy had judged the leap perfectly, and he was now well within the bird's fighting circle, able to punch and tear at its throat without any fear of retribution from its cruel mouth.

Its claws, though. He soon found that the bird could easily twist its claws.

They had landed on the remains of Abby's car, crushing it down into the deck. *Explode!* Hellboy thought, but of course that only happened in movies. As he concentrated on pummeling the creature's throat and sending it back to the Memory where it belonged, he did not see the claw reaching up for him. But he felt it, curling into the flesh of his thigh and meeting in the middle.

"Damn crap shit!" Hellboy screamed. He was tired of being hurt. He wanted to sit down with a beer and a cigarette and kick back, relax, have nothing to worry about for a few minutes. This just was not fun. Fifty miles away the leaders of the world were maybe even now being wiped out by cryptids, and here he was fighting a giant bird instead of beating the life out of the mad mastermind of all this weirdness.

Sometimes he wished weirdness would take a break. Maybe he should just chase thieves and murderers, a much more understandable class of villain.

"Hellboy!" Liz shouted. Looking up, Hellboy could see her head and shoulders silhouetted against the fading daylight. "Close your eyes!"

Cooking again, Hellboy thought, and he squeezed his eyes shut. A blast of heat, a scream from the rukh, the stench of singed feathers, and the claws ripped from his body as the bird retreated to a shadowy corner of the hold.

Hellboy rolled from the ruined car's hood and slumped to the floor, slipping in his own blood. That was never a good sign. He shook his head, felt around in his coat pocket for a cigarette stub, and when he found one, his fingers closed around it like an old friend. The rukh squealed in the corner, and he told it to shut up.

"You OK, HB?"

"Just dandy, Liz." He looked around the hold, hidden in shadow though much of it was, and tried to imagine what had happened to Abby down here. What had held her. Where she had gone. He glanced up again, and past the shape of Liz's head he could see the ghost of the moon forming in the dusky sky. "Abby won't be Abby for much longer," he said. "And the longer we leave Blake, the worse all this could turn out. Time's running out, Liz, and we need to move on. Jump. I'll catch you."

Liz launched herself into space. Hellboy held out his arms to catch her. *Such trust,* he thought. *And that's why we'll win.* He caught Liz and gave her a kiss on the forehead. "Bet Blake doesn't have anyone who'd catch him," he said.

"My hero."

Liz and Hellboy ran from the hold, leaving the squealing rukh behind them. The pain in the bird's voice set them on edge, but they hoped to be able to silence it soon.

If we're right about all this, Hellboy thought. *If Blake really is the center of things. If not . . . hello, new world order.*

The demon stood at the center of the birthing chamber, looking up at the great vat suspended from the ceiling. Abby hung back and watched. It looked very human, yet it exuded something inexpressible, an alien aura that human senses would never understand. She was aware that Leh knew she was there, but there was something about this moment that was very private, very much owned by Leh and Leh alone.

Now I'm being thoughtful toward a demon, she thought, shaking her head. She even smiled. It was a long time since she had done that.

"This is where I was brought through," Leh said. "And this is where I'll leave again. But not alone."

This had once been one of the tanker's great oil cells, and even after so long, there was still a hint of oil on the air. Abby guessed it would never be cleaned away. Behind that, too, the tang of something else, something much more mysterious and distant. She looked up at the vat and the dried, salty crust around its lip. Unused now, perhaps for several years, but like the oil, its presence would always be apparent. The taint of the Memory would never wash away.

"How do you know he'll be here?"

The demon closed its eyes. "Blake is being chased here even now. An old man, a fool, a lamb to the slaughter." It opened its eyes again. "Lamb. I was once an enemy of sheep, but the shepherd put me down. Do I have the taint, Abby? Can you see his mark upon me?" It turned to her, this demon that was her friendly Voice, and she tried to look at its face without falling into its eyes once again. But she could not. She averted her gaze, looked down at her hands, noting how long her nails were now and how badly her body was shaking. She could not fight off the change for much longer. She was going to lose control very soon, and the last thing she wished for—the very last thing she wanted to see—was Blake taken apart. She wanted to do it herself, desperately . . . and yet if fate had decided that a demon would be his end, so be it. Abby had argued with fate many times before, and it was ironic that now, at her strongest moment, she suddenly felt so weak. She could almost feel the puppet strings buried in her mind and soul, guiding her every movement since she had first fled the *New Ark* and leading her back here, now, to this exact moment, with Leh standing before her, blood coursing a monstrous change through her body, and Blake being chased toward them . . .

But chased by whom?

"Who's chasing?" she asked, but her voice crackled from the phlegm suddenly flooding her throat. Saliva dripped from her lips, pink from the blood of her wounded gums.

"Oh, I think you'll know them when you see them," Leh said.

Abe, Abby thought. *Oh, Abe, I never wanted you to see me like this.*

"Not Abe," the demon said. "But close enough."

Abby changed. The world retreated from her for a while, and despite the intense physical pain, this was the one moment when she found true mental peace. She was nowhere for a while, a place without dream or nightmare, with no Memory or reality. Simply a blank.

When she woke up, the world was a very different place.

"I can smell him," Hellboy said. "An old man. A *fading* man. He's almost passed into Memory, but we can't let him get away. Come on, Liz, run!" They pelted headlong along corridors, passing through huge rooms that had once held creatures of untold size and power. *Maybe we've come up against some of them already*, Hellboy thought. *Maybe some we have yet to meet. But if we catch Blake soon, instead of letting him escape into this maze of rooms and corridors, we can hope we'll never have to meet them at all.*

"Stop!" Liz said. Hellboy paused, glanced back at Liz. She was holding up her finger. "Hear that? Footsteps."

Hellboy heard them, racing off way ahead. "Our echoes?"

Liz shook her head. "Only one set. Come on."

The deeper they went, the more amazed Hellboy became. "Has Blake really been here for so long?" he said. "What about fuel, food, repairs?"

"There are a hundred ports where he'd get help with no questions asked," Liz said. "We can worry about the past later, after we've sorted out the present."

"Right," Hellboy said. But as ever, it was the future that worried him the most.

So they followed the echoing footsteps, and soon, far too quickly for Hellboy to think it was luck, they saw the shape of a shuffling man ahead of them. He looked back, eyes going wide, and skirted sideways into a narrower gap between walls. Liz followed him first, Hellboy squeezing in after her.

"Nearly there," Liz said. "Blake! Stop!"

"Yeah, like he'll listen," Hellboy said. "Stop, police!" he shouted, then laughed.

"Sarcasm doesn't suit you, HB," she said.

"I'm just trying it on for size." The smile suddenly slipped from his face, and he was glad that Liz was hurrying on ahead, unable to see his expression. *That's cold*, Hellboy thought. *That's so cold, so empty, so wrong. That's not Blake. He's mad, he has magic, but he isn't . . . evil. I smell evil. Black as pitch and stinking a hundred times worse.*

They emerged into a huge chamber, a place that reeked of old oil and something else, something much more distant and unearthly. "Liz," Hellboy said, "get behind me."

"Don't you start with all that macho—"

"I mean it." The fact that Liz moved quickly behind Hellboy assured him that she had seen the look on his face. "This is so much more than Blake."

At the center of the chamber, suspended from the ceiling, hung a huge vat. Gray stuff had congealed around its rim and dripped down its sides like melted wax. Whatever this thing was, it hadn't been used for a while. It made Hellboy uneasy. He didn't like the smell coming from the thing, or the sight of it, and it felt so out of place in this world. *This is where he brought them through,* he thought. Then he heard the old man scream, and everything began to move very quickly.

"Hellboy!" a voice said. "Long time."

"I've never met you, demon."

Leh shrugged. "Have it your own way." It was standing on the rim of the huge vat, twenty feet above the deck, and it held Benedict Blake in one hand. Hellboy could see the demon's fingers clasped inside the man's throat, as if Blake were becoming transparent.

Hellboy and Liz had rounded the vat just in time to see the demon grab Blake and leap, landing on the vat's rim with uncanny balance. Hellboy had seen a shape slink back into the shadows at the corner of the room, but he wasn't sure Liz had seen, and he did not want to make Abby the center of this. Not yet. Not unless he had to.

"I came here for him, not you," Hellboy said.

"Him?" The demon went to drop Blake into the vat. "He'd make a fine brew, I'm sure."

"Who are you?"

"Leh."

"Leh is dead."

"Really, Hellboy . . . you know better than that. Old demons don't die, they just retire disgracefully." The demon in human form smiled, and its teeth glimmered in the vague light. "Oh, and haven't you seen Abby yet? What a girl she's grown into! Although she's a trifle hirsute, I must say. I pre-

fer my females shaved. Saves on the fur balls." He coughed
and spat, his saliva sizzling on the deck.

"What are you doing here, Leh?"

"So you admit I'm Leh?"

"I admit nothing." Word games pissed Hellboy off. He
clenched his fist, wanting to punch something. The vat.
Maybe that would do.

"I'm here because this idiot's charming sons found me,"
Leh said. "Simple, really. He brought me back, and now
I'm . . . well, I'm not going to tell you."

"You're going to drop Blake into the vat to open a passage to the Memory," Hellboy said.

The demon shrugged. "Good guess."

"I've had a lot of practice. Is this all your doing?"

The demon shook its head, looked around at the grubby
walls and ceiling of the old oil tank. "I suppose you could
just call me lucky," it said. "I've no concern at all about
what this little man is doing, but he serves a purpose. And
now, if you don't mind—"

"You don't want to go back there," Hellboy growled. "I
know demons."

"As well you should," Leh said. "No, I'm not going back
to the Memory. Awful place, so boring, and no ass to be had
for love or money."

"So you're inviting something through."

The demon turned to Blake, pressed its pale visage into
the old man's face, and growled. "You left a friend of mine
in there, when it could have made you a god."

Hellboy shook his head, stepped forward, and then the
room shook as though kicked from all sides by something
with size infinity boots.

For a second Leh's eyes opened in wonder, and the demon turned and looked down into the vat. But Hellboy knew that the impact was from a more earthly source, and the second explosion that followed quickly on the first confirmed it. The *New Ark* was under attack.

Abe must have told them about the ship, Hellboy thought. Hellboy jumped at the vat, clawing his way to the top and reaching for Leh's ankles. The demon sidestepped his grasp with ease and laughed—Hellboy hated demon laughter—before letting Blake go.

A shadow leaped from the other lip of the vat, grasped Blake in its jaws, and tumbled to the deck, rolling into shadow and taking the screaming man with it.

"No!" Leh yelled, and the ship shook again. "Abby!" All the demon received in response was a long, low howl, a haunting noise that filled the room and gave an alternative accompaniment to the sound of continuous explosions.

"Liz!" Hellboy shouted, but he needn't have bothered. Liz was already running after Abby, fire springing alight in her palm to light the way.

"And you," Hellboy said, turning, "can go back—"

Leh was on him, grabbing hold of his right fist and pulling him up onto the lip of the vat. They stood there, demon and man-demon, facing each other as the ship shook and shuddered around them. On Hellboy's left was a drop to the deck. On his right something different. He glanced down, but he could not see the bottom of the vat. It was too dark.

"Like what you've done with your horns," Leh said.

"Thanks."

Leh kept glancing past Hellboy at the doorway Liz had disappeared through. *He needs Blake,* Hellboy thought.

Needs the old man's magic and science to keep the route open from the Memory. But for what? He glanced down again, and the depth of the darkness made him woozy. *Something with tentacles, I'll bet.*

"How's life?" Leh said.

"Just dandy."

"You know I'm going to get him, don't you?"

"I can't let you."

"Think you can stop me?"

Hellboy shrugged. "It's been one of those days. I figure I can give it a shot."

"Oh, by the way," Leh said, then the demon stepped from the lip of the vat.

Hellboy was quick. He grabbed the demon's leg and squeezed, crushing flesh and bone and feeling the warm burst of blood. The demon shouted, but Hellboy was not fooled; this was just a shell. He almost lost balance. Leh suddenly gained weight and tipped them down toward the deck, but then there was a huge explosion from somewhere nearby, the ship tipped, and Hellboy swung his fist behind him, tilting the balance and falling back.

"No!" Leh said.

Hellboy let himself fall into the vat, grabbing on to its lip with his free hand.

"No!"

Hellboy dragged the demon up over the lip and swung it above his head, letting go and watching as Leh fell, and fell, and fell, twisting down into the darkness of the Memory, its screams dying out just as its falling body finally faded from sight.

"Back where you belong," Hellboy said. He groaned. Blood was pulsing from his fresh wounds. And below him something waited. Usually he didn't mind heights, but that endless darkness scared the crap out of him.

He hauled himself back over and fell to the deck, wiping blood from his eyes before taking off after Liz.

He'd only had a fleeting look at Abby—the fur, the muscle, and the teeth—but he knew that he didn't want Liz facing that on her own.

The ship shook again, and he felt the first waft of heat from distant fires.

Damn, he thought, *they sit around doing nothing, and when they do act, they're too damn efficient.*

Hellboy figured he had a few minutes before he became fish food.

Liz found him huddled in a small room with a broken door, bleeding to death. His throat had been ripped out, and chunks of meat were torn from his stomach, legs, and back. Nothing had been swallowed. The werewolf had spat the chunks of Benedict Blake across the floor, as if leaving them as a sacrifice or an offering. To what, Liz did not know. She stood and watched the old man staring at bits of himself as the life slowly bled from him, and when Hellboy arrived, she turned and walked away.

Hellboy took one look into the room and saw that the man was dead. More than dead, he was fading. Becoming transparent. Slipping away into Memory. He should be famous, but he had been shut away in this old ship for so long that, ironically, no one would ever remember him.

"Maybe Leh will have use of you yet," Hellboy said. It

was a pretty uncharitable thought, he supposed, but that's just the way he was feeling.

He ran after Liz, and together they made their way up on deck.

The *New Ark* was sinking. It listed badly to port, the bridge had been all but blown away, and a great slick of debris and fuel had spread across the ocean from the holes in its hull. Several parts of it were on fire, and smoke billowed skyward and merged with that already there from the destroyed helicopter.

The sun was sinking into the land visible to the west.

From the south, two Tornados were streaking across the waves on an attack run.

"I think we should jump," Liz said.

Hellboy shook his head. "I think we'll be OK. Look." There was a helicopter hovering a hundred yards off the bow, and in its open doorway stood Abe Sapien. He waved once at Hellboy and Liz, but he was looking elsewhere, scanning the deck, searching the waves.

Hellboy's satellite phone went off. "Hellboy, where is she?"

"She's still inside, buddy."

"You didn't bring her out? You didn't stay to find her?"

"Abe, I really don't think she wants to be found."

A pause. "That's what she said last time," Abe said. They watched him drop the phone back into the helicopter and dive into the sea. He went in with hardly a splash.

"This baby's sinking," Hellboy said. The sea was now swelling up over the deck, and the sounds of ripping metal and rupturing bulkheads were deafening. He was very tired.

His wounds had begun to hurt for real. Liz held him up and waved the helicopter in, and as the deck vanished below them, they were winched up into its cabin.

Below the surface, the sea was in chaos. Bubbles and wreckage from the ship obscured Abe's view, and the water stank from the ruptured fuel tanks. He pulled himself past floating debris and headed for the sinking vessel, and he did not even hesitate before diving deep and finding his way in. It was suicide, he knew that. But he had found Abby through her own suicide attempt, and there was no option but to try to save her again.

The ship swallowed him up, and he started to feel his way through its ruined corridors and water-filled holds.

Some lights were still working. They cast strange shadows in such turbulent waters. Several times Abe thought something was swimming right at him, but it always resolved itself into nothing more than another surge, another gush of fuel-tainted water being forced along passageways by the pressures of sinking. He forged on, smelling blood here and there and trying to follow its trail. He lost it, found it again, went deeper. The ship was turning as it sank, and he was almost deafened by the sounds of metal twisting and breaking apart. The thumps of distant explosions crushed him against bulkheads. Doors swung open and blocked his way. Something soft and warm grabbed at him, and he kicked out, feeling his feet connect with a slippery thing. By the time he'd turned around, whatever had reached for him had vanished into the chaotic shadows.

He went deeper, sometimes swimming, sometimes rushing through trapped air pockets, always dodging destruction. He looked for Abby. But he found nothing.

The broken ship was way below the surface now, and he could feel pressures building without and within. The sounds of buckling metal grew almost unbearable. And he thought, *Perhaps there's still time.*

They waited while the ship sank, waited some more until Abe finally surfaced, then they winched him up.

"Did you find her?" Liz asked.

"No," Abe said. "But that doesn't mean she's dead." He sat wrapped in a blanket and stared out over the sea. Hellboy sat next to him, scanning the assorted floating wreckage silvered by the full moon. None of it moved except to the rhythm of the waves.

Rio de Janeiro, Brazil—1997

"When we got back to London, we landed right beside what was left of the Anderson Hotel. The SAS were leading the politicians out onto the forecourt and loading them into helicopters. Couple of the presidents saw me and panicked, but I think most of them knew who I was. Big red guy. Easy to identify. But with some of the things they'd seen that day, I'm not surprised I unnerved them. To most people I'm just not natural.

"We reckon that just about the time Abby killed Blake,

the cryptids broke off their attack. Went from trained kill-creatures to . . . well, animals. Some of the more vicious ones kept going, but it was much more random. Lots of them escaped into London and caused chaos on the streets, in the Tube, and beyond. Lots of people died. Even after it was all over and Blake was dead, lots of people died." Hellboy took a long draw on his cigarette and let the smoke out slowly, watching the shapes it made. Occasionally he thought he saw things in there, but most of the time he guessed he was imagining it all.

"But you saved so many more," Amelia said.

Hellboy raised his eyebrows. "We did? I'm not sure. I'm not entirely sure we did much at all. It was Abby who killed Blake in the end. If it weren't for her, Leh would have sent him into the Memory and maybe opened it up. And who knows what else would have come through then?"

"Do *you* know, Hellboy?"

He puffed again on the cigarette, watched the smoke, saw something writhing in there until someone opened the bar door and the breeze blew it away. "I have a few ideas," he said.

"And what of his sons? You saw nothing of them?"

"Nothing on the *New Ark*, at least," Hellboy said. "But I think they're out there somewhere. Always have been. Kate Corrigan is the authority on Blake and de Lainree's *Book of Ways*, and she reckons there's no way Blake could just conjure the cryptids. He must have had some trace, some physical evidence of their existence, to bring them up out of the Memory. She thinks his sons had the book, not him, and they were out there finding the evidence for him."

"What sort of evidence? DNA?"

Hellboy shrugged. "Maybe that's the science part of it, at least."

Amelia finished her beer and ordered two more. "I saw it all on TV," she said. "It looked like a movie. The coverage of the attack was so complete that a lot of people I know still think it really *was* a movie."

"Good," Hellboy said. "It'll help them sleep at night." The new beers came, and they drank in silence.

"So," Amelia said after a while. "Abe?"

Hellboy sighed and shrugged. "Blames himself, of course. But me . . . I think it was inevitable from the start. Abby is one of those people who has a course set in life, and there's nothing anyone can do about it."

"I never feel like that," Amelia said. "Life's what you make it. Living to fate's song . . . that must be awful."

Hellboy drained the new bottle of beer to avoid looking at Amelia. *Yeah,* he thought. *Tell me about it.*

Later they stood together looking up at the statue of Christ the Redeemer. The waning moon hung just over his left shoulder. *Strange,* Hellboy thought. *It all started here for me, and finished with Leh, and Leh was supposedly put down by Christ. Sometimes the turning wheels are just too damn oiled.*

"What now?" Amelia asked.

"Well, Britain's got a lot of new creatures roaming its countryside, and there are those that Blake released around the world as diversions. They'll spread, maybe mate. We've had reports of something huge in the Indian Ocean, bigger than anything ever seen before. So I guess BPRD is going to be busy. In some ways Blake's new world might just come about, only nothing like he imagined. And who knows, maybe people can learn to live with dragons and banshees."

"Hmm," Amelia said. "OK, but . . . I sort of meant, 'what now?' "

Hellboy looked down and returned her smile. "Oh," he said. "I see. Well . . . is there a place around here we can get a good meal?"

"Plenty."

"Good. It's on me."

Amalfi, Italy—2005

Richard visited his brother's grave every month for those first couple of years. As time went by the visits grew less frequent, partly because the grief had lessened and partly because Richard had found a new life. He was living in a leaky old house with a beautiful Italian woman, someone who loved him for what she said he would be rather than what he had been. He adored that idea of falling in love with the future. In a way he supposed his father and brother had done just that, but in very different ways. They had been mad.

He liked to think that through time he had discovered sanity.

But still he sometimes went back to that little graveyard, sat by his brother's unmarked grave, and thought of everything that might have been. Occasionally he read of sightings of strange creatures around the globe, leviathans in the deep, and now and then he would see photographs or grainy footage on TV. As time moved on, he was able to dis-associate himself from these things. In a way, he supposed, there was wonder in the world again.

And he thought of that most of all. Not all the people who had died, or those who had been maimed or orphaned. The wonder. That's what kept him going.

That and the knowledge that if he ever needed it again, the *Book of Ways* was safe and sound in his dead brother's folded arms.

ABOUT THE AUTHOR

Tim Lebbon lives in South Wales with his wife and two children. His books include *Dusk, Face, The Nature of Balance, Changing of Faces, Exorcising Angels* (with Simon Clark), *Dead Man's Hand, Pieces of Hate, Fears Unnamed, White and Other Tales of Ruin, Desolation,* and *Berserk.* Future publications include *Dawn* from Bantam Spectra and more books with Cemetery Dance, Night Shade Books, and Necessary Evil Press, among others. He has won two British Fantasy Awards, a Bram Stoker Award, and a Tombstone Award; and he has been a finalist for International Horror Guild and World Fantasy Awards. Several of his novels and novellas are currently under option in the United States and the United Kingdom. Find out more about Tim at his websites: www.timlebbon.net and www.noreela.com.